———————— ★ ————————

"Sounds pretty premeditated, doesn't it?" he said. "Balancing the concrete on the door and everything, took a bit of thought."

Don waggled a hand. "Maybe, maybe not. For one thing, is it too early to assume that the killer was after a specific victim? If not, if it's a nutter or someone with a grudge against the whole darts team, or the whole bloody pub for that matter, then he could have put the stone up there any time in the evening, and just waited for a random victim to trigger the trap."

Frank thought about that. "Okay, but in that case, he knows he's going to get a woman, not a man."

"Or a transvestite, I suppose. But yes, good point. Anyway—too early for that sort of speculation, Frank. Just check that the uniforms know what they're doing over there, see if they've got anything useful. A confession, for instance, wouldn't hurt."

———————— ★ ————————

"...readers may find themselves portioning the novel out, a few pages at a time, to make it last longer."

—*Booklist*

IN
AND
OUT

Mat
Coward

W🌐RLDWIDE®

TORONTO • NEW YORK • LONDON
AMSTERDAM • PARIS • SYDNEY • HAMBURG
STOCKHOLM • ATHENS • TOKYO • MILAN
MADRID • WARSAW • BUDAPEST • AUCKLAND

If you purchased this book without a cover you should be aware
that this book is stolen property. It was reported as "unsold and
destroyed" to the publisher, and neither the author nor the
publisher has received any payment for this "stripped book."

IN AND OUT

A Worldwide Mystery/May 2003

First published by Five Star.

ISBN 0-373-26456-9

Copyright © 2001 by Mat Coward.
All rights reserved. No part of this book may be reproduced
or transmitted in any form or by any means, electronic or
mechanical, including photocopying, recording or by any
information storage and retrieval system, without permission
in writing from the publisher. For information, contact:
Thorndike Press, 295 Kennedy Memorial Drive,
Waterville, ME 04901 U.S.A.

All characters in this book are fictitious, and any resemblance to
actual persons, living or dead, is purely coincidental.

® and TM are trademarks of Harlequin Enterprises Limited.
Trademarks indicated with ® are registered in the United States
Patent and Trademark Office, the Canadian Trade Marks Office
and in other countries.

Printed in U.S.A.

IN
AND
OUT

ONE

"THERE'S YOUR blunt instrument." Sam Walker nodded towards a concrete block, about the size of a hardback English dictionary, which lay on the tiled floor not far from the dead woman's damaged head.

DI Don Packham leaned forward, hands firmly behind his back, taking pains not to touch anything, not to sneeze alien droplets against the wall, not to spread dust motes where none had been before, and peered at the putative murder weapon. "Not much blood."

"No. She'll have died pretty quickly."

"A heavy blow, then? So—a male attacker?"

The thin, bearded pathologist shrugged. "These days, who can say? Body shapes are changing, the gender difference isn't as important as it was. Besides, after half a century of the welfare state, everyone's taller, bigger, stronger. My granddaughter came to stay with us last week. When I went to wake her up in the morning, her feet were dangling off one end of the Z-bed, and her head off the other. She's taller than me and her father put together."

"But still," said Don, "we can rule out one-armed weaklings and dwarfs, yeah?"

"Well, sorry to complicate things for you, Inspector, but it needn't even have been a particularly heavy blow. Could have been a lucky one—or a very precise one.''

''Oh, great.'' Don was still looking at the concrete lump. ''What is that thing, anyway?''

''Doorstop, I should say. Used to prop the outer door open in the summer, for fresh air.''

Don shivered. It was February, it was the early hours of the morning; the air did not lack freshness. ''You ever been in here before, Doc?''

Mr. Walker frowned. ''This is the ladies' lavatory, Inspector.''

''Yes, very funny. I meant this pub, the Hollow Head. Odd name for a pub; don't think I've ever drunk here.''

''I'm not really a pub man, Inspector. The wife and I tend to make our own wines from our garden produce.''

Don tried to repress a shudder at the thought of parsnip Chablis and pea-pod liqueur. ''So, a white female, average height or slightly less, mid-late forties,'' he said, pointing his chin at the corpse. ''Anything else you can tell me so far?''

''Oh yes,'' said Mr. Walker. ''She's dead. No, nothing much—cause of death was almost certainly the blow to the head, no sign of a struggle. She'd not been dead long before the alarm was raised. But apart from that, you'll have to wait, I'm afraid.''

''Fair enough. The relative lack of blood presumably means the killer won't have left a convenient trail of drips leading to his front door, right?''

''Might not have a drop on him, sad to say. I suspect the blow was to the back of the head, and what blood there was would most likely have been thrown forward. A little nifty footwork by a killer standing behind her as she fell would have kept him clean. Besides," added the pathologist, grunting slightly as he crouched down next to the body, "it may turn out that it was her head striking the floor that actually killed her."

"The blow with the doorstop having stunned her?"

"Right. I won't know until she's moved, but I wouldn't be surprised to discover another wound on the forehead."

"Sir?" A scenes-of-crime officer poked her head around the outer door. "This might be something."

Don eased past the doctor and the dead woman, and moved carefully over to the doorway—a journey of just a few steps. The Ladies at the Hollow Head consisted of three cubicles and a washing area, in a small building separate from the pub. On the other side of a paved courtyard, a similar concrete bunker housed the Gents. Both were reached by either of the pub's back doors. Old-fashioned arrangement, thought Don; not much fun when it's raining. You'd want good bladder control to be a regular at this boozer. The courtyard was more or less empty at this time of year, apart from a few empty beer kegs, but Don could imagine it on a Friday night or a Sunday lunchtime at the height of summer, full of circular tables with sun umbrellas in their middles; full of the smell of bitter and lager and gin and tonic and white wine spritzers and tobacco smoke and sun cream and perfume; full of the sound of laughter and chatter and wasps and kids being told off and men and women briefly relieved from the pressure of the working week, sighing and saying *Blimey, is it hot or what!*

Imagine it? If Don closed his eyes he'd be there.

He opened his eyes, remembered where he was, and spoke to the SOCO. "What have you got for me? If it's a signed confession written in blood, I'll buy you breakfast on the way home.''

The SOCO smiled. ''Not quite that lucky, Inspector. But if you have a little look here…'' With a pencil she indicated the top of the doorframe, before passing Don a small pair of stepladders.

''Thanks,'' he said, as he climbed three steps to look at the point her pencil had indicated. ''Oh yes, good spot. Very good spot. Few fresh scratches and some dust—concrete dust?''

''Tell you for sure when we've tested it, but I reckon so, yes. And if you follow a line down from there towards the victim…just there, you see?''

''I do see: a mark made by a heavy object striking a concrete floor.''

''Having first bounced off a human bonce,'' offered Mr. Walker. ''Yes, that certainly fits with—or at least, does not at this moment seem to contradict—what I've got. And it also possibly explains this.'' He indicated a small chip of stone lying under the hand-drying machine. ''Once the lab gets hold of the concrete block, I'll bet they fit the chip to the main body like a jigsaw piece.''

''Yes indeedy!'' Don clapped his hands together, and beamed at the SOCO. ''Excellent work, well done. That's smashing. So—let's see what we've got here.'' He stepped outside the door, paused to gather his thoughts, running his fingers through his short, thick, night-black hair. ''Okay. The victim—one Yvonne Wood, I am informed by the Hollow Head's landlady—exits the pub via one of those doors over there, crosses the courtyard, comes through this door and into one of those cubicles at the end, intent on widdling.''

The pathologist snorted. ''Widdling, Inspector?''

Don waved an impatient hand at him. "You wouldn't know it, Doc, it's a medical term. Right: she enters the cubicle, locks the inner door behind her, unaware that she has been followed across the courtyard by an unknown other, who quietly takes the doorstop, and balances it between the door and the top of the doorframe."

"Like a schoolboy," said Mr. Walker, "ambushing a maths teacher with a bucket of water."

"Or a geography teacher." Don was momentarily lost in negative nostalgia. "You say that fits with your preliminaries, Doc? The doorstop falling from the door onto her head would be enough to kill her?"

The pathologist whistled silently. "Well, you'd have to be a bit lucky. Or possibly unlucky, if the killing wasn't premeditated—you know, just a nasty joke that went too far. But yes, if the stone hit her in the right spot, at the right angle. You can see for yourself, the door is quite high, the woman is quite low. Besides, as I said, the precise weapon of death might turn out to be concrete from below rather than above."

Finding himself standing outside the Ladies, Don took a small cigar tin out of his pocket, removed a small cigar from it, and lit up.

"I'd rather you didn't, sir," said the SOCO.

"Ah, well," said the DI. "That's life, isn't it?" But he did take two conciliatory paces away from the heart of the crime scene.

"I DON'T THINK we've met," said Frank, showing his warrant card to the uniformed constable charged with corralling witnesses in the Hollow Head's main room. "Detective Constable Frank Mitchell."

"Right," said the uniform, wondering why the

young, redheaded CID man with the Geordie accent seemed so very keen to introduce himself. Common courtesy? Or was he the local recruiting secretary for the Police Christian Fellowship?

"Yeah," said Frank, too busy staring at his own ID in awe to notice that the grey-haired PC hadn't offered his own name. "That's me, DC Mitchell."

"Frank!"

"Over here, sir." Frank watched carefully as his boss walked across the room towards him. He was beginning to learn the signs—the walk, the angle of the chin, the set of the shoulders—which told of the DI's mood. He seemed to be moving jauntily enough tonight, his wiry frame fairly swinging along, but Frank had learned that the signs were only signs; they weren't infallible.

Just as Don reached him however, he took a puff on his cigar—and Frank relaxed. He was sure—he was pretty sure—that Don didn't smoke on the days when he was down.

"Frank, my lad—I won't apologise for dragging you out of bed, because for one thing it's your job, if you want regular hours you can go back to uniform, and secondly, I don't imagine you've slept for more than five minutes at a time since August, have you?"

As it happened, Don was more or less right on that—which was amazing, Frank reckoned, since DI Packham had never had any children of his own (well, okay, none that he knew of, or spoke of; when it came to Don Packham, Frank had long since decided, you did well to surround your assumptions with get-out clauses). Anyway, young Joseph Mitchell was indeed a champion sleep-slayer.

"So, what have we got, sir? Definitely a murder, is it?"

"Oh yes, indeed, Frank. Or at least, put it this way—if it was suicide it took a most imaginative form." Quickly, he filled his DC in on the forensic findings.

"So," said Frank, "not only won't the killer be carrying any bloodstains, he might not even have been missing from the pub at the precise moment of death."

"Right, depending on how long it took poor Yvonne to adjust her nylons, wash her hands and touch up her lipstick, before walking into the unknown's trap."

Frank looked around him, taking in the scene. Not that this was the scene, of course, not the actual death scene; but the single murder case he had previously worked, whilst still in uniform, had convinced him that the concept of "crime scene" covered a greater acreage than merely the spot upon which the corpse was discovered.

It was an old-fashioned London pub, he noted, not tarted up or themed or mock-Irished or turned into a restaurant or a cocktail bar. Not to his taste, really; when he went out for an evening with Debbie—not so often these last few months!—they preferred something a bit more up-to-date, a bit…well, okay, why not: a bit classier.

The Hollow Head didn't look as if it had changed much in forty years. One big room: no family room, Frank thought, with a parent's disapproval, nowhere where women might feel comfortable. A semi-circular bar in the middle, benches and small round tables against the walls, and in one corner a spot-lit dartboard, with permanent raised oche for the players to stand behind, and a printed rubber mat on the floor delineating the seven foot nine-and-a-quarter-inch throw.

Bet they play dominoes here, too, Frank thought. Just like all the old geezers back home.

"Great place, isn't it, Frank? Proper old pub. Not a jukebox or plastic shamrock in sight. Lovely!"

"Yes, sir," said Frank. He looked at his watch: 1.15 a.m. "What do you want me to do—sort out the witnesses?"

Don suddenly leaned in to Frank, and made a great show of peering at his chest. "That's one of the great advantages of being in CID, eh?"

With quiet determination, Frank kept any hint of puzzlement or impatience from his voice. "Sir?"

"It allows you the opportunity to wear to work, ties that your gorgeous wife has bought you for Christmas."

"Right. So, shall I—"

"And how is little Joe? Riding a bike yet?"

"Joseph is very well, thank you. He'd send his regards, I'm sure, if he could talk." The baby had been named Joseph—not Joe, that was a very different matter, in Frank's opinion—after three of his great-grandfathers, two maternal and one paternal. When, in a loose moment, Frank had explained this to Don, the DI had commented: "So why didn't you just call it Granddad, then?" That, Frank had felt at the time, was a Down Sign of unusual clarity.

"Okay, enough chat, Frank—we are here to work, you know."

"Indeed, sir."

"Right. I'll finish up with the prodders and pokers out in the Ladies. You see what we've got with that lot over there." He nodded towards a dozen men and women who sat around tables in the farthest corner of the pub, being interrogated by five PCs.

"Those the witnesses?"

Don lowered his voice. "I think the word you're looking for here is 'suspects'. We'll get a better idea in the daylight, but from a basic recce out back, I don't see us being able to pin this one on the legendary Passing Tramp. Far as I can make out, there is only one way to reach the courtyard, and that's via this room."

"And they were the only ones here?"

"Apparently. So the landlady told the uniformed bloke first on the scene—that grey-bonce you were talking to."

"What were they doing here? Wasn't the pub closed?"

Don nodded. "Lock-in. They were celebrating a big darts win, it seems."

Frank looked at the twelve presumed darts players with new interest. He'd thought they were merely witnesses—shocked, shaken, bored, indifferent, impatient, excited, according to temperament—but now, it appeared, one of them was a killer.

"Any one of them could have done it, you reckon? Lifted that stone up?"

"Doc reckons so. And there are a few empty barrels in the courtyard, which the killer could have used to stand on."

"Sounds pretty premeditated, doesn't it?" he said. "Balancing the concrete on the door and everything, took a bit of thought."

Don waggled a hand. "Maybe, maybe not. For one thing, is it too early to assume that the killer was after a specific victim? If not, if it's a nutter or someone with a grudge against the whole darts team, or the whole bloody pub for that matter, then he could have put the stone up there any time in the evening, and just waited for a random victim to trigger the trap.''

Frank thought about that. ''Okay, but in that case, he knows he's going to get a woman, not a man.''

''Or a transvestite, I suppose. But yes, good point. Anyway—too early for that sort of speculation, Frank. Just check that the uniforms know what they're doing over there, see if they've got anything useful. A confession, for instance, wouldn't hurt.''

Frank sought out the grey-haired PC again. ''Hi,'' he said.

''I know, I know—you're Detective Constable Frank Mitchell. Heard you the first few times.''

For a moment, Frank felt a blush starting, but then he thought—*No*. I'm a DC now, I'm a dad now. I can take a joke. He forced a laugh. ''Aye, sorry about that—I'm new to CID, you see.''

''I'd never have guessed.''

''So you'll have to forgive me if I labour the point a bit.''

''Fair enough, son.'' The uniformed man stuck out a hand. ''Jez Styles, just transferred in from Hackney.''

''Pleased to meet you, Jez. I don't know if the DI's told you, but the witnesses your lot are taking preliminary statements from—''

''One of them is probably more than a witness. Yeah, worked that out myself from the layout out back. I can tell you there's nothing in the statements thus far that's particularly startling.''

''The DI was rather hoping for a confession.''

PC Styles glanced over his shoulder in the direction of the murder scene. ''That's that Don Packham then, is it?''

''Yes,'' said Frank.

"Right... You work with him a lot, do you?"

"Yes," said Frank.

There was a short silence, during which Styles's face twitched slightly, as he tried, Frank reckoned, to find a form of words which would allow him to ask the question that was so obviously burning a hole in his throat: So, is your boss as nutty as they all say, then?

Frank offered no assistance, and eventually the PC said: "No, no confession, no accusation, everyone's story is basically the same. They were here celebrating a darts victory after hours, nobody noticed anyone else going outside. Which is fair enough, really—you don't exactly log people's trips to the bog, do you?"

"And nothing obvious to the naked eye, I gather."

"No; no bloodstains, no signs of struggle, no-one sweating more than they ought to be under the circumstances."

"Okay, thanks. I'll check with the DI, but if all the names and addresses check out we'll probably let them go as soon as your lot have finished." As Frank spoke, Don himself appeared at the edge of his field of vision, waving a mobile phone at him. Frank trotted over to see what he wanted. He needn't have trotted, he could have strolled, he was sure Don wouldn't have expected him to trot. But...well, somehow, since he'd become a father, mobile phones made him nervous. Not logical, of course, but there you go.

"News, sir?"

"Area," said Don, tucking the phone away in his overcoat pocket.

"Ah. So AMIP will be taking over tomorrow?"

Don grinned. "Not at all. On the contrary. Area are more than happy to leave it to us. For the time being, at any rate."

"Blimey!" said Frank. "That's a result. What's their reasoning?"

"Officially? Because we've identified a limited number of suspects right from the start, so the bosses reckon even lowly plodders like us can manage to elicit a confession from one of a dozen half-drunk darts players."

"And unofficially?"

"Well, Frank, you know as well as I do—the brass are all too busy re-investigating cases they screwed up the first time around to bother with actual, present-day killings in pub toilets." DI Packham rubbed his hands together, and danced a few jig steps on the sticky, faded carpet. "Okey-dokey. We'll call it a night, I think, seal the scene, and in the morning, after a decent breakfast, begin afresh and anew. And in the absence of anything useful from forensics, we shall have to do it the old-fashioned way."

Ah, thought Frank, I know what that means: we shall employ the Old Dialectic.

All in all, he decided, he was rather looking forward to tomorrow.

TWO

"So TELL ME, FRANK—you ever had a maximum finish?"

They were sitting in Frank's car, in the car park of the Hollow Head, mid-morning on the first full day of the investigation. The sky was grey, and pregnant with the threat of rain, but as far as Frank could see, Don was still on a high from the night before; leastways, he'd smoked two small cigars since getting into the motor.

Funny effect murder has on some people, Frank thought, before admitting to himself that he, too, felt buoyed by the prospect of getting his teeth into a decent case of homicide.

"I've never really been much of a darts player, to tell you the truth, Don." The DI got annoyed if Frank called him "Sir" when they were alone—at least, he did on his good days.

Now, Don was looking at him as if he'd just admitted that he didn't drink water, or that he'd never seen a bicycle; as if he were an alien from outer space. "You don't play darts? You don't play *darts?* My God, Frank, darts—that's the game of kings, that is! The noblest sport on earth. There is absolutely nothing half as worth doing as chucking arrows at a board—the most important part of a young man's education, darting is. They should include it in the national curriculum.''

''Well, I do watch it on telly. I enjoy it on the telly. Very exciting.''

''Is it? I've never bothered much with sport on TV. I'm not a great watcher, really—I prefer doing to watching.''

I'll bet, thought Frank. ''You manage to get any sleep last night, after we'd finished here?''

''No, didn't bother. Too late. Went off for breakfast at a market traders' café instead.''

''Ah,'' said Frank, who knew all about Don's breakfasts.

''Yes indeed—excellent stuff. Full-scale fry-up, followed by bread-and-butter pudding, all washed down with a pint of cider.''

''Lovely,'' said Frank, feeling slightly queasy. He'd had a cup of black tea and a bowl of muesli.

''Lovely it was. And very healthy—settles the stomach, keeps you going. Have I ever told you my theory of tiredness?''

''I'm not—''

''Sleep, Frank: that's the enemy. I'm convinced of it. Sleep is the main cause of tiredness. You think about it, you're never so knackered as when you've just woken up, are you? Right? So, logically, if you never go to sleep, you just keep going, you can work through the fatigue barrier and come out the other side, fresh as a daisy.''

''Right,'' said Frank, who was far too tired this morning to have the patience to discuss tiredness in the abstract. ''So, any more thoughts on what we're looking at here? We're definitely saying the killer is one of those known to be present in the pub last night?''

"Hope so. If we have to widen the net, then that's going to mean manpower—and manpower means Area. So let's go in there now, beat a confession out of the landlady, and then we can have the rest of the day off. Right?"

"OKAY, NOW WHEN AM I going to get my pub back? I've been told not to open up today, I've got crime scene tape all over the front door, I've got people in space suits cluttering up my courtyard, I've got a brewery delivery for this afternoon I've had to cancel— when am I going to get my pub back?"

Heather Mason, licensee of the Hollow Head, was a small, loud woman of around fifty, with what Don reckoned was a Glasgow accent, and what he was absolutely certain was dyed red hair. Her body was of more-or-less square shape, her head much the same, only smaller. Not a lot smaller, though. Her short, thick limbs poked out at the corners of her torso as if stuck there with hobby glue; her face was roughly the same colour as her hair.

"Not long, Ms. Mason, we're getting on as quickly as we can. The Ladies might be out of action for a wee bit longer, though."

"Okay, but what you don't realise is that 'not long' in your book could be 'out of business' in mine. You see what I'm saying?"

"Loud and clear. I assure you we're going as fast as we can. Now, we need to ask you a few questions about last night. Meanwhile, I wonder if we might trouble you for a cup of coffee? My colleague looks as if he could do with something to perk him up." Don winked at her, and spoke the next words as if imparting a confidence. "New baby in the house, you see."

Heather Mason didn't seem terribly impressed by or interested in DC Mitchell's domestic arrangements, but she did fetch three cups of instant without too much grumbling. "Okay, I hope you don't take sugar."

"Why? Have you run out?"

"No."

Right, thought Don. Interviewing you is going to be fun, evidently.

"I understand that it was you who found the body, Ms. Mason?"

The landlady nodded. "That was me."

"And can you tell us how that happened?"

"It *happened* because I went out to the lavvy and found her there. I don't know what else you want me to say."

"You'd gone out there for what reason?" asked Frank.

She snorted. "Okay, is that a stupid question or what?"

"You'd gone to use the lavatory?" said Don.

"I wasn't there to wash my hair, if that's any help."

If it was any help, you wouldn't have said it, thought Don. "And you were all in the pub at that time celebrating after a darts match. Is that right?"

"Correct."

"Big win, was it?"

"Big enough."

"Cup match?"

"League. Cup's over."

"Home match?"

"Away."

Don sipped at his watery coffee. This woman was beginning to annoy him. "This was a private party? You'd sent the bar staff home?"

There was a slight hesitation, Don noted, before she replied. "Right."

"There were thirteen people present at the time that Yvonne Wood's body was discovered. They were all team members, were they?"

"Okay, yeah, thirteen people in a darts team! That's likely, isn't it?"

The DI flicked a glance at Frank, meaning *You take over for a bit, before I say something the complaints department might live to regret.*

"How many are there in the team then, Ms. Mason?" Frank asked.

"Eight."

He waited, but no elaboration was forthcoming. "Eight. I see. And the other five?"

"Hangers-on of various varieties. Spouses and such like."

"You play for the team yourself, do you?"

The landlady sat up straighter on her stool. "Any reason why I shouldn't?"

Don was pleased to see that Frank didn't react to that, beyond a slight tightening of his jaw muscles. "And Yvonne? She was another team member?"

Mason laughed, producing a sound similar to an elderly car starting reluctantly on a cold, damp Monday morning. "Okay, you're joking! Couldn't have thrown a dart to save her life."

"She came into the category of hangers-on, then," said Frank.

"Oh, yes, I should say so. *Queen* of the hangers-on. They called her Chalkie. You want to know why?"

"Very much," Don assured her, delighted that the one topic which seemed to prompt this unfriendly woman to garrulousness was the one the detectives most wanted to hear about.

"Okay, because she chalked. You know? Scored the matches. Every single leg of every single match. Been doing it forever. Started off because she had a boy-friend in the team, years ago, so they tell me. I've only been here a few years, that Chalkie—she's been here since the place was built, I shouldn't wonder."

Don rewarded her with a smile; the pub building was quite obviously Victorian. "She was older than you, then?" he said, knowing full well that the deceased had been an attractive woman, cut short long before her half-century.

Sure enough, Mason scowled. "Your bobbies last night got all the details. Or does everything have to be done in duplicate?"

"Yes, I understand that. We're just trying at this stage to establish who might have had an opportunity to commit this terrible crime. Assuming it wasn't a passer-by, a stranger."

For the first time, the landlady's eyes brightened. "Okay, it wasn't. Wasn't a stranger, that's for sure. It was one of us. Must have been—here, let me show you."

She parachuted down from the barstool and led them across the room to the nearest of the two back doors set in the rear corners of the pub. She opened the door to reveal three SOCOs still working in the area around the Ladies, with tape measures, powder brushes and plastic bags.

"Better not go out there, Ms. Mason," said Don. "Can you show us what you mean from the door-way?"

"If you can't see it yourself, you're blind. You've

got a courtyard, right? On its right boundary a three-storey wall—the pub's private quarters. On the left, another three-storey wall; that's a bank, believe it or not.''

Don wasn't sure why he shouldn't believe it, so he did. "No windows in either wall," he said.

"Okay, and no windows or doors in the back wall, either. Just a ten-foot-high solid wall, topped with broken glass and barbed wire.''

Lovely, thought Don, most picturesque: they should rename this place The Colditz Arms. "Bet your insurance company loves you.''

"Lot of thieves around these days, Inspector. Lot of vandals. And let's face it, the police are about as useful as a darts player with no arms.''

Don tut-tutted. "Shouldn't knock disabled sportsmen, Ms. Mason. They bring a lot of glory to this country. Matter of fact, I used to play with an armless darter. Chucked 'em with his feet. Had the sixth highest average in the league, two years running.''

The DC gave him a look of frank alarm, while the Hollow Head's guv'nor stared at him as if she couldn't decide whether he was a lunatic or a piss-taker. Don quietly enjoyed both reactions, waiting out the ensuing silence.

"Okay, the point is," said Mason eventually, "the only access of any sort to this courtyard, and to the lavvies, is through the pub.''

"You don't use the courtyard for deliveries?'' Frank asked.

"What have I just said? No, we've a trapdoor to the cellar out on the pavement.'' She led them back to the bar. "It was one of us killed Chalkie, for certain.''

She didn't seem at all put out by this grisly conclusion, Don noted; rather the opposite, in fact. As she climbed back onto her bar stool, he said, "Can you imagine any of the darts crowd having a reason to kill your pal Chalkie?"

"My pal? Okay, that's a laugh. She was no-one's pal. It'd be harder to come up with someone who didn't have a reason to kill her."

"She wasn't very popular, is that what you're saying?"

"Well," Mason began, and then fell quiet for a moment. Don could see, as if it were written on her face, the internal battle he'd witnessed so often before in similar circumstances—between the natural desire to speak ill of the dead, who after all cannot answer back, and the equally natural desire not to give the cops anything other than your name, rank and serial number. "Well, I won't speak for the others. They'll tell you what they'll tell you. Personally, I had nothing against her."

Sounds like it. "Can you provide an alibi for any of the others, Ms. Mason?"

The question seemed to astonish her. "Why would I want to?"

"What I mean is, you were all here together in this room at the time the murder took place. All except Chalkie, obviously, and one other—the person who killed her." Don didn't want to complicate matters at this stage by going into the possibility of the delayed-action concrete booby trap. "Did you notice when Yvonne left the room—and did you notice anyone else leaving shortly after?"

"Okay, no, you can't possibly imagine I was keeping track of people's comings and goings? Keeping a record of every time someone nipped out to the lavvy?

Everyone'd had a few drinks, you understand. Folk were here and there all night.'' She became thoughtful for a while, then added: ''Though maybe one of the others will tell you different. God knows some of them are nosey enough bastards.''

''If you don't mind my saying so,'' said Don, heedless of whether she did mind or not, ''you don't seem to hold your team of champions in especially high regard.''

She slipped down off her perch, and took a couple of steps towards him. ''I'll tell you the truth, Inspector. I don't hold anyone or anything in high regard in this shit-hole of a city.''

''You're not that keen on London, Ms. Mason? Well, I expect you pine for Scotland. You are Scottish, originally?''

''Okay, that's a laugh! What's to pine for? Deep-fried Mars bars and punch-ups and endless whinging, no thank you. And don't call me Scottish, if you don't mind, in that tone of voice. I'm as British as you are. We've got the same Queen up north as you've got down here, get your facts right.''

Don had absolutely no idea what to make of that, or how to respond to it. Luckily, he wasn't called upon to respond, as the landlady continued her tirade for the next five minutes, detailing her contempt for the licensed trade generally, the Hollow Head in particular, her regular customers, her passing trade, her darts team, and the sport of darts itself. She finished by saying, ''I used to live in Sussex. Now that's a nice place, that is. I should never ought to have left it.''

Frank recovered first—perhaps he had an even better breakfast than I did, thought Don. ''Why,'' said the

DC, "do you play in the darts team, then—if you can't stand the game?"

She smiled. "Why do you think, son? To annoy the others, of course."

"You're not much good at the old arrows, then?" said Don.

"Less of that," she replied, the smile vanishing. "I'm as good as any of the others, and whoever tells you differently is talking through his backside."

"I'm sure you are," Don assured her. "You've got a darter's eye and a darter's arm, I can see that. What I don't understand," he added, casually, "is why you hosted a lock-in to celebrate a darts win, when you feel the way you do."

In fact, Don was pretty sure he did know why—and from the suddenly shifty look on the landlady's face, he saw that he was right.

"WHAT WAS all that about?" Frank asked, as they settled down to an early lunch at a nearby pub—one with an over-loud sound system, a limited choice of sandwiches, and expensive beer. But, crucially, one without Heather Mason behind the bar. "I mean, why *did* she stand them a lock-in if they all get on her nerves so much?"

"Simple," said Don, lighting a cigar. "It wasn't a lock-in. Not what you and I mean by a lock-in, anyway. Not what any decent pub guv'nor would mean, or what any victorious darts team would have every right to expect."

Frank pondered that as he chewed on his ham sandwich, which, in accordance with the modern fashion, was ninety-nine percent stale bread to one percent damp ham. "Ah," he said, as light dawned. He was unable to go any further, as his throat clogged with dry bread.

"Exactly! This wasn't an on-the-house booze-up amongst pals, with the landlord as one of the lads. Or lasses, in this case. This was illegal after-hours drinking. She was *charging* them for the drinks. The lovely Heather might not have much time for the pub life, but I don't suppose she's allergic to its profits."

Frank seemed to be remaining silent for longer than was necessitated by his choking fit alone, and Don wondered whether he was embarrassed at not having spotted the lock-in thing for himself. No need, if so: the lad seemed to be settling into CID well enough, from everything Don'd heard. Which wasn't much, admittedly—he tried to have as little as possible to do with his fellow detectives. At any rate, everyone seemed very pleased with Frank's work on that credit card fraud ring.

"That's only my theory, mind," he said. "We'll find out for sure when we talk to the others."

"I wonder how she keeps any customers at all. Being such a miserable old bag, I mean."

"Good point," said Don, nodding his head vigorously. He could do staff morale-boosting as well as the next supervisor. "Bloody good point, Frank, yes indeed—that's one to make note of. So, what have we learned about the victim, that we didn't have last night?"

"Nothing much. Other than that she wasn't very popular. Or rather, that the landlady says she wasn't very popular."

"Yes, we've only Mason's word for that, so far. *Och aye, no' that I've anything against the wee lass myself, the noo.*"

Frank laughed and nearly choked again. "Was that supposed to be Glasgow? It sounded like a Tynesider who'd been raised in Wales!"

"Yes, well, I do have other skills to fall back on if my career as an impressionist doesn't work out. Now—who shall we talk to next? What do we know about our suspects?"

Frank checked his notebook. "All we've got is names, addresses, workplaces and dates of birth. Nothing much to go on."

"Hmm. All right then, do we know the batting order?"

"Sorry?"

"The order they throw in, Frank. In the darts team."

"Well, no—I mean, how would we know that?"

Oh forget it, thought Don. You try to boost the boy's self-esteem, and all you get back is leaden-footed literalism. "Okay. I'll tell you what we'll do. Call Heather Mason on your mobile, and ask her who's the newest member of the team. We'll do him first. Could be enlightening, with any luck—speaking to someone whose loyalties are as yet unformed." Don rubbed at his temples with his fingertips. "And after that, I reckon we'll call it a day. I've got a bastard of a headache coming on."

Frank sighed, as he took his phone from his jacket pocket. "Right you are," he said. "Right you are, sir."

THREE

TO FRANK'S SURPRISE, Kevin Lewis lived in south
London. He'd assumed that the Hollow Head's dartists
would all come from the area around the pub, or at
least from somewhere in the borough of Cowden. Was
it worth mentioning this to Don? Probably not, he decided; the DI had been silent in the car. If he spoke to
him now he'd only get another lecture on his lamen-
table ignorance of the Noble Game.

Lewis's flat was in a smart block in what had obviously been, until recently, a rough area. You can
move in all the young professionals you like, thought
Frank, but the grit of centuries takes more than a year
or two to wash away.

"I'm a barrister," Lewis explained, as he showed
them down an unexpectedly long hall into a large,
open-plan living-room-cum-kitchen with views of the
city from three sides. "I don't work office hours. Besides, late night last night, as you know."

The off-duty barrister was wearing a red silk shirt,
and jeans that looked as if they cost a fortune—which,
to Frank's mind, negated the entire point of jeans. He
was in his late twenties, fairly short—a couple of
inches shorter than Frank—and stocky; a handsome
man, and very black. Of African descent, Frank reckoned, not Afro-Caribbean. He had the presence of a

professional man, his voice accentless—that is, accentless if that happens to be your accent. University but not posh, Frank thought, with approval.

"Transformer," said Don—his first words since they'd parked the car. His nose was in the air, as if he were a hound following a scent. Frank was glad to see him perk up, though he had no idea what the DI was talking about. "Lou Reed, 1972."

Lewis mimed a round of applause. "You've good ears, Inspector. Or a good memory."

Ah, thought Frank. The music coming from one of the other rooms. Don must have good ears—Frank hadn't even noticed the sound, let alone identified it.

"Well," Don said, "indisputably one of the five greatest LPs of all time, right?"

Kevin Lewis strolled into the kitchen area, where he began to fiddle with a flashy coffee machine. Or maybe not flashy, Frank corrected himself; just good quality. The decor of the place generally was more tasteful than boastful.

"Well, yes," said Lewis. "Indisputably one of the five finest. For *Walk on the Wild Side* alone."

"Or *Satellite of Love,*" said Don. "In fact, all around, probably the best album about male prostitution, heroin addiction and transvestism ever recorded."

Bloody hell! thought Frank. Rather have the old sod silent, letting me get on with business, instead of all this embarrassing nonsense. "Lou Reed? Wasn't he the one that did that *Perfect Day* thing for the BBC?"

Don and Lewis chuckled at this, but didn't otherwise reply, much to Frank's annoyance. "You'll have to excuse my colleague," said Don. "He's a parent, you understand." More chuckles.

"But what of the other four, Inspector?"

They sat on large, leather chairs around a small, glass table, sipping their coffee from delicate cups. Frank's sips were less frequent than those of the other two. He knew he was supposed to like this dark, scented stuff, but the truth was he'd been happier with Heather Mason's instant.

"Well," said Don, thoughtfully. "*Clash* by The Clash, obviously."

Lewis waved a dismissive hand. "Obviously. Hardly worth mentioning."

It's just not fitting, thought Frank. Barristers and Detective Inspectors discussing punk music. It's like seeing your dad lusting after the teenage dancers on *Top of the Pops.*

"After that though, it gets a bit more tricky," Don continued. "We shall have to discuss it at greater length some time. But for now, we're here to ask you whether—and if so, why—you killed Yvonne Wood?"

Lewis set his cup on the table, and took a moment to rearrange his features into suitable solemnity. "Ah yes, poor Chalkie. No, Inspector, I did not kill her. Indeed, I am perhaps the only member of the team who could not possibly have had a motive to do so."

"Why do you say that?"

"I only recently started drinking at the Head. I hardly knew the poor old girl."

"Not that old," said Don, as if he felt his rock'n'roll credentials were being questioned.

"No, no, of course—but, you know, a generation senior to myself."

"Tell us how you came to join the darts team. Did you fly in on a million-pound transfer fee from another pub?"

Lewis gave another of his easy, confident chuckles.

"No, it was all quite by chance, in fact. I just happened to be in the area early one evening a month or so ago— I'd been meeting with a colleague locally—and, finding myself in need of refreshment, I simply went into the first pub I came across. While I ate my sandwich and drank my light ale, I chatted idly with three people who were playing darts. When I'd finished eating, they asked whether I fancied a game of doubles."

"And you did?"

"I'd never really played darts, other than the odd game at university, you know, while the worse for drink—but I thought, yes, why not. Make up the foursome."

"So, all quite casual?" said Frank—who was then surprised to see Don giving him a discreet thumbs-up sign. Have I said something clever, then? He'd only spoken to remind them he was still there.

"Yes, Constable, as I say, quite by chance. Anyway, it seemed I had some small, latent talent for the game, or so my companions were kind enough to suggest, and at the end of the evening they asked me if I would like to join their team."

"They were a man short, were they?"

"I assumed so, at first. In fact, it turned out that one of the regular players had been suffering a run of poor form. They didn't tell me that at the time, or else— well, one doesn't like to go around stepping on people's toes."

"And the end of the story," Don suggested, "is that you discovered a great love for the sport, to match your natural talent."

Lewis shrugged. "Not especially. I don't mind darts, it's enjoyable enough. But the partners at my firm work me very hard, you understand, and I don't know a lot of people in London outside the office. So darts seems as good a way as any other of unwinding once a week. Having a couple of drinks, doing something relatively mindless—''

Oh, bugger my cat, thought Frank. Sure enough, Don's mouth was hanging open, and his eyes were popping. He looked like a ferret having a stroke.

''Mindless? Darts? You couldn't hope to find a more cerebral game, for God's sake! The mental arithmetic, the concentration, the becoming-one-with-the-dart... it's an entirely mental game. No-one who once played darts would ever willingly go back to chess.''

The barrister showed no embarrassment, Frank thought, probably because he was used to, in his working life, masking his reactions to the outbursts of police officers. ''My apologies, Inspector, mindless was the wrong word. I meant, rather, that the game of darts employs a different part of the brain to that which I use during working hours, and is thus a refreshing change.''

''They're a friendly crowd, are they?'' Frank asked. ''The matches make a good social occasion?''

''Yes, pretty much. I'm the new boy, of course, not really part of any of the cliques or factions.''

''Are there cliques and factions?''

Lewis nodded. ''Oh, certainly, I should say. Though I would hardly be the best person to ask about all that.''

''Being a newcomer, you mean?''

''Being a newcomer, Constable, exactly. To answer your original question, though—yes, it does make for a pleasant social evening, of an informal, non-intense kind. A chat about trivial subjects—not darts, Inspector, obviously; I mean politics, life, money, that sort of thing—a pint or two, throwing a few darts, a plate of sandwiches provided by the host pub, and then home. As I say, it takes one's mind off work.''

Don was still busy fuming, so Frank continued the questioning. ''I gather from what you said that you're not from around here? So where are you from, exactly?''

''Do you mean originally or lately?''

''Either, both,'' said Frank. ''I meant really, you're not a Londoner.''

''No, not really. But then, is anyone?'' Lewis grinned at Frank, and added: ''Why aye, mon!''

It took Frank a moment or two to realise that this was the barrister's idea of a Geordie accent—and not, as he had first supposed, a symptom of whooping cough. ''Very good impersonation, sir. You're almost as good as the inspector.''

Lewis laughed again, and Frank decided that the regular and easy manner in which the laugh was produced was not, after all, especially attractive. It was a professional laugh to go with the professional voice. ''Well, let's see. I was born in the Midlands, we lived in Wales for a while, and Liverpool, then Mum and I spent a couple of years in Ghana, which is where her father's family originated. Then home, to attend university at Edinburgh…and now London. No doubt I've missed out a few locations along the way, but you get the idea. Rather peripatetic.''

Army family? Frank wondered. Or diplomatic? He was about to ask, when Don jumped in, the singing in his ears evidently having abated sufficiently to allow him speech. ''You'll have gathered that the murderer has to have been one of the people present in your party last night, Mr. Lewis. So: any suggestions? Or is there, conversely, anyone you can alibi? Or, indeed, anyone you think can alibi you?''

"To the last two questions, Inspector, I regret the answer is no. I, of course, had no reason to visit the Ladies, nor did I especially notice anyone else doing so."

"You can't think of a motive for any of your fellow dartists?''

"I'm afraid not. As I say, I didn't know Chalkie very well, but she seemed pleasant enough.''

"And attractive?'' Don asked. "Sexually, I mean.''

Lewis shrugged. "I suppose so. I hadn't really noticed her in that way.'' The twist of distaste around his lips suggested otherwise, Frank reckoned; Mr. Barrister thought Yvonne was tarty. Old and tarty! He wondered about Kevin Lewis's own current romantic status, but again Don gave him no time to speak. *Make up your mind, sir! Are you depressed or manic today?*

"She seemed to get on with everyone okay, did she?'' Don asked.

"As far as one could tell, yes. She certainly did sterling work for the team, all that chalking. I'm sure everyone was suitably grateful.'' Lewis glanced at his watch, in a style which was simultaneously both discreet and obvious. Frank felt a stab of something that was almost envy: the poise of these professional types, but!

"Right,'' said Don, standing up. Frank wasn't sure if this was because Don genuinely felt the interview was at an end, or whether the DI was exhibiting a subliminal response to a gesture he hadn't consciously seen. Bloody Don! He had to cough, to avoid laughing out loud. See what working with you has done to my mind? He couldn't wait for home-time, to tell Debbie about The Case of the Subliminal Barrister. She'd love all that.

"Right," Don repeated. "We'll let you get back to springing villains from the clutches of the justice system, shall we?"

Lewis laughed. "In fact, Inspector, I work in corporate law."

"Ah," said Don, who was never knowingly outquipped. "Defending polluters and union-bashers, eh?"

Still chuckling—though just beginning, Frank thought, to sound as if his air tanks were running low—the barrister ushered them along the hall, and out of the door. They said their goodbyes, and began to walk in the direction of the stairs. ("I don't have anything to do with lifts," Don had told Frank once. "And neither should you, now you're a father." Frank hadn't asked why, and Don hadn't volunteered any explanation.)

They'd only gone a pace or two down the corridor, when Don turned on one heel like an unusually masculine ice-skater, and knocked heavily on Lewis's door.

The door opened, though not very far, and a thoroughly surprised—perhaps even slightly alarmed—face appeared in the crack between door and jamb.

"Yes?"

"Never mind the bollocks," said Don.

The crack between door and jamb seemed to shrink still further. "I—I beg your pardon, Inspector?"

"One of the five top LPs of all time," said Don. "*Never Mind the Bollocks.* Top five on anyone's list, surely."

Light dawned, and the door opened wide. The frightened suspect vanished, and the poised barrister reappeared. "Ah—yes! Of course, the dear old Sex Pistols. Well, yes, absolutely, Inspector. One could hardly argue with that selection." There followed a short period of silence, during which the two men nodded at each other, while Frank stood a few yards away, trying not to shake his head like an exasperated teacher.

"Um…" said Lewis eventually.

Don smiled. "Yes?"

"Well, nothing, I just wondered—is there, ah, anything else at all? Only, I really ought to be, you know…"

"Anything else?" Don repeated, and scratched his nose. "Well, tell you what, Mr. Lewis, if there is— we'll let you know."

As the door to the barrister's flat closed behind them again, Frank noticed that Kevin Lewis had not bothered to turn his music back on.

BY THE TIME they'd reached the car, Don's headache had come back with interest earned, and he felt tired. Maybe he should have got some sleep last night, after all. He wasn't as young as he had once been, that was for sure. Or more than once, even… Never mind the bollocks, eh?

Frank was talking. Don rubbed at his brow, and wondered whether he should stop off at a chemist's and get some headache pills. No; pills never did any good, they were just a con. Just another invention of the advertising industry, like cholesterol and 1990s pop music.

"Sorry, Frank, what did you say?"

"I was just wondering what you made of Mr. Lewis?"

"To be brutal, Frank, I'm not at all sure I approve

of playing that kind of music on CD. You lose the tone, the spirit. It irons out the bumps too much.''

Frank looked at him, sideways. God, Don hated it when people did that!

''Well, no, I really meant what did you think of him as a suspect?''

''I don't know, really. He's a bit of a mystery man, isn't he?''

Frank nodded. ''He certainly didn't seem all that keen to give too much away about his background. I mean, sure, he told us where he'd lived and that, but when you analyse it, there wasn't much there.''

''True. And as for that story about how he came to be on the darts team…''

''Doesn't entirely ring true, does it?''

''Young Kevin doesn't seem all that interested in darts, does he, for a man who spends one whole evening a week playing it?''

''So what do you reckon he's up to?''

''I don't reckon anything particularly,'' said Don, whose head hurt far too much for bloody reckoning right now, thank you very much indeed. ''I'm just wondering a bit—if he's not there for the darts, what is he there for?''

FOUR

"APPARENTLY THERE WAS some mix-up over the keys. Her landlord was abroad and unavailable," Frank explained, but Don wasn't really listening. Visiting a murder victim's home—in those rare cases where the killing had taken place somewhere other than the home—was a duty he always felt ambivalent about. Postponing it by a day or so hadn't upset him especially.

On the one hand, no human yet born could honestly deny the unique thrill of poking around at will in another person's most private world, protected from guilt for such ruthless voyeurism by societal sanction and, indeed, various Acts of Parliament. In purely investigative terms, too, Don had often found such visits quite significant: if the motive for a violent crime was not immediately apparent (as it almost always was), then clues to its perpetrator sometimes lurked amid the visible remains of its victim's life.

On the other hand...well, even when the death had occurred miles away, the dead person's home still smelled of dying. Or so Don found, at any rate.

"Never mind," he told the DC. "We're here now."

Yvonne "Chalkie" Wood had lived—for some years, apparently—in a first-floor flat above an independent jeweller's, which was part of a small rank of shops about ten minutes' walk from the Hollow Head. Further into the city itself, a ten-minute walk would take you past any number of pubs, of course; but in a suburb like Cowden, Don supposed, it wasn't an unreasonable distance to trot for a game of arrows and a spot of throat-rinsing. He wondered vaguely whether suburban pub-goers were therefore fitter than their inner London cousins.

The key, which Frank took from a brown Metropolitan Police envelope, turned smoothly in Chalkie's door, and both men released a tiny breath of relief. It was embarrassing as well as frustrating—though not all that rare—to be unable to gain entry to a premises due to having been issued with the wrong key. Or—also not all that rare—the wrong bloody address. Or both.

"Nice place," said Frank, as they stepped over the "Welcome" mat into the short, cheerfully painted and carpeted hallway.

Don smiled, pleased once more to have it confirmed that he hadn't been mistaken: this boy did have a nose, even if he did his best to keep it to himself. The point about noses—copper's noses—in Don's experience, was that the truly good ones didn't just sniff badness or trouble or lies. What use would a cheese-taster's tongue be, if it could only taste rancidity? What pleased Don so much about young Frank Mitchell was that the boy knew niceness when he sniffed it, and wasn't ashamed to say so.

The actual perfume in that hall was potpourri, emanating from a small wooden bowl next to the telephone table. But above and beyond that, Don detected the scent of a life, which told him that this person did not deserve to be murdered.

He wasn't going to mention that to Frank, though;

he knew his DC's limits. Frank's response to such a comment would be something like ''Nobody deserves to be murdered''—which was more or less undeniable, but entirely beside the point.

So instead, Don said: ''Does look cosy, on first impressions, doesn't it? Well cared-for, lived-in. Not flash, not shabby. Occupied by someone who cared about material things, but wasn't ruled by them.'' He stopped as, out of the corner of his eyes, he saw Frank trying to suppress a smirk. ''Yes, all right, Constable— perhaps we should venture beyond the hall. Never know, might be a sadomasochist's dungeon in the kitchen.''

And so, leaving philosophy behind on the doormat, they began their penetration of this former home in earnest. At first, they proceeded in that manner peculiar to people—even police people—who find themselves in an empty house for purposes which, whilst not nefarious, could hardly be described as respectable. Like astronauts, or deep-sea divers, their movements were exaggeratedly deliberate; their silence was uncommonly profound. To an onlooker, they would have appeared to be more intent on avoiding discoveries than on making them. But after a while, in such situations, confidence grows or else discretion retreats, and the interlopers begin to feel…well, almost at home.

It was a small, compact flat, clearly designed for a single person. There was a comfortable, relatively spacious living-room, a small bathroom, a kitchen big enough for its purposes, and a bedroom in which— unlike some of the places Don himself had rented over the years—it was possible to open the wardrobe door without moving the bed.

''Cuddly toys,'' said Don, pointing at the dozen or

so woollen and fabric rabbits, bears and piglets arranged on the covers of Chalkie's neatly made bed.
"So, I wonder if her married lover was one of our
suspects?"

To Don's irritation, Frank treated him to a blank
look of paradoxical eloquence. "How do we know she
had a married lover?"

"Cuddly toys," Don said again. "On the bed."

Frank looked at the cuddly toys, then at the not so
cuddly DI. "No, sorry—I don't see the connection."

"For heaven's sake, Frank! Don't they do adultery
on Tyneside? Look, it's a well-known fact—well-
known to women, that is—that men never grow up.
Yes? Well, what they don't mention, is that neither do
women. In particular, there is a type of woman who
never recovers from losing the unconditional love of
her daddy. And that—"

"Why did she lose it?" Frank interrupted.

"Lose what?"

"The unconditional love of her daddy."

"Puberty!" Don snapped. "This is very elementary
stuff, Frank, honestly. This is hardly university-level
psychology. When a girl who is her father's pride and
joy starts taking an interest in boys, or just having boys
take an interest in her, her father can't help but with-
draw from her a bit. His love for her becomes more
circumspect, less psychical. Why do you suppose we
say that fathers 'give their daughters away' at weddings?"

"Okay," said Frank, his brow home to one or two
deep creases which Don found rather annoying. "So
where do the cuddly toys come into it?"

Don, his impatience growing by the second, began
to answer that—complete with references to Frank's

slowness—when he suddenly had to stop, having realised that he didn't know the answer. "They just do,
Frank, all right? Just take my word for it. It's a matter
of experience—whenever you encounter a woman over
the age of twenty-three who still has cuddly toys un-
ashamedly displayed on top of her duvet, you may rest
assured that you are in the presence of a woman whose
sexual and romantic interests are directed solely towards married men. Eligible bachelors hold no appeal
for her, even though they look like Mel Gibson, only
taller and richer. Got it?"

"Yes sir, thank you. I'll bear it in mind."

Oh, shit—now I've offended him! He only calls me
Sir when he's sulking. "Right, come on, then. Let's
have a proper look in the living-room."

"What exactly are we looking for, sir?"

Don sighed. "Come on, Frank, don't be daft."

"Sorry, sir."

Another sigh; bigger this time. "We're looking for
anything which tells us what sort of person she was,
what sort of life she led. And at the same time, obviously, we're looking for anything that links her specifically to anyone at the pub."

They searched quietly, and thoroughly, for almost an
hour, but they uncovered nothing startling—or even,
Don thought, mildly titillating. The living-room consisted of a gas fire with a jolly, mock-log surround, a
large but not very new TV, a VCR, a deep, comfortable
sofa and two non-matching armchairs, a couple of
knee-high tables. The bookshelves held mostly large
fantasy trilogies, and the video rack was stocked with
a mixture of thrillers, romantic comedies and Hollywood classics. Don noticed there were no LPs anywhere, and therefore didn't bother even glancing at the

titles on the CD stack: anyone of Yvonne Wood's generation who didn't own any vinyl at all clearly had no real interest in music. CDs, to her, would just be used to provide background music when her borrowed husband came around for the night—or the afternoon, more likely. Torch songs with the pain taken out, country music with the edges smoothed, bland ballads sung by women who didn't smoke.

The small, self-assembly drinks cabinet contained what seemed to Don to be a normal array of bottles. The medicine cabinet in the bathroom held contraceptives, aspirins, and mouthwash. In the kitchen, unsurprisingly, they found food and the implements with which it might be prepared and consumed. Other than the cuddly toys, there was little of a revelatory nature in the bedroom; no love letters, no intimate diary.

Frank did find three photo albums, on a shelf above the bed, two of which were full of family snaps—weddings, birthdays, childhood holidays. The third looked more promising.

"This one seems to be dedicated to the Hollow Head," he told Don, handing him the album. "Look— darts team photos going back a while."

As Don flicked backwards through the album, he saw a few faces he recognised from the current team in the more recent pictures. By the time he'd reached the beginning of the book, however, only Chalkie herself—much younger, but painfully recognisable even so as the corpse he'd seen in the Ladies—was familiar. The first photo was captioned "Hollow Head Darts Team 1979" on a hand-written label stuck beneath it.

"Look at that," said Don. "The fashions are so out of date they're starting to come back in again." Frank, who had never worn sideburns nor a purple shirt, and never expected to do so, said nothing. "She was a good-looker, all right."

In the 1979 picture, Chalkie stood at the centre of a group posed in front of the dartboard, all men except for her, all white except for one very dark, rather handsome black man standing to her left, and all apparently in their thirties or forties, other than Chalkie herself and an older, grey-haired man standing towards the back of the group. In later photos, the average age of the team seemed to drop by a few years—unless that was just an illusion caused by changing fashions—and one or two more women began to appear.

"Wonder which one was her boyfriend? No way of telling from the body language."

"There wouldn't be, maybe," said Frank, "if he was married. They'd take care not to show it."

"True. Well, we'll take the photo albums with us, anyway. They might come in handy. But other than that, I don't think there's a great deal here for us." Don look around him at the comfortable little flat, and thought that there wasn't a great deal here for anyone anymore, not until it was cleared and re-let. And yet, until not many hours ago, it had been someone's home. By ending the existence of its tenant, the murderer had ended the existence of the home, too. Anyone who believes in an afterlife should come and have a look at what coppers see—what remains, after life. That'd soon cure them. "How about you, Frank? Seen anything else that tickles your fancy?"

"Well, there was one thing. Sort of."

"Spit it out."

"If your theory about her and married men is correct, well—I don't think there was anyone steady in her life. I mean, not judging from this place, anyway.

There's no His and Hers feel about this flat, is there? Which you'd maybe expect, if—''

"If she'd been performing the time-honoured role of the ever-faithful mistress—you're right, Frank, good spot." Don ran a knuckle back and forth across his upper lip, and mentally replayed their search of the kitchen, the bathroom, the bedroom. "No, this wasn't a love-nest, was it? It was the home of a single woman. No extra toothbrush, no male clothes or toiletries, no out-of-character books by the bedside. So, her affairs—''

"If she was having affairs," said Frank, with what sounded to Don very much like stubbornness.

"Oh, she was, Frank—the cuddly toys cannot lie. No, what this means is that she wasn't a married man's mistress; she was a serial thriller." He paused to allow time for Frank's appreciation of his pun. When this was not forthcoming, he continued, "She slept with married men on her own terms. Without illusions, even, if that's ever possible."

"One-night stands?" said Frank, and Don had to laugh at the DC's unhidden disgust.

"Not necessarily. But brief affairs, I would guess, not intended—on either side—to lead to anything more permanent."

"Seems a sad way to live."

"Perhaps. But not uncommon. She worked in a betting shop?"

"That's right. Bo's Bets."

"As good a place as any to meet married men, I suppose."

"Not much help to us if she did," Frank pointed out. "If her sex life is a motive in her murder, then she has to have been sleeping with someone in the darts team, doesn't she?''

"I don't doubt she was. More than one, quite possibly. That's what got her interested in darts in the first place, remember, from what Heather Mason told us." Don tapped his left foot on the carpet for a while, then shifted position and tapped his right foot for a while longer. "There's nothing here that points at any of the Hollow Head men?"

Frank shrugged. "If there is, I haven't seen it. Nobody in the darts photos seems singled out at all."

"No violently inked-out faces, or rows of kisses, you mean? No, there's nothing like that. We'll have a closer look at them all the same, you never know. Meanwhile, where's her address book? It wasn't amongst her effects, was it?"

"Debbie keeps ours by the telephone," Frank said, and went off to look. He was back a moment later, waving his trophy. "Aye, here we are."

"Well done, Frank. From thesis to synthesis in one easy move—first-rate detecting." Frank's face fell, as if he suspected he was having the urine extracted from him. "No seriously, mate, nice one. That's what detective work is all about. Stating the obvious and then acting on it. Let's have a look."

It would be too much to hope, Don realised, that the padded notebook, embossed with the golden words "Telephone numbers," would carry an entry under M for Married Men, or B for Bits of Trouser, but he hoped nonetheless. Of course, he'd been right the first time— it *was* too much to hope.

"Got that list of suspects' names, Frank? Ta. Right, let's see which of the men is in here."

To his further disappointment, he discovered that all

of the suspects—men and women—had entries in Chalkie's little red book.

"No addresses for most of them," Frank said, reading over Don's shoulder. "Just home phone numbers."

"Perhaps Chalkie was in charge of ringing around if there was a glitch in the arrangements for a match. Change of venue, cancellation, whatever. She wouldn't have needed addresses, anyway, she saw them all at the pub at least once a week."

"Just a thought," said Frank, "but is there one entry where she's got more details than the rest? Like, if one of them was her lover, then maybe she couldn't have rung him at home, so—"

"Good thinking, Frank, very devious—we'll make a bastard out of you yet!" Frank's lack of response to this piece of casual badinage, beyond a slight stiffening of his aura, was so concrete that Don reckoned he'd be lucky not to stub his toe on it. For God's sake, if you can't take a joke... He felt his headache coming back. Or had it ever gone away? He couldn't remember, which probably meant it hadn't. Frowning slightly with eyestrain, he went through the book once more. "No, no such luck. A lot of them have got work as well as home numbers—some have faxes, most have mobiles." He handed the book back to Frank.

"Except your friend the barrister," said Frank, turning to the Ls. "Kevin Lewis has only got a mobile number listed."

"I don't suppose he wanted calls about a pub darts team coming through the office switchboard," Don said, rubbing at his brow, trying to get at the pain beneath the skin. "And at home, he quite possibly has only got a mobile."

Frank was maddeningly reluctant to let his pet theory

be put to sleep. "And under Luke Rees's name, she's crossed out the home number and put a question mark in its place. Four question marks, in fact."

"There are two Reeses, aren't there?"

"Yes, two brothers." Frank checked his witness list. "They live together and work together, according to the details. And, same phone numbers in both cases. Same fax, too, but different mobiles, obviously."

"They're not actually Siamese twins, then? Thank Christ for that. Look, Frank, she obviously wasn't sure whether they still shared a home number or not—I mean, they share an address, but they're grown men, they might have converted it into separate flats or whatever. She put a question mark next to one of these guys, knowing she could get in touch with him if needed through his brother, then she never got around to checking with him. It doesn't matter anyway, because if they're not married they don't come into the present debate, do they?"

"Yes, sir," said Frank, putting the book in his pocket.

Right, thought Don. If he's going to start with his *Sirs,* it's time to call it a shift. With my head splitting open like this, one thing I cannot put up with is moody DCs.

"We've done all we can here, Frank. You go on home and change your babby's nappy. We're owed a bit of sleep for our disturbed night."

"And what are you going to do, sir?"

"What do you think I'm going to do, Frank? I'm going to go and do some road-training for the bleeding London Marathon!"

Frank bounced Yvonne Wood's keys in his hand once, and then said: "Right, sir. Hope the rain holds off for you."

FIVE

THE FOLLOWING MORNING, Frank was making break-fast—not that it took much making; this had been a toast-and-cereal household even before Joseph's arrival—while Debbie fed the baby. Both parents had been awake all night, or as near all night as made any difference, for the usual progeny-related reasons. An uncle of Frank's, a man not much given to joyful optimism even by the standards of the Mitchell tribe, had warned them of this, while offering his commiserations on the safe delivery of their firstborn. "The only time they don't demand attention at one end," he'd ruled, "is when they're demanding attention at the other end. There again," he'd added, after a moment devoted solely to the hum of the long-distance phone line, "that's not always true. Sometimes the little sods demand it at both ends simultaneously."

"Poor Daddy," Debbie told her son. "He's got to go to work soon, and he hasn't even been to bed yet. Now, whose fault do you suppose that is?"

Phurrrrrrrrrrt, Joseph replied, without moving his lips.

In fact, Frank was feeling surprisingly fresh. "I reckon I'm getting used to it. Perhaps Don Packham's right—don't go to sleep, and you won't get tired."

"Is that why Daddy's just poured boiling water onto the muesli, do you suppose?"

"Oh, shhhhugar!" Frank opened the kitchen door and flung the soggy cereal onto the back lawn. Something would eat it, surely? A bird or a squirrel. Or a rat… Ah well, if it was still there tomorrow, he'd scrape it up and stick it in the bin.

Debbie was laughing, causing Joseph to jiggle around like a jockey on a three-legged mule riding over uneven terrain, and Frank knew what she was laughing at, too. He didn't care, though: Frank Mitchell was not going to swear in front of his baby and that was that, no matter who laughed at him. Why, man, you don't know what they take in at that age, do you?

He didn't bother putting this to Debbie, because he'd already heard her reply. "Swearing's still swearing," she argued, "whether you say sugar or shit. It's not the words that makes it swearing, it's the way you say them." All the same, Frank reasoned, no kid ever got kicked out of school for saying "Sugar" to his English teacher.

Breakfast for three was prepared and consumed without further distractions. As he swallowed the last of his tea, Frank looked at his watch, glanced at the phone extension on the kitchen wall, and looked at his watch again.

"When do you think he'll ring?" said Debbie.

"I'm not a hundred percent sure he will," Frank replied, looking at his watch again, but without taking in what it told him. "He's been—well, up and down the last couple of days, but I definitely got the impression he was going down properly yesterday afternoon. He kept rubbing his head, like he had a headache."

"Perhaps he did have a headache."

Possible, thought Frank. Perhaps he was looking for symptoms of his boss's depression where none existed.

By nine o'clock, the DI still hadn't rung, and Frank began to assess his options. What he ought to do, of course, was report to his CID skipper for assignment, but if he could avoid that, he would. His association with Don Packham hadn't made him, as he had at one time feared, into a departmental pariah. Hell, he'd gone to great lengths to ensure that it wouldn't—assiduously cultivating fraternal relations with colleagues, always making sure he took on his proper ration of dull or unpleasant jobs.

Nonetheless, the unpopular, misunderstood, distrusted DI's spectre haunted all of Frank's other relationships within the office. How could it not? Snideness and wise-arsedness are the coin and the lingua franca of detective life the world over—and the moody, detached, unpredictable Don made a better focus for such attention than anyone Frank had ever met. Some of this rubbed off, inevitably, on the young man who was so obviously Packham's favourite constable.

All said, though—for all his faults, life with Don was not dull. Especially when they were investigating a murder.

By ten past nine, Frank'd made his decision. "I'll phone him," he announced. Debbie smiled and kissed Frank on the back of his head. "Yeah, I know," he said. "You're always saying I should do that. Well, you're right." Of course you're right, he thought. But that doesn't make it an easy thing to do.

Don took ages to answer, and Frank found that he was chewing his lower lip, while listening to the endless rings. That annoyed him: he'd never been a lip-chewing sort of bloke. Not until he'd met Don Packham, at any—

"Yeah?"

"It's Frank here." Not *It's Frank here, Don* or *It's Frank here, sir*—not until he knew which Don he was dealing with today. Although, from Don's initial monosyllable, there didn't seem an awful lot of doubt about that. "I was just wondering where you wanted me this morning."

A pause, and then: "What sort of music do you listen to, Frank?"

"Music? Well...all sorts, I suppose."

"All sorts, for God's sake! That's what people who don't listen to anything say. People who don't like food always say 'I'll eat anything, me,' and they think it's a good thing, they say it proudly. All it actually means is they've got no taste."

Frank realised he was chewing his lip again, and that decided him—perhaps it was the lost sleep, after all, but whatever it was, suddenly he wasn't in a pussy-footing sort of mood. "Well, I'll tell you what, Don. You come round here for a meal one night—" *like civilised people do* "—and you can have a good root through my record collection, and then after dinner you can tell me what it says about me. All right?"

There was a long pause this time, long even for Don, and then the DI said just one word: "When?"

"Whenever you like, you just give us a shout." Even as the words set off on their irrevocable journey along the wires, Frank realised that he'd bottled out. Damn! He should have named a date, but he'd been caught off balance by Don's response. The dinner would never happen now; on the new middle-class estate where he and Debbie now lived, he'd learned that

"You really must come around some time" meant "We'll say it instead of doing it, okay?"

In that same instant, it occurred to him that Don's "When?" had been spoken in a voice which could only be described as...shy.

To cover his embarrassment—and because he had always had, even as a child, the knack of banishing from the front of his mind things he didn't want to think about—Frank said: "Meanwhile, I thought maybe we should speak to the captain of the darts team. This guy Brian Gough. If you agree."

"Yes, right," said Don. "Meet you there." And he hung up.

"Well," said Debbie, sympathetically, "you're certainly learning plenty of useful management skills. You could become a personnel officer when you retire from the service."

"I'll be a basket case long before then," said Frank.

The baby belched.

SITTING WAITING in his car—*Why are people with babies always bloody late? Because they choose to be, that's why*—Don took out a cigar, put it in his mouth, then removed it unlit and replaced it in its tin. Come on, Frank! Where the hell are you?

A rap on the near-side window made him jump so violently his right foot almost went through the dashboard.

"Christ alive, man!" he yelled, opening the door. "You half killed me—I didn't hear you creeping up."

"Sorry, sir," said Frank. "I'll try to make more noise next time."

Sir, is it? So Frank was in one of his moods again.

"I suppose he's likely to be at work, isn't he? The skipper."

"I took the precaution of ringing him at work," said Frank. "He said he'd come home for the interview—wouldn't be convenient to do it at the office, he said."

"What is it he does? Do we know?"

"Retail management, apparently. Stock manager for a small bathroom fittings chain."

"How small?"

"Three stores, all in Herts."

"I got the impression the other night he was from Yorkshire."

"I don't know," said Frank. "I didn't hear him speak."

"Oh, you don't need to hear the accent," said Don, shaking his head. "You can always tell a Yorkshireman." He got out of the car and stretched. "But you can't tell him much."

The Goughs lived in a good-sized, three-bedroom, ground-floor flat in a tree-lined residential road of mixed properties—purpose-built blocks, conversions, semis and a few detached houses. The door was answered by Tess Gough, Brian's wife, a pretty if rather harassed-looking woman in her mid-thirties, with Indian colouring and a Scottish accent. She explained that she wasn't working today because of a training day at school.

"You're a teacher?" Don asked.

"A teacher's aide."

"That sounds interesting."

"Well, it is! I work at a junior school in south London, helping with the children who don't speak English."

"Are there many of those?" asked Frank.

"Enough to keep me busy! We have children from every continent on earth, and just about every country. Refugees, immigrants, people whose parents are working here, what-have-you. Between them, they speak more than fifty languages, and three times that number of dialects."

"Blimey," said Don, genuinely impressed. It sounded a lot more interesting than his old village school, where they'd had two dialects—local and incomer.

"Indeed, Inspector. Not many know that a third of all children starting school in London in any year don't speak English as their first language."

"And do you have any children of your own?"

"We don't," said Mrs. Gough, and the way she said it made it clear that this particular avenue of conversation was at an end.

Her husband arrived while she was pouring them all a second cup of tea. He looked flustered at the sight of two police-men sitting chatting with his wife, drinking tea and eating biscuits. Typical Yorkie, thought Don; doesn't think womenfolk should talk to strangers unaccompanied, in case they say anything…well, anything *womanish*.

"They don't mind you taking the time off, your employers?" Don asked him.

"They can hardly complain, can they? Murder inquiry. I told them, I said, one of my people has been killed unlawfully, it's up to me to assist the police in whatever way possible."

"Right," said Don, reckoning he'd got this one pegged, met this sort before. Early forties, junior management—very junior management—always getting himself elected captain or secretary of every organisation he joined, every committee he ever sat on, from school onwards. Rather officious, not naturally humorous. The perennial prefect.

"Now, Brian, my colleague here doesn't know very much about darts—he's only young, of course, and he's got a new babby to worry about—so why don't you talk him through it? What does it actually entail, being the skipper of a trophy-winning darts team?"

Gough shoved a biscuit into his mouth and swallowed it. He was a big fellow, in what Don reckoned a typically Yorkshire way: a pale-skinned, sandy-haired mixture of dough and muscle. "Well, what *doesn't* it entail, more like. It's more workload than one man can rightly carry, to be fair."

"But you do carry it?"

"Well, it's a case of got to, isn't it? Someone has to do it. None of the others could manage it, that's for sure."

"I imagine Chalkie must have been a great help to you, though."

Gough looked puzzled. "Yvonne? In what sense?"

Don noticed that he called her Yvonne, not Chalkie; he also noticed that at this point, whether coincidentally or not, Tess Gough rose from her chair, and left the room without a word. *Don't blame her. He hasn't addressed a word to her since he came in, bloody caveman!*

"She's got to get ready for work," Gough explained, a slight flush rising in his cheeks.

"Of course," said Don. "No problem. About Yvonne Wood. I understand she did all the chalking for you at every match, home and away?"

"Yes, that's correct." The flush had faded, and he

seemed altogether more relaxed now that it was just the three of them—the three men.

"In my experience of darts teams," Don said, "which I might say without immodesty is considerable and extensive, one of the hardest parts of a skipper's job is dragooning folk into taking their turn at chalks. Everyone's happy to play, but chalking—no-one wants to do that, do they?"

"That's true, I can't deny that."

"So Yvonne was a very valuable member of the squad, I should think."

"She did her bit, I suppose, yes. But look, the real work takes place away from the oche. Fixture lists, team selection, arranging transport to and from away games. Meetings of the captains' committee, duplicating and circulating results sheets. Arbitrating disputes—I don't often get a night off with my feet up in front of the telly, I can tell you that!"

"Sure, sure, I can see all that. But," Don persisted, "you'll certainly miss Chalkie—that is, Yvonne."

"I suppose I—well, yes, obviously." Gough seemed suddenly to remember the purpose of the interview, and what nature of event had prompted it. "Yes, indeed, very sad, very bad business. A *very* bad business."

Which was one way of describing the bludgeoning to death of a friend, Don supposed. "Tell me about her. What sort of person was she?"

"Very pleasant. A popular and respected member of the team," said Gough, and to Don it sounded as if the man was reading from a job reference.

"Very keen on darts, I suppose?"

"She didn't actually play herself. I mean, not even in the pub, in casual games. You know, she just liked chalking. Seemed to enjoy that, certainly."

"It was more the social side that attracted her, perhaps?"

Gough gave that more thought than, in Don's opinion, it merited at face value. "I suppose that's right, yes."

"What about her private life, Brian? We believe she lived alone—have you ever been to her place, incidentally?"

"I... Yes, yes. Yes, in fact I have, as it happens. We all went back there once a few months ago, after a match. For a nightcap, you know."

So—if that's true, any suspects' fingerprints found there will be meaningless. Bugger! "And did she have a boyfriend?"

"I wouldn't know. No way that I would know that, I didn't know her that well."

"Well, come on Brian, you must have noticed whether she ever had anyone with her, at matches and so on, or just drinking in the pub."

"I don't go to the pub much except for when there's a match. You know how it is." He tilted his eyes in the direction of the living-room door through which his wife had departed.

"Okay, but you never saw her with anyone at the darts, in any case?"

"No, I did not. I got the impression she preferred her own company, sort of thing."

Ask him who he thought might have killed her? No, Don decided, better for the moment to let him think we already know. He turned to Frank, who had been busy writing in his notebook. "You have anything else for Mr. Gough, Constable?"

Frank shook his head. "No, sir, not at the present

moment. No doubt we'll wish to see Mr. Gough again in due course.''

"Oh—right, of course. Certainly, any time, I am always available to the police."

In your capacity as Minister of State for Darts at the Department of Hollow Heads, thought Don. You pompous prat.

They rose, and walked through to the front door. Mrs. Gough appeared, on cue, to show them out. "Anyway, Brian, it's a pretty good outfit you've got there, I gather. Win more than you lose, right?"

"Why don't you see for yourself, Inspector? As it happens there's a friendly match at the Head tonight."

"And it'll go ahead will it?" said Frank, not bothering to disguise his amazement.

For a moment, Gough obviously had no idea what he was talking about. Then light dawned, and he made a fair effort of looking sombre. "Well, you know—it's what she would have wanted."

"Well," said Don. "We might just take you up on that. It'll be an education for my young colleague, if nothing else."

In the open doorway, Don asked: "And did she do anything else for you?"

"What? Who?"

"Chalkie. That is, Yvonne. Apart from scoring, did she assist in any other ways?"

"No, not really," said Gough, but Don hardly heard him. His attention was fixed on Tess Gough, who had evidently forgotten her manners, as she retreated to the kitchen, and slammed the door behind her.

SIX

FRANK HAD NEVER BEEN to a darts match before, not deliberately at any rate, so he wasn't sure what time it would start. He could ring the pub, of course, or the team captain, and ask—but he didn't fancy that. Even less did he fancy ringing DI Packham at home and asking him. So instead he sat at his desk in a CID room from which all but the night crew had already departed, and he ate a tuna salad sandwich, sold in a plastic container which weighed more than the sandwich, and tried to figure it out.

Most people would have their evening meal more or less as soon as they got home from work, he guessed. He and Debbie didn't fit that pattern: for one thing, they'd both been in jobs which involved shifts and unpredictable hours, but in any case, they liked to sit on their big sofa and talk for a while before their mouths filled with food. Things they might buy for the house during their next out-of-town shopping experience— that was a favourite topic of conversation for two people whose working lives revolved around hate, loss and boredom. Nowadays, of course, they just talked about (and frequently to) the baby.

But okay, people come home from work hungry, they want to get the meal out of the way before the kids are off out for the evening, or whatever. So say that's some time around five-thirty to six—or for those who commute a fair distance, say seven to seven-thirty. In which case, if you were organising a darts match, you'd reckon to kick off at…eight? Eight-thirty?

Frank got to the Hollow Head at half-seven, just to be on the safe side—and because, though he wasn't a great pub-man, even he would rather be in a pub than a CID office at seven o'clock on a winter's night.

He didn't fancy the bitter. He wasn't an overly nostalgic person, Frank Mitchell, nor a big drinker, but he did miss the rugged beers of his birthplace. Even when you could get them in London, they didn't taste the same; they lacked the metallic tang of heavy industry. There again, these days so did Tyneside.

"Pint of Guinness, please."

Heather Mason served him, and gave no sign that she had ever met him before in her life. Fair enough; that was not an unusual manner for a copper to be greeted, especially in a boozer.

The pub was filling up already. No sign of Don yet, but Frank recognised many of the faces of the team members or hangers-on from the night of the murder, and at a couple of tables in the far corner, he could see what he took to be tonight's opposition: all blokes, all in their twenties or thirties, most of them drinking lager. There seemed to be no fraternisation between the rival teams at this stage. The visitors looked nervous, excited, even though Gough had said this match was a "friendly." Frank had never really had the appetite for games, but he supposed that, if you were that way inclined, a competition was a competition, whether it was a so-called friendly in a local pub, or the final set of the World Championship. Probably more so in the former than the latter, in fact—at least if you lost at the

Embassy, you got a runners-up cheque by way of compensation. But in a pub match all you were playing for was personal pride and the honour of the team, and there were no second place prizes in that competition.

Still no sign of Don. Frank took a pull on his Guinness. His stomach cramped slightly, and he wished he'd had something a bit more substantial than a tuna sandwich for dinner. The box it came in, for instance.

"Good evening, Constable. Are you here to make an arrest?"

Frank turned to find the young barrister, Kevin Lewis, standing at the bar alongside him. "Evening, Mr. Lewis. No, no arrest as yet—we're just here to learn a bit more about the set-up, familiarise ourselves with the players, as it were."

"We?"

"Mr. Packham will be along presently." *I hope.* Frank moved to one side as Brian Gough, scribbling on a clipboard as he approached, almost walked into him. "Evening, Mr. Gough. I—"

"Kevin," said Gough, ignoring the DC. "I'm putting you in at number six, okay?"

"Fine, Skipper. Whatever you say."

The team captain tapped his highlighter pen against his teeth, and returned to scrutiny of his papers. He looked anxious, but he also looked like a man who rather enjoyed anxiety.

Glancing around the room, Frank saw that many of the pint glasses, on the bar and on various tables, had darts cases laid across their tops; little stitched leather holders, about five inches long by two inches wide, with a tuck-in flap at one end, and a small pocket on the front to take detachable flights and spare shafts. This was something he'd seen in pubs many times be-

fore, Frank realised, without having noticed it. Now
that he thought about the practice, its purpose was obvious—one pint of beer looks very much like another,
but every darts case is individually identifiable, if only
by its contents. A neat way of making sure you didn't
drink out of someone else's glass. Or, perhaps more
importantly, that someone else didn't drink out of
yours.

"I *always* play at number six," Kevin Lewis told
him, with an amused shake of the head, as they
watched the captain march over to the opposition table
where he engaged in a formal and solemn handshake
with his opposite number. The toss of a coin, carried
out by Heather Mason, was followed by another handshake between the skippers.

"They take it all pretty seriously, don't they?"

Lewis looked thoughtful. "I'm not sure about that.
Not in the sense you mean; which, if I caught your
tone correctly, was a pejorative one. They know it's
only a game, and to them, this formality—the hand-
shakes, the team lists, the tactics and the coin tossing—
it's all part of the enjoyment. The thing is, Detective
Constable, if you play a game, you must take it seriously, else why do it? You are not fighting a war, or
building a house, or selling a basket of apples. You are
doing something that has no real purpose: if you don't
take it seriously, stick to the written and unwritten rules
and so on, then it becomes pointless as well as pur-
poseless."

He speaks of "them," not "us," thought Frank. So
still the question remains—what is he doing here? "So,
Mr. Lewis, who's going to be keeping score for you
tonight?"

"Ah, what a mournful thought," said Lewis, not

sounding very mournful at all, to Frank's mind. "The question hadn't occurred to me. I believe the usual custom is for every player to take his turn at chalking." He grinned, and added: "Oh, dear! It's been rather a long time since my maths O Level, I'm afraid!"

Sometime during this conversation, Don had entered the pub, and was now at the other end of the bar, being served by a barmaid. Frank was about to go over to him, when he saw the DI's order arrive—a glass of red wine.

Oh, bloody hell! Bet he's not smoking, either...

Frank watched as Don settled himself at a table in the Hollow Head's remotest and most gloomy corner. He wasn't speaking to anyone, or even looking at anyone. Frank didn't bother trying to catch his eye.

He was still wondering whether he ought to greet his boss, or whether he could put off the evil moment for a little longer by ordering another pint, when he was distracted by an argument taking place over by the dartboard. They were too far away for Frank to hear anything above the pre-match hubbub, but it was clear that Brian Gough was annoyed with the man he was talking to, or being talked to by, more like: a bloke in his late fifties, with nicotine-coloured hair, big eyebrows, and a generous ration of protruding nasal hair. The skipper held his clipboard and his highlighter crossed defiantly over his chest, as he endured what looked to be a pretty serious verbal onslaught. Gough's side of the exchange consisted mostly of almost uninterrupted head-shaking.

Checking his witness/suspect list, Frank guessed that the man with the hairy conk was probably Billy Page. He looked over at the dartboard; its cover consisted of twin doors, the insides of which were lined with blackboard. The doors were open now, as members of both teams tossed practice darts, and the two sides had been chalked up, "Home" on the left and "Away" on the right. The name "Billy" did not appear in the lists.

After a final, furious round of negative body language, Brian Gough strode over to the bar, to put his clipboard on a shelf above the optics.

"Mutiny in the ranks, Mr. Gough?"

"Not an easy job, this," Gough replied. "None of this lot could do it. And if they think they could, then why don't they? I'm not stopping them."

I bet, thought Frank. He paid for his second pint, and then decided he couldn't put it off any longer—it was time to brave the bear.

As he'd feared; the ashtray was empty, the red wine merely sipped at. Don's eyes were heavy, his lips thin.

Maybe a pre-emptive strike—I've not tried that before.

"Evening, sir. You look like you've got a touch of the flu coming on, if you don't mind me mentioning it. Perhaps you'd be better off in bed? I'm sure I can manage here."

Don grunted.

Fine. Right. "Right, well, I'll just mingle, sir. Chance to fill in the gaps in my darting education. Ah, look—I think we're about to get underway."

Frank returned to his position at the bar, from where he had a decent overview of the action, and from where he wasn't too close to Don Packham. He'd done his bit; let the old sod look after himself for a while.

First up to the oche were Brian Gough and a young lad with cropped hair and an earring. They both threw "three at the board" by way of getting their eyes in— Frank congratulated himself on remembering the jargon—until a very small, grey-haired, old man, "made of poor stuff,'' as Frank's gran would have said, and dressed in a shiny blue suit, called out ''Game on, ladies and gentlemen, please!'' in a surprisingly strong voice. That'd be Cliff Overton, Frank deduced; another non-player judging by the team list. Presumably he'd taken over the late Yvonne's chalking duties. His manner suggested that he was delighted to do so.

It was all a bit different from watching the professionals on the telly, Frank quickly realised. Professional players looked agonised every time they scored less than a hundred, and reserved their air-punches for ton-forties and ton-eighties. Here, the average total from three darts thrown seemed to be around forty-five. Throws of sixty—three darts in the single twenty bed— brought yells from the onlookers of ''Darts!'' while successful penetrations of the tiny treble-twenty area inspired actual applause.

The Hollow Head's captain got down to his out-shot first, after a good cover shot on the treble-nineteen at the bottom of the board, but missed the double sixteen with all three darts. His opponent stepped up and speared the middle of the double-twenty—the outer ring, at twelve o'clock on the dartboard—with his second arrow. The defeated Gough shook hands with his opponent, looking thoroughly unconcerned with this reversal. Obviously, Frank thought, it's the admin that matters to him, not what happens on the board.

During that first leg, Frank had acquired a personal commentator: a man of about thirty, slim, with thinning fair hair and thick glasses. He spoke with an Essex whine. ''Got no finish, the skipper. He can throw all right, but he's got no finish. All comes down to bottle in the end.''

''And Mr. Gough hasn't got it?''

"It's like Eric Bristow used to say, isn't it? 'Tons for show, doubles for dough'. No good scoring, if you can't hit the double."

"So why does he play at number one, Mr....?"

"Sean Hall."

"DC Frank Mitchell." The two men nodded at each other, very briefly, in lieu of a handshake.

"Yeah, well, good question, Constable. Stands to reason, doesn't it—you put your best player on first. All the other teams do, you can count on that. But, well, he's in charge, isn't he? He can do what he wants."

"And who is your best player, Mr. Hall?"

Hall sipped from a pint glass of orange squash. "Well, depends who you ask."

Ah, thought Frank, trying not to smile. Modesty forbids, eh?

Next up for the home side was one of the Rees brothers—Frank could tell that by the fact that, over the other side of the room, not watching his sibling's game, was another man who looked almost identical to the player on the oche, other than being entirely bald instead of having a head that was neatly enveloped in bushy black hair. Both men were in their late thirties, solidly built, and bearded. The only obvious difference, other than the hair, was that the hairy one seemed to take more care over his attire than did the bald one; his beard was much neater, too.

He won his game with ease, scoring two tons along the way, as well as a shanghai on twenties—single, treble, double—before finishing on his fourth attempt at double-ten.

"He's good," said Frank.

"Luke? Yeah, he's not bad. The bald one's better, though."

Sure enough, Lee Rees left his opponent standing in the next leg, opening his account with a ton followed by a second throw of one hundred and twenty-one, which only missed registering the maximum score by a couple of millimetres.

"See what you mean, Mr. Hall. He is good."

Hall nodded and smiled. "He's my doubles partner," he said, with evident pride—though pride in his own superb taste in partners, Frank felt, rather than in his mate's abilities.

"He doesn't pair up with his brother, then?"

"Those two?" Hall laughed. "Not likely! No, Baldy Bro and Bushy Bro don't even speak to each other, let alone play doubles together."

Frank was about to ask the obvious question, when Lee Rees checked out with his first attempt at double-sixteen.

"Right," said Hall, after gulping a couple of mouthfuls of orange squash, like a Wimbledon challenger. "That's me—I'm on."

Sean Hall's style, Frank was not especially surprised to see, was rather less graceful, less natural than that of the man he called Baldy Bro. His face earnest—earnest like someone with constipation, if the truth be told—he seemed to force his darts through the air by willpower.

It was a close game—in which, Frank noticed, most of the Hollow Head team seemed to take little interest—with no high scores. In the end, Hall was beaten on the doubles, having missed double top, double ten and double five in three consecutive darts, the last of which bounced off the board to land on the rubber mat. Despondent, he returned to the bar.

"Tough luck," Frank commiserated. "That double ten bent the wire, I reckon. And the double five was in and out."

"Feel those," said Hall, handing the DC his darts. "See? They're the wrong weight. I reckon the bloke in the shop got them mixed up. These are twenty-one grammes, far too light for me. I prefer a twenty-four."

"Ah, right, yeah." Frank rolled the arrows in his palm, simultaneously pushing his lips out into an expert's silent whistle. "Yeah, see what you mean. So, two-all. Who's on next?"

"Superdart," said Hall, taking his darts back from Frank and giving them a speculative palm-roll of his own. "Clive Callow."

"Sounds promising, if they call him Superdart!"

Hall shrugged. "It's what Yvonne Wood used to call him. She was being sarky, I presume—she usually was. Anyway, he used to play county darts, years back, but he's nowhere near that standard now."

Once again, Frank opened his mouth to ask about the rift between the Rees Brothers, when out of the corner of his eye he caught sight of the bald one of the pair, making what could only be described as valiant attempts to engage DI Packham in conversation.

Oh, Christ—who knows what he might say or do in his mood? "Excuse me, Mr. Hall. I'd best have a quick word with my boss."

As FRANK REACHED Don's table, Lee Rees was saying, "When I say the word 'America' to you, Inspector, what's the first thing that comes to your mind?"

If there was one thing Don hated—and there was

more than one, in actual fact—it was stupid questions. Silly guessing games. If you've got something to say, just say it! Without hesitation, he answered: "Guns."

"Ah," said the bald man, "but—"

"Guns." Don hadn't quite finished. Another thing he didn't like very much was being interrupted. "Shootings, violence, drive-bys, murder, manslaughter, school massacres, death row, lynch mobs—"

"Red wine, sir?"

"What?" Didn't Frank know better than to interrupt his superior officers?

"Can I get you another drink, sir?"

Don didn't so much shake his head as rattle it. "And the electric chair," he said. "That, since you ask, is what I first think of when you say to me the word 'America'."

"Oh," said Lee Rees, after what sounded suspiciously like a stunned silence. His mouth was hanging open slightly, and he seemed somewhat unsure of where he was or why. Especially why. "Oh...I—I was rather hoping you'd say 'hot dogs'."

"And why the hell would I say hot dogs? I don't believe I've ever said hot dogs in my life. The hot dog does not feature in either my vocabulary or my diet." Don picked up his wineglass and drained it. Why the hell had Frank been so desperate to buy him another drink, when he hadn't even finished the first one? He didn't want another one, in any case—stuff tasted like dog's blood.

"Nothing important," said Rees. "No offence intended—I'm just doing some, you might call it, informal market research for a new business venture I'm hoping to invest in. A small sideline. Genuine American-style hot dogs, based on a genuine American recipe sold from a genuine American hot dog van that I've recently been offered by a geezer who imported it from America and then went bust.''

"Oh, great idea," said Don. "Yes, indeed—give our kids genuine American junk food and with a bit of luck they'll start genuinely shooting each other as well."

The bald dartist looked at Don, looked at Frank, then looked at his pint. "Right," he said. "Well, nice to meet you. Cheers." He retreated to the bar.

Prat, thought Don. Or *said,* possibly—he wasn't sure if he'd said it out loud or not. Didn't much care, either.

Frank sat beside him. "Something interesting about those two."

"What two?"

"Baldy Bro and Bushy Bro—the hot dog man and his hairy brother."

Don snorted. "I can't imagine anything being interesting about that prat."

"Well," said Frank, "apparently they don't talk to each other. I'm not sure why, yet, but—"

"Why? It's because they're siblings, Frank—good God, you don't need to be a detective to figure that out! All siblings hate each other, that's a given, that is."

"Well okay, sir, but in the present situation, surely any source of hostility within the group of suspects is—"

"Oh do shut up, Frank. It's far too early for theories." Theories are a total load of crap, anyway. There's no mystery about why people murder each other; the only puzzle is why some people *don't* murder each other. This case would turn out to hinge on something petty and pathetic and grubby, just like every other crime he'd wasted the best years of his life investigating. Investigating! Cops don't investigate. They just loiter around waiting for someone to confess or get grassed up. The whole concept of detection is a fraud, made up by bloody Hollywood. Poor old Frank, wasting his life on this rubbish—I must be kinder to him, poor sod.

To his horror, he felt his eyes filling up with water—must be the smoky pub atmosphere. "I think I have got a bit of flu as it happens, Frank. Reckon I'll sod off early. What's happening in the match?"

"Well, the one they call Superdart just won his singles, so that's three-two to the Hollow Head."

"Who's on next?"

"Heather, the lovely landlady."

"Oh, God, I don't think I can bear watching that." They did, however, watch the landlady's first couple of throws—a twenty-six and a forty-one. "She's crap. She throws like she talks: aggressive, nasty, suspicious, paranoid. Hurling her darts. You don't throw darts, you let them go. They're not bloody javelins. Stupid woman." He stood up. "I'm off, Frank. See you tomorrow." He thought Frank looked relieved. Kind of him, to worry about my health like that. He'll make a good dad. Or he would, if such a thing existed.

"Okay, sir. You'll ring in the morning?"

"Don't I always?" Don't fuss!

Outside the pub, Don found the barrister in conversation with a young woman who he introduced as Gail Webb. Taking the air, he supposed. Didn't blame them, it was like a smog sauna in that bloody place, with the heating turned up and the windows all closed.

"Has Heather finished?" the woman asked him. "Am I on?"

"No, you're all right, love. She'll be a while yet. You two not watching?"

"Well, it's only a friendly, isn't it?"

"True. You bring up the tail do you, Mr. Lewis?"

"That's it, Inspector. New boy's prerogative."

"Oh, it's not that," said Gail Webb, punching the barrister lightly on the arm. "It's because we need someone solid down the order, to rescue us if the top players don't perform."

"Well, I'm off. Good luck." How lonely must these people be to spend their evenings doing something they obviously have no interest in?

"You're not staying for the sandwiches, Inspector?"

"She makes them, does she? Ms. Mason?"

"Cheese and pickle, and ham and pickle," said Lewis.

"Thanks, don't think I'll bother."

He started walking, and having walked a few yards, decided he'd walk all the way home. After a few more yards, he remembered he'd left his car in the pub car park. Oh well, he'd walk anyway. Clear his head. He'd been going for nearly ten minutes when he remembered that these days he lived miles away from Cowden, and it'd probably take him half the night to get home.

Cursing, but without much force, he retraced his wasted steps, comforted by the knowledge that, when you get right down to it, all steps are wasted. Why did human beings insist on rushing around all over the place, as if they were expecting to reach a destination eventually? Why not just stay wherever they happen to be when they're born, and wait for it all to be over?

SEVEN

BEFORE THE PHONE had rung twice, Frank had slid out of bed, located his feet—conveniently positioned at the ends of his legs, but less conveniently wrapped inside a duvet cover—picked up Joseph, and commenced a structured programme of *There, there-ing, Shush-ing* and *That's a good boy-ing*. It was only when the phone rang for a third time that he realised it wasn't the baby that was making the noise.

We're going have to get a baby that doesn't sound like a phone, he thought. No, wait a minute…

Joseph slept on, bubbling happily.

Halfway through its fifth impatient trill, the bedside phone was silenced. Debbie closed one eye, in order to see the clock better: five a.m. At that time, a call could only mean disaster—or Don. She chuckled, as she picked up the receiver; realising that, of course, it could be both.

"Mortuary, Expecter Disaster," she said, carefully articulating each separate syllable, though not to any great effect. Once, working night shift at a general hospital, she'd fallen asleep in the restroom. When her colleagues woke her, her apologies were so nonsensical that she'd been taken down to Casualty for a look-at; it took her a while to convince them she hadn't had a stroke.

"Debbie, my darling!" Don replied, on a roar of delighted laughter. "Look, girl, this can't go on—either you marry me or you don't, but I'm not willing to see you behind Frank's back any more. Can't we at least send him out of the room?"

"He's hiding the bobby, Expecter. Just a moppet."

She and Frank swapped: baby for telephone. At that moment, Joseph woke up for the first time that night and started crying—somewhat to Frank's relief. He didn't like silent babies, they gave him the shivers. Especially silent noisy babies.

"Morning," he said, checking the clock as he did so. Five a.m.!

"Ah, Frank, I can hear by the background sound effects that I didn't wake you. It's as I suspected, you were up already, thanks to Citizen Joe. Right?"

"Yes, sir," said Frank.

"Oh, it's *sir,* is it? I see, Frank, not at your best in the mornings, eh? Well, never mind, we've got to make allowances for you new fathers and your mood swings."

"You're feeling better this morning then, Don?"

"What? Better?"

"The flu."

"Oh, yes, right. No, wasn't the flu at all as it turned out, just some twenty-four hour thing. Shouldn't have let you talk me into thinking it was flu, you'll turn me into a hypochondriac. That's the trouble with you parents, you're all fusspots."

"Yes, Don. Sorry, Don."

"Never mind, no harm done. Takes more than a bug to knock me out. Now listen, Frank, I've been thinking about this case, and why it is that I don't seem to be able to get a grip on what it's all about. And I know now what it is that's been bothering me."

Frank coughed, partly to clear his throat and partly to wake himself up, as he suspected he might be asleep though he couldn't prove it. "Right," he said.

"It's the victim, Frank. Chalkie. We know next to nothing about her. Do we? Except that she worked in a bookie's, lived alone, and quite possibly wasn't very popular with women."

"True."

"I didn't hear anything terribly useful last night, did you?"

"You did say we weren't to ask direct questions last night, just to observe."

"Don't be so bloody defensive, Daddy! I'm not criticising, just saying. All right? So, the upshot is that we—and I blame myself—have been going about this arse-forwards. We need to know something about poor old Chalkie first, so that we know what questions to ask. Makes sense, yes? Right, so, hence the early call: we're going to go and visit her poor old mum. Can you be ready in an hour? I'll pick you up."

Being the home of a policeman married to a nurse, and that marriage having produced a baby, the Mitchell household was very used to hurried mornings. Shift workers, and those who work an on-call system, know well how to shave, shower, and otherwise scourge and ablute, in double time and with little fuss or mess, while almost simultaneously pouring their breakfasts into mugs and bowls, and from there down throats and into guts. Those who are able to survive, and even to thrive, in such a way of life, soon learn how to evacuate their bowels smoothly, and their homes punctually. They may even, with practice, learn how to converse with each other during some (if not all) of the above activities, pitching their voices over the noise of the washing machine, the baby, the running water, the humming shaver, the steaming kettle.

Could he be ready in an hour? Hah! Frank could have been ready *twice* in an hour.

Sitting in the kitchen with a final cup of tea, watching Joseph power-snooze on his mother's shoulder, Frank said: ''What's the first thing that comes into your mind when I say the word 'America'?''

Debbie gave a sad sigh. ''Guns, I suppose.''

''Oh. Yeah, that's what Don said.''

''I think it's what most people would say, isn't it? Nowadays. Who asked him, anyway?''

''Bloke in a pub. A witness in this murder case.''

''And what did you say?''

''I wasn't asked.'' Frank laughed, softly. ''Don answered at somewhat greater length than you did, and by the time he'd finished the poor bloke didn't have the will to continue. So he never got around to me.''

''What would you have said? What is the first thing comes into your mind when someone says the word 'America'?''

Without hesitation, Frank answered: ''Space.''

''Space? What, you mean as in wide open prairies and Yellowstone Park and the grass is as 'high as an elephant's eye?''

''No, no. I mean space as in the moon and dehydrated foods and 'Houston, this is Lunar Module One'.''

''You mean outer space? The space race? But that was more than thirty years ago, love, that was all before we were born.''

Frank shrugged. "Aye, well. Better than guns, though, isn't it?"

Debbie put the baby down, and walked round the table. She stood behind her husband's chair and put her arms around him, and laid her cheek against the top of his head. "Rockets to the moon," she said. Joseph cried. She took her arms away from her husband and put them around her baby instead.

DON DIDN'T COME IN, he just honked outside—somewhat to Debbie's annoyance. "Have a word, love. There's folk trying to sleep around here."

It was a cold morning, as it had every right to be, so early in the day and in the year. But it was dry and windless, and the air tasted crunchy, the way a tight lettuce smells when you first slice into it with a big, friendly knife.

"Shall we take mine?" Frank suggested, leaning into Don's car window. "I know you don't like driving and talking at the same time." And I don't like being driven by someone who thinks the Highway Code is only there to keep learner drivers out of his way, and who is quite likely to start thinking "What's it all about, Alfie?" whilst doing 70 mph down the motorway.

"Fair enough, Frank, if you're sure you don't mind."

"Not at all." They left Don's car and got into Frank's. Frank closed his door as quietly as he possibly could. Don didn't.

"Where are we off to, anyway?"

Don settled comfortably into the passenger seat and lit one of his miniature cigars. "Ah, Frank, what treats I bring you—a day by the seaside, no less. Bognor Regis."

"That's where Chalkie's mum lives?"

"It is, in as much as anyone who lives in an English seaside town in the winter can be said to be living. You ever been to dear old Boggy, Frank?"

"No, bit far south for family trips when I was a kid. And Debbie and I prefer to get abroad when we can, in search of a bit of sun. How about you?"

"Well, when I was a nipper, it was Weston-super-Mare, of course. The great West Country resort, where else? But as it happens, I do know Bognor a bit. When I was somewhat younger than I am currently, I spent several brief, romantic interludes there."

"Dirty weekends, Don? Well I never."

Don frowned at him. "The phrase 'dirty weekend' is only ever applied to others, Frank, not to one's self. And certainly not to one's superiors."

"Beg pardon, Inspector."

"Hmm."

"Why Bognor?"

"Yes, odd choice, I know, but you see, her husband owned a guesthouse there, so we got a discount. Take the next left here, Frank."

AT FRANK'S INSISTENCE, Don had phoned Mrs. Wood from the car to alert her to their imminent arrival. "Who cares if she's not there?" Don had argued. "We can spend the day playing bingo and eating whelks."

"In February?"

"Ah yes, fair point. Give us your mobile."

Having paused along the way for a cup of tea, they arrived at Mrs. Wood's bungalow on the outskirts of the resort just after nine. They were admitted by a woman in her early sixties, dressed in what Don recognised as the modern uniform of British women in their early sixties—jeans, floppy top, trainers, black hair tied back with a multicoloured, tie-dye bandanna.

Mrs. Wood had a Midlands accent, and a face that showed some suffering; most of which, Don instantly decided, came from the inside out, rather than the outside in.

"We weren't close," she said, before they'd even taken their coats off. "I might as well tell you that now, and get it over with. I hadn't actually seen her, not physically, in more than a year, and we only spoke on the phone about three times a year. Christmas, her birthday and mine. Shall I put the kettle on?"

"If it's no trouble, Mrs. Wood, thank you. Had you and Yvonne had a falling-out, if you don't mind me asking?"

"Not as such, no. Not really. We just weren't close, if you want the truth." She led them through to a large kitchen at the back, and they sat at a Formica-topped table while she made tea. "The fact is, she was always a bit jealous of me. Sounds awful, I know, but there you are. We were so close in age, you see—I had her young—and, well, if I've got to say it myself because there's no-one else to say it, the fact is I was always the pretty one."

"I'm sure you were, Mrs. Wood. More like sisters, eh?"

She made a face at him, as she poured boiling water into three cups. "If you mean in the sense of not getting on, you could say that, yes."

"Did she have a lot of boyfriends?"

"Not until she left home." Now there's a surprise, thought Don. "But later, she made up for lost time, from what I could gather."

"When did she leave home?"

"As soon as she could, Inspector! As soon as it was legal. I was still married then—I'm a divorced widow, currently, or vice versa, whichever you prefer. I mean, we were divorced, but then he died. Of course, he was older than me." She distributed the teas. "Where was I?"

"You were saying," said Frank, "that Yvonne left home."

"Oh yes. Well, before that, the three of us lived around Birmingham, mostly. Moved around a bit. My husband—my late ex-husband, or ex-late husband, whichever—was a salesman. Anyway, once I was on my own, I came down here. It's nice by the seaside." She dunked a dead-fly biscuit in her tea. "She specialised in married men, I can tell you that."

"Yvonne did?" Wonder who she learned that from; Mum or Dad?

"Oh, yes. Mind you, so many of the girls do these days, don't they? And I can't say I blame them really, I mean—lot easier all around in the end, isn't it?"

Don hated dead-fly biscuits, even the sight of them made him feel queasy. Since childhood, he'd never quite been able to convince himself that their nickname actually contravened the Trades Descriptions Act. "Was she with anyone recently, do you know?"

"I wouldn't know. She wouldn't tell me anything, except bits and pieces that she let drop over the years."

"Or any particular friends?"

"Like I say, we didn't really talk about things like that. It was her jealousy, you see? She didn't want to compare her life with mine." Mrs. Wood patted her hair, and kissed her own lips as if checking the taste of her lipstick. "Silly, if you ask me, but there you are."

"You can't remember anyone that she mentioned more than once, or even hinted at the existence of?"

"There was someone special years ago, because I remembered that when the local police told me she'd been found dead at a darts match." She took a tissue from her sleeve and blew her nose. She wasn't crying, Don noticed; it was a blow of disgust, not grief. "A darts match! Honestly, I mean, how tacky can you get! I know it sounds awful to say it, but honestly…"

"Why did her being found dead at a darts match remind you of her having someone special?"

"Well, that was it, you see. When she first went to London, we kept in touch a bit more. I suppose she was lonely, before she found her feet, needed someone to talk to, even if it was only poor old Mum. And I remember that she'd met someone—the first boyfriend she ever mentioned, as far as I can recall—and how she'd met him in her local pub. He'd joined the darts team, and she'd taken up keeping the score for them, or something pathetic, just so as to be near him." Mrs. Wood sniffed again. "Married, of course."

"She told you that?"

"She didn't need to, Inspector. I'll tell you this for nothing—there'll be a married man at the bottom of it, and that's for sure."

"It?"

"It!" she said. "My daughter getting herself murdered, like a tart."

"SHE DOESN'T SEEM to be greatly mourned anywhere, does she?" said Don, as they buckled their seat belts. "Poor old Chalkie."

"We don't know that, though, do we? Not for sure. We can't get inside people's heads."

They drove in silence for a moment or two—going the long way around, because according to the DI, only a crazy man would drive all the way to Bognor for the day without getting a glimpse of the sea—until Don said: "That's a very good point, Frank. As well as being a comforting thought. Well said. Anyway, from our point of view, that was a highly fruitful morning."

Frank had just been thinking the precise opposite. "Seems to me she didn't know much more about her daughter than we did."

"No, no, can't agree, Frank—she gave us a solid motive, and one that fits with what we already knew about Chalkie."

"She did?"

"The married man, Frank! Cherchez le married man! I'll bet the horrible old cow's right about that. Plus, Mrs. Wood has confirmed our suspicions concerning why Chalkie might have been unpopular—unpopular with women, at any rate. And, as icing on the cake, we now know that she had an unhappy family background. Come on, Frank—the bloody FBI couldn't have given us a better psychological profile than that."

"I suppose so."

"Definitely so. No, mate, that was time well spent. Besides, I do love to be beside the seaside, especially out of season. Clears the tubes out." To Frank's alarm, Don rolled down the passenger side window, and stuck his head out. He began sniffing loudly, like a bloodhound with polyps.

"Feeling all right, Don?"

"Hey?"

"Everything all right? Do you want me to stop the car?"

"Not yet, I'm still— *Yes!* Pull over, pull over!"

The tyres on Frank's car shrieked as he responded to the urgency in his boss's command. Don leapt from the car, still inhaling energetically. "Just up that alley there, if I'm not mistaken."

"What is?"

"Didn't you ever do that as a kid, Frank? On the way back from a day at the beach, the whole family sticking their noses out of the window, sniffing out the best-smelling chippy?"

Sure enough, there was a chip shop in an alley leading away from the seafront, and, yes, just for a minute, Frank did feel a tiny stab of nostalgia, for days gone by and grandparents never again to be seen. There was something special about a seaside chippy, he admitted to himself; the scrubbed tiles on the walls, with their marine motif; the gleaming stainless steel counter behind which stood a smiling, red-faced woman wearing a crisply-starched hat and overall; the shining jars of pickled eggs and gherkins and onions; above all, the smell of freshly fried potatoes and battered fish.

Don ordered a bag of chips, open, plenty of salt and vinegar. "Better make that a large one, in fact, I didn't have much breakfast. No, hold on—how big's your large? All right, tell you what, make that a large-and-a-half. That's it, don't spare the vinegar, keep going…keep going. I want to see it leaking through the paper underneath. You haven't had a proper bag of chips unless your hands pong of vinegar for a week afterwards."

Although it was barely lunchtime, Frank would have been happy to eat a fish supper at one of the tables in the small restaurant, but he didn't fancy a takeaway. The fact was, people like him and Debbie just didn't eat their food from paper bags.

As they drove towards London, via a leisurely route of Don's choosing, the DI scoffed his chips, every now and then offering Frank one. "You sure? They're bloody good." He sighed happily. And frequently. "Good day out that was, Frank. A very nice morning indeed. You want to do that with your family some time, you know—a day out by the seaside for you and your lovely wife and your gorgeous baby. It's a most underrated resort, is Bognor."

It took him a while but, to Frank's amazement, Don eventually consumed every scrap of his enormous portion. With a final sigh of contentment, he balled the paper, shoved it under his seat, and lit a cigar. "You missed out there, Frank, those were first rate chips. We could always stop again if you've changed your mind?"

"No, you're all right, thanks. I'll have a sandwich when we get back to the office."

Don laughed, blowing smoke out between his teeth and through his nostrils. "Tell you what, I should have asked the chippy, shouldn't I?"

"Asked her what?"

"Whether they did deep-fried muesli!"

EIGHT

HE LOOKS HUNG OVER, Frank thought, as he and Don met on Friday morning in a public car park on the edge of Cowden's largest and oldest light industrial estate. Not hung over from booze, though; more like…well, maybe it was all that sea air yesterday.

He remembered when he was a kid, snoozing all the way home in the car after a day out on the golden beach at Cullercoats, smelling the sand and the salt and the hot plastic of the back seat, and being just awake enough to hear his gran's voice, tuned in with the hum of the engine, saying: "Aw, little pet, look at him. It's the fresh air knocks him out, little lovey."

Anyway, fresh air or whatever, Don seemed deflated today. Not *Down,* exactly, not in the Capital D way that Frank had learned to recognise, but flat, sort of. Flat, but making an effort. A kind of *morning after the night before,* maybe.

"Who are we seeing next, then?"

Don lit a cigar, to Frank's considerable relief. After a few unenthusiastic puffs he extinguished it, to Frank's considerable confusion. "You fancied those brothers, didn't you? You said there was something funny about them."

"Yeah—Bushy Bro and Baldy Bro. Apparently they're not on speaking terms. Haven't been for a while; two or three years, it seems. But they live together and work together.''

"Right," said Don. "That's sounds promising. In fact, it sounds very much as if there's a woman at the bottom of it, which is more than promising. Yup, good: we'll have a word with the Brothers of Perpetual Silence."

That's not what you were saying the other day when I tried to tell you about it, thought Frank. There again, be fair: Don did hear everything eventually, even if it wasn't always quite when and where and how you intended him to hear it.

"What kind of business is it?" Don asked.

"They run a garage."

"Petrol station?"

"No, a repair garage. They're motor mechanics."

"Ah, are they, indeed? That sounds good, doesn't it—a motor mechanic would certainly know how to balance a concrete block on a door frame at just the right angle."

Frank couldn't imagine quite the circumstances in which a motor mechanic would need to perform such a task within the normal run of his professional duties; nor did he reckon you'd necessarily need to be a skilled engineer in order to shove a lump of rock on top of a plank of wood. But never mind—it all seemed to be waking Don up a bit, for which he was duly thankful.

DON WAS FEELING a bit tired, just a bit shagged out, as he and Frank walked through the open gates of Rees Brothers' Motor Repairs & Parts. He'd been doing too much thinking lately, that was the problem—excessive thinking always made him tired. That was the trouble with police work: most of it was routine, robotic, so that your brain got lazy. Then, when you were faced with some actual headwork for once, you weren't up to it.

The garage wasn't on the industrial estate itself, but just across the road from the car park, one of several units built underneath railway arches which looked cavernous from the outside, but were actually rather poky. A humble affair, Don thought, though no doubt it made a reasonable living for two single blokes working alone.

"Hello—anybody home? I've got a horse needs shoeing."

This would be Bushy Bro, he decided, as a broad-shouldered man with voluminous, but well-cut hair emerged from underneath an ancient, maroon Jaguar.

The mechanic wiped his right hand on his blue boiler suit, which left it even oilier than it had been before. He shook hands with Don; Frank managed to stay back, out of hand's way.

"Mr. Rees?"

"That's right. Luke Rees."

The voice was quite soft, though firm enough; the accent typically, and to Don's ear delightfully, north London. All south Londoners sounded like thugs, he reckoned, even if they were vicars. But north Londoners—well, a lot of them sounded just like south Londoners these days, as did half the nation, from Cornwall to Edinburgh. Those who still sounded like north Londoners, though, they had an accent Don had taken to immediately, back when he'd first moved to the capital. Unpretentious, but always holding something back; a plain, working-man's voice, carrying a hint that mischief was available at a moment's notice, should it be required, but only at the management's discretion. Erudition, unashamed yet not paraded, filtered through home-rolled cigarettes and pints of light-and-bitter. It was the accent in which The Kinks had written and sung their songs.

He heard Frank cough, and realised that he had not yet responded to Bushy Bro's short speech. "Pleased to meet you, Mr. Rees. And your brother, Lee—that's your older brother, I take it?"

"No, I'm the elder."

Bit hard on the lad, Don thought—being dramatically balder than your older brother. Other than that, they looked pretty similar. "Is Lee around?"

"I don't think so."

"You don't *think* so? You don't know?"

Rees shrugged. "He has his jobs, I have mine."

"I see. Well, never mind—we'll catch up with him later. Perhaps you could tell him we want to see him."

"Best you tell him yourself, Inspector. Leave him a note if you like, I'll put it on his desk."

*Well, well…*so it's true. They *literally* don't speak, by the sound of it.

"Looks like you're busy enough, Mr. Rees," Don said, gesturing about him at the Jaguar and the three further cars which stood outside the garage, presumably awaiting collection or attention. "Do you own the place?"

"I'm joint owner."

"With Lee?"

Rees nodded. "Our parents are both dead—they married quite late in life—and they left everything to me and Lee, half-and-half."

"Everything?"

"This business, and the family house. They were very keen on family, you see, my parents. My father was an evacuee during World War Two. His close relatives were all killed in the Blitz, and he lost touch with the rest. While my mother had effectively lost all her family, back in Ireland, due to some terrible feud about money.''

"They were wealthy people, then?''

Rees laughed. "Christ, no! I shouldn't think any one of them left more than a sack of spuds in his will. But bald men do fight over combs, you know. It's sad, it's stupid—but it's human nature.''

"Hence the joint custody of their worldly goods. Well, you can see their point.''

"Sure, sure.'' Rees rubbed his hands together; Don was fascinated to see that, against all the known laws of physics, this appeared to increase the total amount of oil involved. "Anyhow, family history aside, I know what you're here to talk about, obviously. And I'm afraid I won't be able to help you much. I didn't really know Chalkie all that well.''

"I see. And your brother, did he know her better?''

"You'll have to—''

"Yes, I know: we'll have to ask him. We will.''

"She seemed a nice enough sort. As far as I know there was nothing that—''

Don interrupted him. "No, it's all right, I don't want to know about the deceased, as it happens. I want you to tell me about your darts game.'' Because Don's theory—and he couldn't immediately remember whether this was one of his long-standing theories or whether it was one he'd just this minute come up with, but either way he knew it was a good one—Don's theory was that if you got people taking about their passion, they'd tell you a lot more about themselves than if all you asked them was their whereabouts on the night in question. Besides, he was a bit weary of hearing about poor old Chalkie and her lonely life.

The mechanic laughed and scratched his hairy head. "Oh. Well, I suppose you know what you're doing, Inspector."

"Interesting you should say that, Mr. Rees, because I sometimes suppose that, too. My colleague here has, to my knowledge, never yet supposed such a thing, though I live in hope."

"Well, why don't you both come out back, I'll put the kettle on."

He led them to a little kitchenette at the back of the unit, next to the office. Don's eyes met Frank's—and each set was rounder than usual—as they saw that both the kitchenette and the office were divided in two, by means of partition walls running down their middles. Instead of two small rooms, therefore, there were four tiny rooms. Both of the kitchenettes contained, amongst other things, an electric kettle—and a dartboard.

They had to go through the bisected doorway sideways and in single file. There were no actual doors; if there had been, Don thought, they'd not have been much bigger than cat flaps. Luke's half of the bisection, at least, was clean and tidy; not bad for a bachelor. Don himself managed *clean,* most of the time, but he found *tidy* a bit of an effort. It wasn't a matter of men being unable or unwilling to do domestic chores, he reckoned; simply that, as a generalisation, when you lived alone, you got into male habits—when you lived with a woman, you saw things more through a female prism.

"This is where you do your practising, is it? Would you mind?" Don picked up a set of darts lying on top of a mini fridge. "I don't carry my own with me these days."

"Let me guess," Rees laughed. "Spoils the line of the suit?"

"Hardly. No, it's just that they could be construed as an offensive weapon, under the regulations." Don threw three darts at double sixteen, retrieved them, and threw three more. Throws four and six were right on target.

"Not bad," said Rees, spooning instant coffee into three pristine china mugs. "I see you're like me—you don't just practice on the twenties."

"No point, is there? Treble twenty's the number you throw at most, so logically it's the one you need least practise on." He turned to look at the DC standing by the door, with his arms crossed. "Fancy a chuck, Frank? I'm sure Mr. Rees won't mind."

Frank shook his head. "No, you carry on, sir. I'll look and learn."

Silly boy. Don had wanted to know whether Bushy Bro would, in fact, mind sharing his darts with not one, but two strangers; some players were very possessive about the tools of their sport.

"You'll have to forgive my colleague, Mr. Rees. He doesn't get much time for darts. He's a new daddy."

Rees looked at Frank as if noticing him for the first time, giving him a broad, clearly genuine smile. "Congrats, Constable. Nice one. What breed is it?"

"A boy," said Frank—and said nothing else. Don wished he wouldn't be so po-faced about everything. *Can't he see I'm trying to get the witness to open up?*

"How about you, Mr. Rees?" Don asked. "Any children yourself? Any nephews or nieces?"

The smile vanished from Rees's face. "Not that I know of."

"That's the answer in both cases, is it?" Don joked, to ease the sudden tension. "Ah well, same for me, I'm afraid. We can't all be so lucky. How do you practice, then?"

The sharp change of subject brought a puzzled frown to the mechanic's face. "Pardon?"

"The darts—what do you do, go round the clock?"

"Oh, right. Round the clock, yeah. Singles, trebles, doubles, twenty-five and bull. Miss two in a row, I have to go back to the beginning. Also, if that gets boring, I have this." From a shelf above the fridge he took a powdered milk tin, full of slips of paper. "All different finishes written on them, see? I pick one out of the hat at random, go for it."

"Right," said Don. "Neat idea. Let's have a look, then."

Rees dipped his hand into the tin, and passed a slip of paper to Don.

"Oh, dear," said Don, reading it. "One-two-three, never won a game."

Rees shrugged, as the DI handed him his darts. "So they say. But they're all the same size, aren't they?"

"Course they are. My view precisely."

"You play for a team, Inspector?"

"Used to. Don't have the time now. Might take it up again someday, though—I miss it."

Don sat and watched as Luke Rees set the outside edge of his right foot against the oche (in this case, a line chalked on the concrete floor), and leaned his body into the throwing position. *Not bad.* His balance was good—some players lean over too much, straining after the advantage of every extra inch cut from the distance between dart and board. Rees's grip was light but firm, the thumb and first finger holding the shaft of the arrow, while the second finger just touched the barrel, for additional stability. He drew his forearm back towards his shoulder, the movement pivoting nicely on a stationary elbow, then forward again, culminating in a smooth release and a flowing follow-through. The dart missed treble nineteen by about four inches.

"Oh, shit!" He bunged the last two darts randomly in the direction of the board, then picked up his coffee and took a slurp. "I'm not used to performing for an audience of coppers, no offence."

Don smiled. "Just goes to show, you should never scoff at old superstitions. You chuck at number two, don't you, for the Hollow Head?"

"Mostly, yeah."

"With the skipper at number one, leading from the front."

There was no reply to that; Rees just drank his coffee.

"So," said Don. "In my experience, number one is for show, and number two is the top player in the side. That you, is it?"

Rees rolled a cigarette, though he seemed to be having some trouble with it. Perhaps because his hands were still oily. Or perhaps for some other reason. Did he seem nervous? More nervous than was natural under the circs?

"I don't really think about it like that. Most of us in the team can play a bit."

"Perhaps you and I can have a game some time, Luke. I'd enjoy that."

"Sure, why not," said Rees, his smile open and friendly.

"Of course," Don added, "that depends on how things turn out in this investigation."

Rees gave up on his cigarette, and crushed it into a tin ashtray. "Yeah, I suppose so."

"Well." Don stood up. "We'd better be getting on. This has been a pleasant interlude—keep practicing those big finishes."

"Will do."

"Just before we go, tell me one thing—are you really worried that your brother might have killed poor Chalkie, or are you just naturally tense?"

This time, Luke Rees's face didn't freeze. He smiled wryly, but easily, and said: "I have no idea why anyone would kill her, Inspector. But if it was my brother...well, you'll have to ask him about that."

Back in the car, Frank said: "So, you reckon it's the thought of his brother as a suspect that's making him nervous, not himself?"

"Not especially," said Don. "Could be both, after all. Or neither. But I will be interested to hear from the others whether Chalkie had been taking an interest in the brothers' feud lately. Mind you," he added, lighting a cigar, "we don't yet know whether this is a *lately* murder, or a *festering* murder."

"How do you mean?"

"I mean, was Yvonne Wood killed because of something that's just happened—or because of something that's just happened once too often?"

NINE

NOT BRUNCH—just an early lunch. That was how Frank preferred to look at it, anyway; brunch, after all, was a whole extra meal, which could hardly be healthy. You saw far too many fat, sweaty cops, even these days, and not all of them old fellers, by any means. To be fair, though, Don Packham enjoyed his grub at any and every opportunity—when he was in the right mood, at any rate—and no one would ever call him fat.

So, after a modest plate of beans on toast for the DC, and the usual belly-buster for the DI, they sat in a Chinese café in a street mostly full of Indian shops, and considered their next move. All that dart chucking at the garage seemed to have woken Don up nicely, Frank was glad to note, and what the darts began, the nosh had completed. *Simple medicine's the best*, Frank's granddad used to say, before downing his nightly scotch.

"Where to next, then? Straight on to Baldy Bro?"

"No, he'll wait. I think it's time to get a woman's perspective on the character and habits of the late Chalkie Wood. And when I say a woman, I don't mean a pub landlady."

"Or a mother."

"Obviously not a mother, Frank—mothers aren't women."

"Although, I think the one in this case might be," said Frank. "What I mean is—you're saying that women aren't mothers, meaning that in the context of their daughters, they're not in competition for men—"

"Am I? I thought I was just popping out a wisecrack purely for the sake of it." Don lit one of his small cigars. "But do go on."

"Well, only that Chalkie and her mother were—according to Mrs. Wood—more in competition than you would normally expect."

Don tried to blow a smoke-ring. Or else tried to do an imitation of a deaf goldfish speaking to a room full of lip-readers, Frank wasn't sure which. "And that tells us…what, exactly? In relation to today's tasks, that is."

Well, sod you, then. "Nothing in particular, I dare say. But you have told me, more than once, to mention things which strike me as significant, and not to be afraid of being shot down or making a fool of myself. 'Say what you see' was, I believe, the precise idiom you employed."

"And I was absolutely right when I said those wise words, Frank, and you are absolutely right to remind me of them, and you will kindly remember to remind me not to forget them in future. Does the smoke bother you, by the way? I never thought to ask." He stubbed out his half-smoked cigar, energetically.

"Not at all," Frank said, thinking *Oh all right, then—un-sod you.* "All the men in my family smoked pipes, so it would take a fair-size bonfire of old car tyres to offend my nose."

"Men?" said Don, standing up, and rattling his

pockets for change. "I thought it was the women smoked the pipes in the north-east."

I won't tell him about great-granny Mitchell, Frank decided. *Not just yet.*

THE CALL CENTRE, which employed Gail Webb and several hundred other non-unionised workers, most of them married women, was part of an unfinished greenfield development just outside the Cowden borough boundaries. It consisted of one enormous building—a temporary-looking, single-storey structure that reminded Frank of a poultry shed he'd worked in during school summer holidays—and an even bigger car park.

At reception, they were told they could not speak to a member of staff who was "currently committed" unless concerning a "legitimate family emergency." When Don's reply to this was the single word *Arseholes,* uttered in conjunction with a dazzlingly broad smile, the receptionist summoned a supervisor, whose objections were blunter.

"We do have targets to meet, you know," the harassed young woman with the lorry-wide hips and hunched shoulders of someone twice her age, told them. "This isn't a holiday camp."

Frank opened his mouth to point out, in time-honoured fashion, that *This is a murder inquiry, you know,* but Don had obviously had enough clichés for one day.

"Yes, we have quotas too, love. In the police service. If we don't catch one murderer a week we don't get our Friday bonus. I'm sure you understand. So fetch Ms. Webb, yeah? Round about now, please."

Wearing a huff the size of a small continent, the supervisor did as she was bid, and after a further wait of almost ten minutes ("Always got to make a point, these types," said Don), Gail Webb arrived at reception.

She led them to a small rest room, furnished with soft chairs and a coffee machine, but empty of human beings. "The rest room's always empty," she explained, "because we don't get rest breaks."

She was tall for a woman, Frank noted—as tall as him—but, although quite slightly built, she didn't appear out of proportion. Most of her height seemed to be in her legs. She had lively eyes, slightly wild brown hair, and a rather large nose. Don had once told him— actually, it had been more than once—that women with large noses tended to be keen on sex. Not that Frank believed such daft generalisations, but all the same he hoped the heat he could feel in his face was not outwardly visible. *Why should I be embarrassed, but?* Don's the one that said it, not me.

All in all, she was an attractive, friendly-looking woman of about Frank's age, mid-twenties—and of about Don's type, judging by the way the DI was smiling and laughing with her. Her generous smile was contagious, Frank admitted to himself, and an impressive testament to her character, given that she was obviously nervous about the coming interview.

"Nice to meet you again, Gail," said Don. "Did you win your singles the other night?"

"No, believe it or not, I miscalculated a finish— went for the double sixteen instead of double ten. Very embarrassing!"

"Ouch," said Don. "I've done that myself before now. You feel a right idiot, don't you?"

Time for business, Frank reckoned. "Thanks for seeing us at short notice. I hope we don't get you in trouble with your boss.''

''I hope we do,'' said Don. ''You'd be better off out of this dump. Slavery was abolished in 1833, has nobody told them?''

The curve of her nose increased a little when she laughed, Frank noted. Not that it was of any significance, of course. ''No, word hasn't reached them yet. Perhaps I could raise it at one of our Focus and Target Sessions.''

Don lifted an interrogatory eyebrow.

''Don't ask!'' she said.

''Why do you stick it? Or is that a daft question?''

''Well, we need the money, basically. My husband—you haven't met Stuart yet?—well, he's a fitter, very skilled, but he was made redundant a couple of months ago and he hasn't found anything decent yet.''

''So money's tight?'' Frank asked.

''We're not desperate or anything, but we have got some shockingly expensive tastes, I'm afraid.''

''Hand-made darts?'' Don guessed.

''No, travel. For instance, we went to Cuba last winter. It was fantastic, everything we'd hope it'd be and more. But a bit pricier than a fortnight in Spain.'' She sighed, and added, almost to herself: ''We've had to cancel India this summer. Anyway, Stuart's redundancy came out of the blue—his company relocated to Germany, with virtually no warning. Luckily I've got several part-time and casual jobs in addition to this, and we've got no children yet, so we get by. But there never seems to be much left at the end of the month, if you know what I mean.''

''Oh, I do indeed,'' said Don. ''And my colleague

is learning, if he didn't already know. He's a new daddy, you see, got a lovely little babby called Joe.''

"Joseph," muttered Frank.

"Oh, lovely—congratulations!"

"He won't let me be a godfather, unfortunately, on account of me being a Satanist," said Don. "But there you go—you meet prejudice everywhere, don't you?"

She positively roared with laughter at that, while Frank cringed, and thought that, one day, Don was going to say something like that to someone who wasn't certain whether or not he was joking. *Someone like me, for instance.*

"How well did you know Yvonne Wood?" Frank asked.

"Not well, really. I only saw her at the darts. She chalked for us, as you probably know, she didn't actually play."

"It's strange," Don said. "Everyone says she was always there, but no-one seems to have known her all that well."

"She'd been there forever—the rumour is that she got involved with the team twenty-odd years ago, when her boyfriend played for it. Then he left, presumably, and she never did. So I suppose she's just part of the fittings, in a sense. Seems awful, now she's dead, doesn't it? But I don't know that anyone really knew her as such. You could try asking Cliff Overton, he's been around almost as long."

"Yes, we'll be talking to him soon. Now, I understand that your husband was also present on the night Chalkie died. Does he generally attend games?"

For the first time, the balance of Gail Webb's body language tilted from nervous-but-friendly to nervous-

and-guarded. "Yes, he usually comes along. Well, not usually—always in fact."

"So he's a darts fan, is he?"

"Not really, he's more into football."

"I see. So he's just a loyal hubby, likes to support your team?"

She pulled at a strand of loose hair that was hanging over her eyes. "Sort of. Look, you'll hear this from other people, so…the thing is, Stuart is rather possessive. I think to be honest he comes along because he doesn't like the idea of me being alone with a roomful of men." She smiled, without conviction. "I suppose I should be flattered, really, after four years of marriage."

"Common enough, these days, isn't it—women playing alongside men in darts teams? Not like when I was a lad. We had separate ladies' teams, and God help the poor bloke who got beaten by a woman in a practise game!"

Her expression serious, she replied: "I hold my place in the team on merit, I will say that. I'm not the best player in the world, or the best in the Hollow Head, but I am not the token woman in the team."

"No, well, you wouldn't be, would you? Because of your landlady, I mean."

She put her hand up to her mouth as if she'd just burped. "Oh, God yes! I wasn't counting Heather. Probably because—no, forget that, I'm sure you don't want to hear gossip."

"I'm sure we *do*," said Don.

"No, really, no. I don't know what I'm talking about, I only know what I've overheard. You know what people are like."

Never mind, thought Frank; if I know my DI Packham, we'll be coming back to that in the days to come. "Does it bother anyone, you being a woman?"

"Some of the more old-fashioned people, maybe. Who are just as likely to be young as old, incidentally. Mostly, I think it's what the Inspector just said—some guys get upset if they're beaten by a woman."

"Whereas some guys pay good money for the privilege," Don interjected, eliciting another round of breast-quivering laughter. From Gail Webb, and from himself.

"But really, if playing a woman puts them off—well, that's an advantage to me, isn't it?"

"Quite right," said Don. "If they don't understand the spirit of darts, then that's their problem. Tell me, in recent times have you noticed anyone arguing with Chalkie, or falling out with her, or on the other hand, spending a lot of time with her?"

She nodded. "Yes, quite a few people, in fact."

"Really? That's most helpful. Who, for instance?"

"Well, Cliff and Chalkie were hardly on speaking terms—but that wasn't just recent, that had been going on for ages, I think. And she never got on all that well with Heather Mason. But I did see her chatting with the Rees brothers at the last couple of matches, more than she usually would."

"Both of them?"

She thought about that. "I'm not sure, to be honest. I tend to think of them as a pair, despite—well, despite their obvious differences."

"Excellent," Don said. "You do keep your eyes open, don't you?"

"I'm nosey, you mean," said Gail, brushing an invisible fleck of dirt off the tip of her nose with an index finger. "Well, I am a bit, to be honest. I find people interesting. Don't you?"

"Certainly," Don agreed. "Anyone else you can think of?"

She shook her head. "No, no that's it. That's the lot."

Oh no it's not, thought Frank. He caught Don's eye, and could tell that the DI was thinking the same.

"Okay," said Don. "But was there anyone in the team that she was particularly chummy with? Generally, I mean. What I'm getting at is, is there someone who might be able to tell us more about her?"

Gail Webb shrugged. "I suppose the skipper, Brian. I think she helped him a bit with the team sheets and that, so they probably spent some time together."

They left it at that, but five minutes later, as the two officers sat in the car comparing notes, there was a tap at the passenger side window.

"Yes, Ms. Webb? Did you forget something?" She looked flushed, Frank noticed; from running after them, perhaps.

"The thing is, I want you to hear this from me, not from someone else." She spoke quickly, as if to get the words out before she had time to change her mind. "I was expecting you to ask me if anyone had a motive for killing Chalkie."

"We should have," said Don. "We forgot. So, who've you got in mind?"

"Me," she said. "And if you want to know why, you'd better ask my husband." She turned and trotted back across the car park in the direction of the turkey shed.

"Leave her," said Don, as Frank opened his door to go after her. "Ask her husband, she said. And that's what we'll do."

TEN

FROM THE WAY Don sat in the passenger seat as they drove away from the call centre and back towards Planet Earth, Frank could tell he wasn't too good. His bum was way down in the seat—like he was a fifteen-year-old in a maths lesson, first period after lunch—and his shoulders were up around his ears. Frank couldn't have said whether the DI was depressed, precisely, but he was certainly not (as one of Frank's late great-uncles, the one with the wart, used to say) "Cheerful as a piglet in a tit factory."

Still, he had to say something: he didn't know where he was supposed to be driving to. "I suppose we'll be wanting to see Gail's husband next, then?"

"Poor bloody woman." Don was staring out of his side window as he spoke, and his chin was still on his chest, so that Frank had to concentrate hard in order to catch his words. It was like trying to listen to a radio when the batteries were almost dead.

"Do you reckon? She seemed to be coping with life pretty well, I thought. Not one of life's losers, that one."

"Why do people get married, Frank? Honestly, you'd think after a million years of evolution, we'd have learned our lesson by now, wouldn't you?"

Sometimes, when Don was having one of his rants,

Frank wondered if his boss even knew who was in the car with him. Anyway, there was no direct answer that Frank could give to Don's question which involved neither dissent nor dissembling, so he made no attempt to provide one. Instead, he said: "These are points we might put to her husband, I suppose, if that's who we want to see next."

"No, I do not bloody well want to see him, Frank! Loathsome little man. Probably knocks her about."

Because he gets a bit jealous when she plays darts with blokes? *Dear oh dear, that sexy nose has done for you, hasn't it!* "We are going to have to see him sooner or later, though, in view of what she—"

"Yes, thank you, Constable, I do realise that—I am a fucking detective, you know."

"Yes, sir."

Frank turned left and then right and then right again, driving as slowly as he reasonably could without running the risk of getting nicked for kerb-crawling. He still had no idea where he was supposed to be going, and the atmosphere inside the car just now was not one that encouraged questions.

"Look, I'll tell you what," said Don, after the car had covered two miles in what might well have been a new world record for Slowest Motorised Journey. "We'll forget about lunch, all right? I just can't be bothered with lunch today."

Oh bugger my cat, thought Frank; that is bad. Not that he wasn't relieved in a way, since as far as he was concerned they'd already *had* lunch, and he really didn't think he could face another—you didn't get much exercise in CID, not compared to uniform. But even so, Don not wanting lunch, that was not a good sign.

"Okay, sir. So where are we going?"

"I want you to go and see Chalkie's employers. I know uniform have already done it, but we might as well cover everything."

"Right you are, sir." He didn't dare ask *And where will you be, meantime?* in case such a query was taken as impertinence, insubordination, or a personal attack. Or, even worse, as the nagging of a substitute spouse. There were moments when that did not seem too absurd a fear to Frank. He thought about it for a moment, and eventually came up with: "Where shall I drop you—back at the office?"

"Sod that. No, take me back to my car. I'm going to get my head down for a couple of hours, then I'll see if I can't track down this old geezer—what's his name? Gail mentioned him."

"Cliff Overton? I've got a work address for him here."

"Sounds like the sort who should be willing to speak ill of the dead. And you know what these old buggers are like—once they've started, you can't shut them up. Well, not since they brought in the Police and Criminal Evidence Act, you can't, anyway. I reckon it's because they know they're going to die soon, so they want to use up all their air. You know, like a holidaymaker spending his last few drachma on bubblegum at the airport on the way home."

"Yes, sir," said Frank. "That's the thing about the old 'uns—they do go on a bit."

EVERYTHING'S GETTING bigger, thought Don, as he parked his car outside the out-of-town DIY superstore where Cliff Overton worked. But sooner or later people are going to realise that bigger doesn't always mean better. Or maybe they're not...

Wide-eyed and horrified, he wandered around the great acreage of the superstore, with its aisles upon aisles of drills and curtain rods and plumbing bits and bobs and compost bins and lengths of plastic and racks of pre-packed grommets. *Grommets?* Weren't they the baddies in *Lord of the Rings?*

This wasn't really Don's sort of place at all. As far as he could remember he'd never been in one before, although he was aware that just about every town and suburb in Britain was now ringed with such sites. He'd never had much occasion to Do It Himself; never lived anywhere long enough for the need to arise. That was the great advantage of renting, he reckoned; if the sink got blocked you just handed in the keys and moved on to somewhere else.

He couldn't remember what Overton looked like—he must have seen him, at the original crime scene or at the darts match, but if so he hadn't registered particularly—and he was surprised to discover that most of the staff here seemed to be old folk, well past retirement age, he'd have guessed.

Don shuddered, as he passed yet another skeletal ancient with snowy hair and fingers twisted like tree roots, pushing a trolley full of duct tape. It gave him the creeps, truth be told, seeing all these geriatrics shambling purposefully around, doing slow-motion imitations of working people. He began to feel quite claustrophobic, in this enormous, spacious room—trapped amongst the coffin-dodgers in CrumblyWorld. *Middle age is bloody frightening enough without being constantly haunted by the ghosts of your future.*

On the pretext of inquiring about a cordless screwdriver ("Do I need one of these? What does it do, exactly? So how does it get its power, then, if it's cordless? It goes *backwards?* Blimey!" Don enjoyed a brief vision, like a film run in reverse, of using a backwards screwdriver to unassemble whole cities. An anarchist screwdriver!), he asked a teenage assistant, one of a rare breed in this place, how come so many of his colleagues were senior citizens.

The boy—who enjoyed the crack about the anarchist screwdriver, which Don hadn't realised he'd said out loud—explained. "Company policy, yeah? Fighting ageism, and that."

"I suppose that's fair enough," said Don, though he reckoned the best way to guarantee someone a happy retirement was to give him a decent pension, not pay him minimum wage to push grommets around a warehouse until he dropped dead.

"Maybe. But I reckon if the bosses take up an *ism,* it's because there's something in it for them."

"Too true," said Don. Ah, the cynicism of youth— what a breath of fresh air it was! "And what's in it for them this time?"

The lad leaned in to Don, as if to speak confidentially. The effect was rather undermined by the loudness with which he spoke; perhaps, Don thought, he was used to talking to people whose hearing wasn't all it might be. "Well, for a start, old people never take sick leave. They just come in and moan a lot. And they never ask for pay rises. They never take their holiday entitlement. They work through their lunch hours, they do free overtime. They're just basically so bloody grateful that someone has been kind enough to give them somewhere to go during the day."

"You're not keen, I take it?" said Don, thinking that

ageism worked both ways: weren't all these old folk, who'd already had their turn, pinching jobs from youngsters who actually needed to work?

The young assistant shook his head. "On the contrary. I love working here. I mean the job's shit, obviously, but the old people—they're brilliant. I love talking to them, listening to them. And they all look after me, you know? Like, there's only a few of us young ones working here, so we get treated as if we're their grandchildren. Imagine going into work every day and spending eight hours being spoilt by a dozen grandparents! I'm hardly allowed to lift a finger—'You sit down there, Sonny, you look tired, I'll fetch you a nice cup of tea.' No, the only thing I don't like is it costs a fortune working here."

"How do you mean?"

The boy smiled. "Well, let's just say that staff turnover is higher than average."

"Ah," said Don. "I see. You mean mortal turnover."

"Right. Think about it—all those collections. I'm dipping in my pocket twice a week for bloody funeral flowers!"

Don laughed. He didn't always feel like human company, and he hadn't thought he felt much like it today, but this kid had something about him. "Tell you what, I'll take the anarchist screwdriver. Now, can you direct me to a fellow called Cliff Overton?"

At the enquiry desk—Customer Service Point, actually—Don took his place as third in a queue of three, behind a man of about thirty and a young woman with a baby, and watched Overton in action.

The young mother got little joy from the little, grey man, who treated her with something approaching disdain—as if, Don felt, he didn't really think women should be buying tools at all, especially not women with babies. The man behind her wanted advice on which electric drill he should buy. Overton asked him questions that he obviously found incomprehensible, but even when he admitted this the old bastard was plainly unwilling to tell him what he wanted to know in plain English. Don reckoned he knew why: Overton was of a generation and a type who believed that every man of marriageable age should be able to turn his hand to every manner of job about the house himself, and that any who couldn't—any who needed advice—had no business being let out on their own. Cliff Overton was a DIY Nazi.

"Can I help you, sir?"

"You can, Mr. Overton." Don showed his warrant card. "By having a bit of a chat with me."

Overton was outraged. "I can't leave my post. I have responsibilities!"

His patience finally expended, Don replied: "Oh bollocks, Cliff! You're not an ambulance dispatcher—you're leaning against a counter in a suburban tool shop telling people how to use their screwdrivers backwards. Come on now, we'll go for a walk around the car park."

He allowed the fuming Customer Service Operative to ring for cover, then more or less marched him out of the shop and into the cold sun of the outside world. Don's own sun had set again, the pleasant chat he'd had with the younger assistant almost forgotten. *I've spent the best years of my life being polite to miserable old sods of all ages, sexes, classes and races.*

And ranks, he added. And if they were the best

years, I'm not looking forward much to the rest. So—
straight in with this old sod. No messing.

"Who do you reckon killed Chalkie, Cliff?"

Overton made a face like a cat tasting curry for the
first time. "Chalkie! Stupid bloody name for a grown
woman."

"Yvonne, then. Who killed her?"

"Well, don't look at me—I haven't had an erection
in ten years."

Don blinked, and forgot what he'd been going to say
next. It wasn't only what Overton had said that had
caught him by surprise; it was also the fact that he said
it with such evident pride.

"Sorry to hear that, Cliff. And on top of everything,
you're going deaf, aren't you?"

"No, I'm not! What do you mean?"

"Well, you yelled that bit about your floppy knob
so loudly, a bloke driving a lorry down the far lane
over there turned to stare at you and nearly ran over a
nun walking her Doberman." Now it was Overton's
turn to look as if he couldn't quite believe what he was
hearing. *Good,* thought Don, who was a strong believer
in "Do as you've just been done by".

"You're a bloody odd sort of policeman, aren't
you?"

"Me? You're the one going on about erections—
what have they got to do with anything?"

Shaking his head with irritation—but slowly—
Overton said: "Obvious, isn't it? You ask anyone.
Yvonne Wood was a tart, plain and simple. She'd sleep
with anything in trousers. And that's what got her
killed, sure as eggs."

Tart, Don assumed, meant that she wasn't married

and had more than one boyfriend. "You ever marry, Cliff?"

"I am a widower, if you must know."

"Oh, I beg your pardon. Were you together long?" And if so, did the poor cow top herself?

"Not long. My wife was killed in the war."

"Your wife was killed in the war?" said Don, thinking that this was an unusual bit of role-reversal. What was she, a paratrooper?

"Yes, she was as it happens. She was killed in the Blitz, while I was away fighting for your blooming country. That's amusing to you, is it?"

Don held up a hand, and looked down at the tarmac. "I apologise, Mr. Overton. I sincerely apologise. I misunderstood. But listen, this is important: do you actually know—not suspect, but know-of anyone in the darts team, or associated with it, who had an affair with Yvonne?"

"More like who *didn't!*"

Right. So, nothing in fact, just rumour. No, less than rumour—just mucky imaginings from a jealous old lemon-sucker. "What, you're saying she slept with all the men in the team? And the women, too?"

Overton flushed, his grey face turning an unappetising shade of pink. "Don't be disgusting! I'm going back in now."

"All right, just one more thing—what do you actually do for the darts team? I know you don't play, and you didn't chalk, because they had a chalker. So what are you—the lucky mascot?"

Overton, who had begun walking away from Don, stopped and turned; clearly, this was something he was more than happy to discuss. "If you really want to know, I think you might justifiably describe me as a kind of coach, trainer, manager, and non-playing captain all rolled into one. If it wasn't for me, I may say without false pride, that team would collapse. The landlady doesn't give a damn, the so-called skipper's too busy filling out flow charts and pie diagrams and filing his clipboards in alphabetical order to actually get anything done. Yes, sir, if it wasn't for muggins, here—''

Ah yes, thought Don, as the old man continued to itemise the many facets of his indispensability; now I've placed you. You're the Hollow Head's official Pain in the Bum. Every team's got to have one—it's probably listed as Item Five in the league regulations.

ELEVEN

WHILE DON WAS stocking up on DIY gear, Frank was sipping strong, black, rather sweet coffee in the tiny, intimate, chaotic office of the owner and manager of Bo's Bets. The day was dry and chilly, and Frank was happy enough to be sitting in front of an electric fire, sunk in an ancient armchair. The electric fire might have been an antique, if there were such a thing as antique electric fires. It was at least as old as the chair, and, with its three glowing bars, almost shockingly effective. Frank had taken his coat off as soon as he came into the room, and was now thinking seriously about removing his suit jacket, too.

"Call me Bo, please," said the manager, lighting a foreign-smelling cigarette. He didn't quite light it from the butt of its predecessor, but the pause between them could not have been measured in any unit larger than seconds. "Everyone does. It's not my name, but then, you know, names aren't all they're cracked up to be."

By his accent, look and manner, Frank took him for a Greek; probably Greek Cypriot, in this area. With his dark skin, generous features, and luxuriant grey-black hair, he could be any age from forty to seventy. *Could be any age he wanted to be,* Frank decided. Women would go for him: ever since he was Joseph's age he'd have had women all over him. Frank didn't approve of envy—and more than that, he found it distasteful—but he couldn't help envying men like Bo a little; the sort that looked like pirates and behaved like gentle-men, and did both naturally, without effort or apparent thought. Not that Frank had ever been without a girl-friend, from the time he was fifteen onwards but, well, until he'd met Debbie, he'd always been aware that he wasn't *attractive* to women, even though he had no difficulty *attracting* them.

"Very nice coffee, Bo. Hits the spot on a day like this." Bo had put a plate of small cakes next to the coffee pot, but Frank didn't fancy them. They'd be too sweet for him, he'd had them before in Greek restaurants and hated them, so he just ignored them. His host didn't push him to eat one; he'd offered them once, and left it at that. This was another thing Frank'd noticed about Greeks, since moving to London: the wholly unembarrassed and unforced way in which they offered hospitality. Where he came from, you did your duty as far as guests were concerned, and you put a brave face on it, but nobody said you had to enjoy it. "How long did Yvonne Wood work here?"

"She was with me for many years, Frank. I don't have to call you Detective Constable Mitchell? My coffee will go cold if I have to keep saying that."

Frank smiled, and drank some more coffee. Actually, he thought it tasted pretty awful, but since he couldn't bring himself to eat the cakes, he had to drink the coffee. Nobody said he had to enjoy it, mind. "Frank'll do fine."

"Okay. Good. Well, Yvonne—a lovely woman, re-ally lovely—she pretty well ran this place. Without her, I don't know, maybe it's time to call it a day."

He sounded more upset by Chalkie's death than anyone else they'd spoken to so far. Was this one of her famous married men? And was there a subtle way of asking that? "Sounds like she was one of the family, Bo."

The bookmaker waved his coffee cup in one direction and his cigarette in another. It was an expansive gesture, one that spoke eloquently of loss, and even more so of Bo's balancing skills. If Frank had tried it, he'd have been lucky to get away with first-degree burns and a dry-cleaning bill.

"Oh, she was, Frank, she was! She used to have Christmas dinner with us, you know, me and my wife. Ah, my poor wife is inconsolable. Well, so am I, if it comes to that." He leaned forward. "But this is what is so strange, you know, everyone loved Yvonne—you must have heard this, I'm sure, from everyone, yes? She was such a friendly, good person, no-one could have hated her enough to kill her."

"I have to say, in all honesty, that we have found, from talking to her friends at the pub and so on, that she was possibly more popular with men, as it were, than with women. On the whole, like." *Was that subtle enough?*

Bo put his cup down, and stubbed out his cigarette. "Ah. You are very tactful, Frank. Yvonne…I think we could say that dear Yvonne was, you know, unlucky in love. You understand? She always went for the wrong men, to put it plainly." He shook his head, sighed, and lit another cigarette.

"To put it even more plainly," said Frank, "you mean married men?"

Bo nodded; his nod, if anything, even more sad than his headshake. "Yes, I am afraid that was mostly the case. But you know, Frank, for a woman who gets to a certain age, it is not so easy to find a loving partner. Not so easy at all. But, of course, married men—well, they are always easy. There is never, since the world begins, a shortage of married men willing to play away from home. It's sad, you know, but it's the way life is.''

Frank wasn't daft: he knew that the bookie's remarks provided an opening for an obvious question. But somehow, he just couldn't bring himself to ask it, not right out. Not sitting here, enjoying the man's fire and his horrible coffee, and sharing his sad nods and sighs and headshakes and hand gestures. This, he thought, is why most detectives prefer to do their interviewing in bare rooms, in brick-built police stations.

He comforted himself with the thought that it couldn't really be relevant, anyway; Bo was not a suspect, no matter how many away games he might or might not have played.

''What you're telling me is very helpful, Bo, and you will understand that it is an aspect of the case that, necessarily, we are looking into very closely. Adultery is not an uncommon motive for murder, as I'm sure you know. Was there ever, as far as you were aware, an occasion of a wife or a girlfriend who found out about one of Yvonne's, ah…''

''Dalliances?''

''Precisely. Her dalliances.''

''Well, there was nothing that I knew of, but although we were close, we were maybe not close in that way. I feel that perhaps Yvonne was not happy about this aspect of her life. You understand? It wasn't something she preferred to talk about too much.''

That *is* sad, thought Frank. All that trouble and guilt, and she wasn't even enjoying it. ''Do you happen to

know if she was seeing anyone, in the weeks just before her death?''

"Yes," said Bo, ''there was someone. But in answer
to your next question—no, I don't know who it was.
Don't know his name, or anything about him. Only that
once or twice lately, Yvonne would say at closing time,
Must rush, got a date tonight—wish me luck. Something like this.''

"I see," said Frank, giving his fingers time to catch
up as they wrote in his notebook. "Could it have been
someone from the darts team?''

Bo shrugged. Even his shrug was sad, or perhaps
apologetic. "Quite possibly. I just don't know.''

"Or one of your customers perhaps?''

"Well, this is possible, of course, but I would say
probably, no. I think that Yvonne did not wish to…''

"To mix business with pleasure?'' Frank suggested.

"That, yes, but even more I think that she would
perhaps not have gone out with someone from here,
because of me, you see. She would not have wished to
embarrass me like that. You understand?''

So many rules, thought Frank; Chalkie's love life
was governed by so many rules. "In that case, if her
boyfriend wasn't from the darts team, let's assume, and
wasn't a customer of the betting shop, then where else
might she have met someone? What else did she do
with her life?''

"I think, to be truthful, that outside work she did
not have much except the darts team. She loved that
team, you know—it was a family to her, in many
ways.''

"She didn't have any other hobbies, belong to any
other clubs?''

"I think not, no. She never mentioned anything else, and I think she would have."

"It sounds as if she led quite a lonely life," said Frank.

Bo wiped his eyes on the back of his hand. "Ah, Frank, it is sad—such a friendly, intelligent, attractive woman, not so old, with so much to give—to talk of her in this way, it is sad. But lonely: yes, I think she was lonely." He took a cigarette from the packet, but instead of lighting it, rolled it between his fingers for a moment. "Listen, I will tell you the truth, what I think is the truth about poor Yvonne, only because she is dead now, and you must find who killed her. You understand? I think perhaps the one thing she really wanted, more than any other thing, was a husband. Of her own, I mean, of course. Yes?"

"I understand what you mean, yes."

"And in her life, she had Bo's Bets, and she had the Hollow Head, and so, if she couldn't have the one thing she really wanted, a family of her own, then she would have these two good things that she really loved. She would make do with those two good things, which she loved for their own sake, and not because they were pretend families, not substitutes. You understand, Frank? She would not settle for anything that was less."

"Except her married men."

"Ah well, you are young and you make judgements. But we all have our needs, no? And we all keep hoping, don't we? No matter how many times it does not work out. And, you know, the great sadness of this whole situation—well, we are both men, we know this to be true: these married men, they always go back to their wives in the end. Yes? Whatever they say, these men, they always go back to their wives. This is the one thing that I could never say to her, to poor Yvonne— but then, I suppose, she must have known it, if anybody did.''

Frank sipped some more coffee as he digested all that. What the bookie said made a lot of sense, and it seemed to lead to only one logical conclusion. ''Then her current boyfriend almost certainly would have been a member of the darts team.''

''Yes, it seems likely to me.''

Frank wondered what Don would make of that. He'd be pleased, surely? Further circumstantial evidence that Chalkie had been having it away with a married man on the darts team gave them a good, solid, understand-able motive to work with. On the other hand, it didn't narrow things down all that much: husbands and wives, boyfriends and girlfriends, could all be in the frame for a murder inspired by adultery.

He had said his goodbyes to Bo, walked out through the shop and into the street, walked twenty yards to where he'd parked the car, and was just about to press the button on his key fob when a thought struck him.

''Shit,'' he muttered, and walked back along the pavement, and into Bo's Bets. The assistant on duty gave him a puzzled look, but buzzed him through the security door into the office, even so. The bookie was still sitting where Frank had left him, smoking and star-ing into the fire. *Someone loved you, Chalkie,* thought Frank.

''Look, Bo, I'm new to this detecting lark,'' he said, having declined further coffee, or even a seat. ''There's an obvious question I should have asked you, except that it only just occurred to me.''

"Sure, go on," said Bo, drinking coffee and smoking simultaneously, whilst standing up.

If it's not sex, Frank was thinking, then it's likely to be money. Could be both, of course. Money; gambling; Chalkie Wood worked in a betting shop. *Idiot!* Don would've spotted that right away. No matter what bloody mood he was in. Ah well, better late than never, as the undertaker said to the doctor when they met on the dead man's stairs.

"Did Yvonne ever recognise any of the betting shop customers, as far as you know? Recognise them from elsewhere, I mean."

"Well, yes, certainly. She had lived in this area for many years, she knew many people to say hello to. From the pub, from the shops, and so on."

"Right, but what I'm getting at is, did she seem to know anyone in particular—as more than a casual nodding acquaintance."

Bo smoked his cigarette in silence for a moment, before replying. "Ah. Yes, I see now what you mean, Frank. Or rather, I think I must call you Constable now, because you understand that what you're asking me, it raises certain ethical matters."

"Ethical matters?"

"There is between a bookmaker and his client an unwritten contract of confidentiality, you understand. Of course, you are looking for a motive, I see that. A secret gambler. I can tell you now, that if you had known Yvonne, you would realise that she was not the sort who would...*use* information improperly, in any way."

"Of course, sure, I understand that—but these things have to be checked out, eliminated, so that we can concentrate on what's left."

The bookie walked around in small circles, smoking and sipping his coffee. He didn't bump into anything, which Frank found pretty impressive, given the cramped nature of the surroundings. Eventually, he spoke—with his back to Frank, as if to underline his reluctance.

"I do not know the man's name. All right? I do not know it, simple as that, he is not a client with an account, only a casual customer. But yes, a few weeks ago, there was someone who I felt, perhaps... He only came in here three or four times. The first few occasions, he dealt with me. Yes? I was on the counter. But the last time he came in, it happened that Yvonne was out front. He saw her, and I am sure this was the first time he had seen her here, and I felt, yes, that he was not pleased to see her."

"When you say he wasn't pleased, how displeased was he? Like, slightly embarrassed—or something more?"

Again, Bo paused before answering. His easy hospitality of earlier had evaporated in the heat of his ethical dilemma. "Well. Okay, yes, I would say it was more than that. He looked—his expression was one of almost, I would say, panic. He left without placing his bet."

"I see," said Frank, his heart beating faster, while he rushed to get everything down in blue ink. "And this man—"

"I have already told you, Constable, I do not know his name."

"That's understood." Frank felt in his jacket pocket for the team photo. "But you would maybe recognise him from a picture?"

Bo sighed, and took a pair of reading glasses from the pocket of his shirt. "Let us sit down, Constable. If I must do this, I want to do it properly. No mistakes, you understand?"

TWELVE

SITTING IN HIS CAR, Frank phoned Don for further instructions—and got no reply from Don's mobile, other than a network message telling him that the number he was calling was currently unavailable. *Uh-oh*...

He called the office—a thing he generally tried to avoid doing on Don-related matters—but he needn't have bothered, as it turned out; DI Packham hadn't been seen in the CID room all day. "You want us to dredge the canal?" one evidently underemployed wit asked him.

For a few minutes he simply sat there, drumming his fingers on the steering wheel, occasionally tapping his mobile phone on his knee, somewhat in the manner of an absent-minded doctor testing his own reflexes.

After a while, though, no amount of drumming and tapping could protect him from an inescapable conclusion. *Ah, shit!* It's no good, I'll have to go around to his flat. The DI had said he was going to "get his head down for a couple of hours"; perhaps he was fast asleep at home, his alarm clock lying atomised on the floor around him.

Hell, but he'd rather not visit the man at his place of residence! He'd only ever been there once before, and although, in fairness, Don had been pleased to see him, and had made him very welcome, it had still been an unusual and even unsettling experience. Unusual and unsettling were not terms of approval in Frank's language.

He tried Don's mobile one last time—"The number you are calling is…"—and then pointed the car towards West Hampstead.

As he parked, almost dead opposite the conversion in which Don rented a studio flat, Frank noted that the DI's car was nowhere to be seen. He looked up the street, he looked down the street, but no—no car. And he was damn sure these little flats didn't come with garages.

Still, since he'd come this far, he might as well see the thing through to its anti-climax. The street door was open (they always were, in Frank's experience, and even if the Met were to employ ten thousand extra crime prevention officers, they always would be), so he climbed the stairs to the first floor. On the landing he paused, and took out his mobile. One more go, he reckoned; anything to put off the moment when he would have to hammer on his boss's woodwork. No reply, of course—he hadn't for a second thought there would be, but there again he'd never heard of anyone coming unstuck by being too thorough—so he took a deep breath, and banged on the door. One, pause; two, pause; three—

The door opened, and there standing in the doorway was a figure wearing something that looked a bit like a sari, in bright orange, a floral headdress, huge orange earrings and a four-inch layer of multi-coloured makeup.

Oh my God! Don's wearing earrings! Don's wearing makeup! Don's a—

"Can I help you, young man?"

At the sound of the voice, panic receded sufficiently to allow Frank's senses to come into operation; not at full speed, perhaps, but at least his mind had returned from its brief visit to the ceiling and was once again resident in his head.

Don is not a five-foot-tall, seven stone, elderly Chinese woman. No matter how much slap he's got on, or what he wears in his earlobes, he just *isn't*. So who the hell's this, then? His girlfriend?

"I said, can I help you? You look as if you've seen a ghost."

"Yes, I... Yes, right." Frank was acutely aware of a small quantity of sweat that needed wiping from his forehead. There was no way he was going to run his sleeve across his brow on a cold February day, standing on this draughty landing, in front of this citizen who, from her frown, already thought she was dealing with a man trapped without a visa on the wrong side of the border between Eccentric and Odd. He let the beads of sweat go where they would, cleared his throat, and started again.

"I'm very sorry to trouble you, ah, madam. I was actually looking for Mr. Don Packham."

The old woman's face cleared. "Ah, yes. Please wait here." She shut the door. And put the chain on, Frank couldn't help noticing. Presumably, she had gone to fetch Don. *Oh, hell, I hope he's not naked.*

After a few seconds, the woman returned carrying a pile of envelopes. "These are for Mr. Packham, I think."

"For Mr. Packham? Oh, I see—he doesn't live here anymore?"

She gave Frank the kind of look that one might give an idiot; which, as the rational part of his brain finally caught up with and overtook his imagination, he decided was fair enough. "No, of course he doesn't live here. I live here. I've been here for three months. The previous tenant didn't leave a forwarding address, according to the landlord, so I've been keeping his post in case he turned up to collect it. But he never has."

No, thought Frank; he's probably forgotten the address by now. "I see, of course. That was very kind of you."

"Kind? It is normal, surely. However, if you are a friend of his, perhaps you could take them?"

"Certainly, yes. I'll see he gets them." He held out his hands to receive the mail, but the Chinese woman kept hold of it. She was looking at him with fresh suspicion. He reckoned he could guess what she was thinking: *If you're his friend, how come you don't know his current address?*

Frank showed her his warrant card. "I work with Mr. Packham, you see."

"A policeman? The previous tenant was a *policeman?*"

"That's correct, madam."

She gave him the post. "Well, that is a surprise, I must say. A policeman—I would not have guessed."

Frank decided he didn't want to know what she meant by that, so he tucked the letters into his overcoat pockets, and thanked her for her trouble.

"Not at all, Constable. From your face, I would say rather it was I who had troubled you."

Back in the car, he took a moment to wipe his brow—at last—and catch his breath. Bloody Don Packham! Couldn't he be normal about *anything?*

Once again, he dialled Don's mobile number.

"Yeah?"

"Oh—sir?" said Frank, taken by surprise. He'd almost forgotten that people sometimes did answer phones. "It's Frank here."

"Yeah?"

Frank battled on, in the face of overwhelming monosyllables. "I've spoken to the bookie. Yvonne's employer?"

"Yeah."

"Quite interesting, in fact." He waited. Nothing; so now it was zero syllables, was it? "And I was just wondering what to do next."

"Use your initiative, Frank."

Listening to the silence of a unilaterally ended phone call, Frank thought: "Right. I bloody will." He started up the car and drove home, where his welcome would be more certain.

THE NEXT MORNING, Saturday, having overslept, Don arrived at the Hollow Head at half-past nine, and was annoyed to find Frank not there. Surprised, too, because he wasn't a bad lad, really, not by a long chalk. And reliable enough, no question about that.

He suddenly had a nasty thought: it definitely wasn't like Frank to be late. Supposing he was ill? Now Don came to think about it, the young DC had sounded a bit odd on the phone yesterday.

"Hello, is that Debbie? It's Don here, love, Don Packham. Yes, I'm fine thanks, I was just a bit concerned about Frank. Is he all right? Are you sure? Because if he's unwell, then obviously he must on no account... Well, okay, you're the nurse, I suppose you know best. But you're absolutely certain he's well enough to come to work today?" Don shifted the phone to his other ear, and began searching his pockets for his cigar tin. "He's absolutely fine is he? Well in that case, why isn't he here?" He put a cigar between his lips, and then began going through his pockets again, looking for something with which to set light to it. "'Here' as in the pub, the Hollow Head. The murder scene. Right, well look, send him on his way, will you? Fast as possible. He'll just have to finish whatever he was doing on his own time."

The pub wasn't open yet, and he didn't fancy disturbing that dragon of a landlady quite so early in the morning, so he decided to sit in the car and have a smoke while he waited for Frank to come dawdling in. Upon tobacco-assisted reflection, he further decided that he wouldn't give the lad a bollocking for being late. Everyone's entitled to a bad day now and then—especially if they've got a new babby to deal with, that can't make life any easier.

Bloody hell! The cigar dropped from his mouth. Supposing it was the baby that was ill? He should have asked!

Frank had scarcely finished parking his own car before Don was upon it, yanking open the driver's door to demand: "Is he all right?"

"What?" said Frank. "Is who all right?"

"The baby, for God's sake! Is Joe okay?"

Frank blinked, scratched his nose, and said: "Well, yes, he was when I left home. Thanks for asking."

Don exhaled deeply, breath and smoke indistinguishable on the frosty air. "Well, thank heavens for that. I mean, you can't be too careful, can you?"

Still blinking, Frank got out of the car, then reached back in to retrieve a bundle of envelopes secured by two rubber bands. "I've got some post for you here."

Now it was Don's turn to blink. "You've what?"

"Got some post for you. I went around to your flat yesterday—to your old place, I mean, in West Hampstead."

Don looked at the post, then at Frank, but couldn't make a lot of sense out of either of them. "Why on earth would you do that?" he said, as the two of them walked over to his car. "I don't live there any more."

Frank sighed. "No, I realise that—now. But I didn't realise it when I went around there. Which was why I went around there."

Don shook his head. "You're not making any sense, Frank. You went around to my old place because you didn't realise I didn't live there any more? That's not much of a motive, is it?" He took the bundle of post and chucked it on the back seat of his car without glancing at it. "I haven't lived in West Hampstead for ages. Do try and keep up."

"You didn't tell me you'd moved, sir."

"Oh, I am so sorry! Obviously, in future I shall report my every movement, of residence or of bowel, directly to you, Chief Superintendent Mitchell!"

They got into Don's car. Don smoked a cigar. Frank looked out of the window.

Eventually, Don said: "Okay, so what did we get yesterday? I spoke to this Overton bloke, he certainly wasn't keen on poor Chalkie. He's another one who had a lot to say about her and married men. Nothing specific, but the more we hear, the more I reckon we're looking for a woman."

"As the killer?"

Don nodded. "I reckon so. The female equivalent of a cuckold, whatever that is. Cuckoldess, possibly. Cuckoldette, I don't know. Anyway, Chalkie was knocking off some married bloke, his woman found out, and decided to put a stop to it.''

"Well, yeah, maybe. But I got something interesting from her employer, too.'' Frank took his notebook out of his pocket, which struck Don as mildly pretentious, though he certainly wasn't going to say anything about it. Not with Frank in this mood. "Now, Bo—that's the bookie—he too confirms that Yvonne's boyfriends tended to be married. But he also gave me something that might point in a different direction.''

"Such as?''

Frank took the team photo from his pocket. What's he going to bring out next, Don wondered—a sodding rabbit?

"Gambling,'' said Frank. "Like, a motive for murder—if it's not sex, it's probably money, isn't that right?''

"Can be, yes. That's what they say on the training courses, anyhow.''

"Right. Well, I showed him this picture, and asked if he recognised any of the darts people as his customers. And he did.'' Frank pointed at one of the figures gathered around the Hollow Head's dartboard. "He'd placed a few bets at Bo's, and had dealt with Bo himself. Then the last time he came in, only a couple of weeks ago, he found himself face to face with Yvonne Wood.''

"That is interesting,'' Don admitted. "How did he react?''

"He bolted, basically. Turned tail and fled. He was obviously shocked to see her there, from what Bo says.''

"Yeah but hold on, Frank—he knew the woman. He must have known she worked there.''

"Not necessarily. He's not a member of the team himself, remember—he's only what the landlady calls a hanger-on."

Don took out his cigars, discovered that he'd only got one left, and put them away again. "Even so…"

"Also, don't forget that Chalkie was chalking every game. So it's quite possible that he'd never had much of a conversation with her, not at a personal level, at least. Besides which, even if she had happened to mention she worked in a bookie's, she might not have said which one."

Don thought about it. "I suppose that's possible. Darts is like any other hobby, you go there to get away from work, not to natter on about it."

"Either way, when he did see her working there, he wasn't best pleased."

Don took the photo from Frank. "Well, given that your Mr. Webb's name has already cropped up once in this investigation, we should certainly reckon on talking to him at our earliest convenience. He doesn't look exactly full of the joys in this photo, does he? Very much the pose of a man doing his duty."

"His wife said he wasn't much of a darts fan, didn't she?"

"One thing I will say for this case—we've no shortage of motives."

Frank grinned. "Aye. Adultery and blackmail, and that's only so far." Don started to speak, but Frank interrupted him. "And, of course, Stuart Webb fits into both categories. Sorry, Don, what were you going to say?"

He's all smiles now that I fancy his theory, thought Don. Detectives! They're all kids at heart. "Only that we shouldn't rush to assume that the gambling angle automatically leads, if it leads anywhere at all, to black-mail. We've heard nothing to suggest that Chalkie was that sort, at all.''

"If not blackmail, then what?"

"Simple fear of exposure. Assuming his wife doesn't know about his gambling habit, which is a fair old assumption on its own, and one we'll have to check out.''

Frank shook his head. "I'm dead sure she didn't. She can't have done, otherwise his behaviour at Bo's Bets makes no kind of sense.''

"Now, Frank—makes no kind of sense that we can yet see, you mean.''

"Aye, fair enough. But think back: Gail Webb did say that they were always short of money these days, didn't she? And, plus, he's out of work—I mean what kind of wife is going to be happy to see her man gambling when he's not bringing in a wage?''

Don decided to light up anyway. They could stop at a tobacconist's on the way. He got out of the car. "Come on, you're driving.''

Frank slid over to the driver's seat. "Where to?''

Don hoped his laugh was lost in the noise his shoes made on the gravel as he walked around to the passenger's side. *Ah, shouldn't laugh at the kid for being keen!* "We'll go and have a word with your pal Stuart Webb, the man with the pony fixation. But when we've done that, we'll get back onto the Avenging Missus scenario.''

Frank sounded slightly deflated as he asked: "You still reckon that's more likely then, do you?''

"I won't say it's more *likely,* Frank, not necessarily.

But you've got to admit, if it comes to a choice between sex and money, then sex has got to be more *fun*." He belted himself in. "Any bloody day of the week."

THIRTEEN

"BIT ANONYMOUS," said Don. "I mean, I'm sure they're not cheap, these houses, and I daresay they come with two of everything, but I wouldn't like to live on an estate, all the houses exactly the same. And if I did live on an estate, I'd want it to be a working-class one, where at least your neighbours might say good morning to you occasionally. Don't you reckon?"

Frank restricted his reply to a single syllable: "Mm." The truth was, though, that he didn't agree, not even nearly, and his disagreement began with the simple fact that this was not an estate. It was a development. Completely different matter; Gail and Stuart Webb might be short of income, but they were a long way from poor, and they lived in a very new, semi-detached, three-bedroom house on a highly respectable-looking *development*. Anonymous—yeah, okay. But cheerful, too, to Frank's eye.

Anyway, not an estate, not by any stretch of the imagination: two or three cul-de-sacs, separated from (or, depending on which way you looked at it, linked to) a couple more cul-de-sacs by a hard-surface playground and a green playing field. Oh yes, and—he saw now as the car turned the final corner into the Webbs' street—linked to, or separated from, another cul-de-sac development in the other direction, by a small shopping precinct.

Very nice, thought Frank as he parked and unbuckled. Sort of place where people wash their cars every Sunday, even if it's raining, taking all day about it—but don't have their radios on max while they're doing it. His sort of place, in fact; not the sort of place he came from, sure, but certainly the kind of place he was going to. He hoped neither of the Webbs would need nicking before this case was finished; wouldn't be fair to such a nice development.

Stuart Webb met them at the door wearing an apron and rubber gloves. *I'm having one of those days,* thought Frank. *I'm just thankful he hasn't got his hair in curlers.*

''You'd better come, in, I suppose.'' His accent was Welsh—south Wales, Frank guessed—which tallied with his stocky body and dark hair. He was a few years older than his wife, though not yet thirty. His expression was one of dissatisfaction, of annoyance at the universe's shortcomings, and from the way the lines of his face fell, Frank suspected it was at least a semipermanent feature.

''Sorry to disturb you, Mr. Webb,'' said Don, as they walked through to the kitchen. ''You're obviously busy.''

He'd been cleaning the oven, that was clear—and really cleaning it, too. Frank saw the bucket full of blackened, soapy water, the selection of old toothbrushes, the wire scourers and drying rags, and the pattern in which these accoutrements were arranged on the kitchen floor suggested that Webb had been lying on his back to do his cleaning, as if he were underneath a car raised on blocks. Frank smiled; he'd been married long enough to know that when men did women's jobs, that was how they did them. He remembered his grand-dad doing the ironing when his gran was poorly: "It may take longer my way, son, but it's a damn sight more thorough than what your gran does." Even as a kid, Frank had understood one advantage of such thoroughness: it could only be contemplated once or twice a year, not on a weekly basis.

"I bet your wife's delighted to have you helping out, isn't she?" said Don.

"I'm not *helping out*," Webb replied. "I'm *doing* it. She works, I look after the house. I'm not doing her some sort of *favour*, you know. It's not her bloody *birthday*."

"No, right," said Don. "Absolutely. All I meant was—"

"When we both worked, we split the chores in half. Now I'm not working, I do this and she does the earning. It's only logical." He picked up one of the grease-encrusted toothbrushes, looked at it for a moment and then dropped it. "I'm sure my wife will have told you how I'm redundant."

Funny choice of words, Frank thought.

"Absolutely," said Don. "Logical, as you said. And very sensible. All I meant was that perhaps not all couples would work things out so sensibly."

"Well then, they're idiots, aren't they?"

Frank had a feeling they weren't going to get a cup of tea at this house. No biscuits, either.

"Mr. Webb, we have two good reasons for treating you as a suspect in the murder of Yvonne Wood," said Don, somewhat to Frank's surprise, because in the car earlier, Don had said *We'll go in soft, see if we can't get him to trip himself up*. There again, when the DI felt that one of his suspects was behaving in an unnecessarily impolite manner, he did tend to lose patience with them quite rapidly.

"Do you indeed," Webb replied, still sounding annoyed rather than worried. "And what are they when they're at home, then?"

Don nodded at Frank. *Ah—time for table tennis, is it?* Taking his lead from his boss, Frank went in hard and low, hoping he'd got it right, that he'd interpreted the signals correctly; but at the same time knowing that, whatever his other faults, DI Packham at least wasn't one of those guv'nors who thought constables shouldn't think.

"Your wife believes you were having an affair with Chalkie." She hadn't quite said as much, not in so many words, but this was the interpretation Don and Frank had agreed to put on what she'd told them in the call centre car park. If she *hadn't* meant that, Don had said, or if she hadn't meant them to mention it to her husband—too bad. She should learn not to speak in riddles during a murder inquiry.

Stuart Webb smiled for the first time since he'd opened the door to them. The first time that day, as far as Frank knew. It was—no getting around it—a smug smile. *"Feared,"* he said. "Not *believes.*"

"I beg your pardon?"

"My wife feared I was having an affair with Chalkie. She doesn't believe I was doing so. You see the rather crucial difference, from a police point of view?"

"And how do you know what is in your wife's mind, sir?"

The brightness of Webb's smugness intensified, as if from sixty watts to one hundred. "Gail told me about all this last night. She told me what she'd said to you, and warned me that you'd be round to see me about it.''

''And what did you tell her, Mr. Webb? In answer to her allegations.''

''They weren't allegations, Constable, they were *fears*. And I was able to reassure her that her *fears* were unfounded.''

''I see,'' said Frank, and then found that he couldn't come up with anything to follow it. He was, no two ways about it, floundering. If the Metropolitan Police Sports & Social Club gave prizes for impressions of flatfish, he'd be up on the podium, no trouble. ''I see,'' he began again, and almost sighed with relief when Don interrupted.

''You've reassured your wife, Mr. Webb, but of course as far as the law's concerned, what you tell your wife is entirely your own affair. Nothing to do with us.''

Webb's frown was back, Frank noted with some pleasure; the smugness must have found Stuart's face a nice place for a holiday, but not somewhere it would wish to live. ''What are you suggesting?''

''You've told your wife one version, Stuart. Now perhaps you'd like to tell us another version. The two versions don't have to match in every particular, is all I'm saying. But,'' and here he leaned over and tapped Stuart Webb very lightly on the shoulder with the tip of one finger, ''the version you tell us has to be the truth. That's the crucial difference.''

Irritation, smugness, and now anger—the reddening of the face, the spreading of the shoulders; that was anger, all right, Frank reckoned. He doesn't mind being accused of murder, but he gets all steamed up if you say he's been lying to his wife. Interesting; though

from the point of view of Webb being a potential murderer, not entirely encouraging.

"The truth, Inspector, is what I told my wife. I have
not had any kind of sexual or romantic liaison with
Yvonne Wood at any time. Ever. And if you want me
to make a formal statement to that effect..."

"Not at the moment, perhaps later." Frank was impressed by his boss's smoothness; by the way he managed to suggest that Webb's answers were precisely
what he'd been hoping for. "It depends on how our
inquiries progress. We will of course be talking to others connected to the deceased—"

"You can talk to who you bloody like, pal, your
inquires won't progress in that direction, because
there's nothing there to discover!"

"Fair enough," said Don, taking out his cigars.
"Mind if I smoke?"

Webb took two audible breaths, right down into his
lungs. "No, I don't mind. There's an ashtray up on
that shelf behind you."

"Thanks. Got it. Now, the second thing." As Don
lit up, he nodded once more at Frank. *Ping pong; ping
pong.*

"Your gambling, Mr. Webb," said Frank. "Has it
become a problem?"

This time, Frank was pleased to see, Webb did look
shocked. He'd been expecting the questions about him
and Chalkie—but he certainly hadn't been expecting
this. He managed to say, "Gambling?" But then he
had to stop, to clear his throat.

"What is it you bet on, Stuart?" Don asked.
"Horses, dogs? Football? Tell me, do you go in for
that spread betting at all? Lot of money to be made
that way, if you really know your sport." He blew a

jet of aromatic smoke at the ceiling, and watched it disperse. "I haven't got the bottle for it, though, to tell you the truth. I mean, ten quid on a nag's one thing, but those spread betters—they can lose thousands in an afternoon. No limits."

Webb picked up the electric kettle and shook it. Apparently satisfied that it contained sufficient water, he clicked the switch to set it humming. *Oh, hello,* thought Frank: suddenly he wants to make friends with us.

"Who says I gamble?"

Don gave him an avuncular smile. "Come on, Stuart. Don't be silly. We wouldn't be asking if we didn't know about Bo's Bets, would we?"

With a shrug, Webb said: "I like the odd bet, sure. Horses, mostly."

"Point is, Mr. Webb," said Frank, who had lost track of the ping-pong, but thought it must be more or less his turn, "Mrs. Webb doesn't know you bet, does she? It's a secret, I reckon."

Webb turned the kettle off, then on again. "I don't see what this has got to do with murder, which is what you're supposed to be investigating."

"Motive," said Don. "Simple as that. You saw Chalkie at Bo's Bets. You recognised her, she recognised you. You needed to silence her before she told Gail. Or before she told someone who in turn told Gail. Or perhaps she was blackmailing you?"

Webb laughed. "What for? I haven't got any bloody money, we're broke. Didn't you hear me say? I'm on the dole."

"All right then," said Don, stubbing out his cigar. "So you killed her to protect your secret from Gail."

"Oh, for God's sake! That's ridiculous. Nobody's going to kill someone over something like that."

"Sir," said Don, in serious tones. "Most of the murders in this city, in this country—probably on this planet—are over much less than that. A husband kills his wife because she's put the tin opener in the wrong place once too often, a wife kills her husband because he snores—"

"Ah, yes—but!" Webb took a half step across the kitchen towards Don, and brought his finger up in a gesture half triumphant, half lecturing. "You're talking about domestics. We weren't married, me and Chalkie, were we? Hardly knew each other, in fact. Also, you're talking about people driven mad for a moment, losing control, but at the same time you're accusing me of a premeditated murder. A premeditated murder, that is, over a wholly trivial matter. Make your bloody mind up, man!"

"Saving your marriage," said Frank. "That's not trivial."

Webb turned to him. "Look, matey, I don't know about you, but *my* marriage won't stand or fall on whether or not I have the odd bet. Believe me!"

Quietly, Don asked: "So what would you kill for then, Stuart?"

Stuart Webb gave the Detective Inspector a long, even look. "I don't know. About the same as you, I expect."

Don clapped his hands together, once, and stood up straight. Frank knew what that meant: a sudden change of direction. "You attend all the Hollow Head's darts matches, don't you?"

"Most of them, I suppose. I try to, anyway."

"Right. So you're a big darts fan, then?"

"No, not really. But Gail's very keen, I just don't want to be a darts widow."

"Widower," said Frank.

"Whatever. Besides," added Webb, with a note of pride in his voice—a note which Frank found bordered on the insufferable—"I think it's important in a marriage for the husband and wife to do things together."

"Do you?" said Don.

"I do, as it happens."

"In that case, perhaps you should take her down the bookies with you."

"Oh, that's it, right! If you've got any sensible questions to ask me, I'll answer them—I'm a law-abiding man, and I respect the police. But if you're just going to go round and round in daft little circles of bloody irrelevance..."

"Don't worry, Mr. Webb," said Don. "We'll see ourselves out. And I'm sure we'll be talking to you again, irrelevant circles or no."

FOURTEEN

"DO YOU FANCY a game, Frank?"

"Sure, why not."

The pub in which they'd eaten their lunch was modern in design and attitude; a large, spread-out building, divided into distinct "areas" rather than bars or rooms, and designed to attract a different type of clientele at different times of the day—business people at lunchtime, pensioners in the afternoons, high-spending youngsters in the evenings, and families at weekends. It was air-conditioned, carpeted, well staffed and scrupulously cleaned. Don had made it perfectly clear that he despised the place—"About as much character as a Swedish hotel"—but even he had to admit that the lunch menu was extensive, the food fresh, hot and tasty, and the prices reasonable. The range of well-kept beers was also pretty impressive. And then, of course, Don had noticed the dartboard, on his way back from the Gents.

"One thing about these modern boozers," said Frank, "they cater for all sorts."

"Even old duffers who want to play actual pub games in a pub, you mean?" Don snorted. "It's all a bit of an add-on, though, isn't it? Their core business isn't selling beer to working men, thirsty and in need of entertainment—not in places like this. It's lasagne and deep-fried mushrooms and feta salad. And bleeping computer games and what-have-you; bet you anything that's where half their profit comes from.''

"Be fair, though," said Frank. ''You can't complain about the facilities. Look at that, we've got a nicely cordoned off throwing arca. Wc've got a brand new rubber mat on the floor, a proper little raised oche, an electronic scoring machine, and the lighting is superb.''

"Exactly! And that is all wrong.''

"It's wrong to have good facilities?''

"It's wrong to have the bloody light turned on when there's no-one playing. For heaven's sake, Frank, there are rituals, there are traditions, there are ways of doing things. Look, you're in an empty pub, you're having the first pint of the night, you fancy a game of darts. So you go up to the bar and you say to the landlord, 'Packet of peanuts, mate—oh, and could we have the darts light on, please?' And the guv'nor replies, 'Certainly you can, sir. There'll be a few more in later, if you fancy some competition'. And he reaches behind the bar to the light switch, and the dartboard clicks into life, and you take a first sip of your beer, you light a fag, you take your darts out of your pocket and assemble them. You have that first, tentative chuck at the bull's-eye—"

The man was babbling, as far as Frank could see. ''Yeah, but if the light is already on when you get there, that's more convenient isn't it?''

Don closed his eyes for a moment. ''No, no, Frank—look. This isn't about convenience, all right? It's about...well, if you like, it's about martial arts.''

A small amount of beer became entangled in Frank's nasal hair.

"When you've finished choking, I'll explain," Don continued. "It's like martial arts in the sense that—"

"What is? What's like martial arts?"

"*Life* is," said Don, with the impatient air of a man fed up with stating the obvious. "What you're doing, when you ask for the light to be put on and so on, is you are concentrating on preparation. Right? You are doing something step by step, instead of trying to do it all at once. The way a judo geezer concentrates on *that* muscle and then *this* muscle, *that* movement and then *this* movement."

"But what are you building up *to? A* game of darts?"

"*Life,*" Don repeated. "An evening out after a hard day's work. If it's to matter, if it's to be real, if it's to count, it's got to be done *right.* Yes? Okay, look—you go into a crowded pub on a Friday night. How can you tell which of the men at the bar spend their days getting covered with oil and grease and dust?"

At last, a question that made sense. "Easy. They're the ones wearing collar and tie, with clean hair and scrubbed fingernails and a fresh shave."

Don made an affirmative gesture with a small cigar. "Right. You see? Being spruce on their own time matters to them, because on the boss's time they have to be dirty."

"I don't see what that's got to do with whether the darts light is on or off," said Frank, but he was careful to say it without any hint of impatience or scorn. He was enjoying this; he'd worked with DI Packham a fair bit in the last few months, but he still couldn't quite get used to the concept, let alone the reality, of a boss who thought enough of him to argue with him. And not just about matters related to work, either…unless this *was* related to work. One thing Don was good at, Frank had seen, was getting into the minds of a group of people, seeing how they related to one another. Perhaps, in some unfathomably roundabout manner, that was what this was all about.

"It's all about moments in time, Frank, that's the best way I can explain it: separating them out so that you can experience each one, not letting the universe get away with what is its natural tendency—to run all the moments together until you can't tell one from the other and suddenly they're all used up. It's like the first morning of a Test Match at Lord's; a blue sky, but the dew still on the outfield. People settling in their seats, or queuing at the bars, the radio commentators clearing their throats. It's all still, and slow, and quivering with possibilities. In those last moments before the first ball is bowled, everything is possible. And that is my point about the darts light being on when nobody has asked for it to be on—it's a detail they've got wrong, you see? It makes me realise that this place is basically a theme park, and that this corner here is labelled *Ye Traditional London Pub.* But because it's not real, they get little bits of it wrong."

Sometimes, when Don went off on one of his verbal rambles like this, some of the stuff he said transported Frank back to his childhood, and he could never quite figure out why. He looked at the offending dartboard light, and said: "I could ask them to turn it off if you like. Then you can go up and ask them to turn it on."

Don laughed at that—a great roar that had people on the other side of the room turning around to find out what was happening.

Frank did have to go up to the bar, to fetch some house darts. They were short, brass jobs with moulded plastic flights—a long way from the three-part, leather-encased wonders of engineering which the Hollow Head's chuckers used.

The longer they played, the more cheerful Don became. Perhaps I should play darts with him on a regular basis, Frank thought: Arrow Therapy. *Must tell Debbie that, she'll like that! Wonder if you can get it on the National Health?*

"Not bad," said Don, as Frank landed all three darts in the largest section of the twenty bed. "But you're still gripping it too tightly. Just let it rest on your fingers—if you can divide the weight more evenly between your front and rear foot, you'll find the grip comes easier, too."

The lesson continued through successive games of 301, double in, double out, as Don lectured the DC on the subtleties of grip and stance, of aiming the dart and drawing back the arm, of release and follow through. "This is only the easy stuff, of course," the master informed the pupil, as the former took his score to four-nil with a double top out-shot. "The physical stuff. Anyone can do that, with a little practice. It's whether you can manage the headology that decides how good you're going to be."

There was a moment during the fifth leg, when Frank suddenly underwent a flash of self-understanding. The thing was, having hardly thrown a dart in years, and never with any serious intent, he did seem now to possess some natural talent for the game. He wasn't a darts genius, but he could do it—he was getting the hang of it quite easily. Mind, he always did pick things up rapidly, had done ever since school. But he also understood, as he tried to relax his arm (not easy to do when your boss is standing behind you, telling you over and over to *Relax your arm, Frank! Just relax your arm!*), that he was too self-conscious ever to make the leap from *okay* to *good*. He wasn't quite sure why that should be, or what it meant—and he certainly wasn't sure that it mattered a damn—but he knew that he was too conscious of how daft he looked, of people watching him from the bar, to ever achieve the state of union with the arrow that Don was urging on him.

If he could just disappear—if he could be deaf, dumb and blind, and not even exist, except for his fingertips holding the dart aloft—he was sure he could place the arrow anywhere he wanted, with no effort at all. And for a moment—not longer, but a moment even so—he admitted to himself that he would like to be able to do that; would like it quite a lot.

The lesson completed—"Sufficient unto the day," Don declared—they sat down at a table in the café area of the pub, Don with a fresh pint, and Frank, the driver, with a cup of coffee.

"So what about Stuart Webb, then? Does he still have two motives?"

"Not sure," said Don. "He was certainly more convincing about the adultery than about the gambling."

"Then we do still fancy him for the gambling motive?"

"Well, either that, or else the motive is still sex, and we're looking for someone else. And don't forget, there's still his wife."

"His wife? We're seriously looking at her as a possible killer?"

"Think about it, Frank. The key point about adultery as a murder motive—*anything* as a murder motive, really—is not that it happened, but that someone thinks it did." He put down his pint and lit up a cigar. "For instance, suppose a Geordie mistakes me for his oldest pal, who he hasn't seen since army days, and calls over to me *How are you, me old mucker?* And because the acoustics aren't very good in there—''

''In where?'' said Frank, who liked to get the details straight when Don was off on one of his flights of fancy.

''In this knife shop, House of Sharpies,'' Don replied, with a chuckle. ''Do pay attention, Constable. Because I can't hear him very well, I think he's said something quite different, so naturally I—''

''Stab him to death.''

''No, no chance of that—the knives are all chained down, in accordance with safety regulations. I smash him over the head with the cash till. Now, the fact that he *didn't* subject me to unprovoked obscene abuse doesn't alter my motive. Which is, that I *thought* he did.''

Frank blew on his coffee to cool it. It was a rare luxury, in the life of a busy copper and young father, to be able to drink a cup of coffee without scalding his mouth. ''You're saying that if Gail thought Stuart was having it off with Chalkie, even if we believe him that he wasn't—even if *she* believes it now—that doesn't rule her out, on account of what she believed at the time of the murder.''

''She's still on the list, Frank. That's all I'm saying. They both are.''

''Do we know of anyone who definitely had an affair with Chalkie?''

Don nodded. ''Right, that's been worrying me, too. From what your bookie said, particularly, we assume there was someone recently, but we still lack absolute confirmation. I'd say we make finding that person a priority."

"Aye, agreed," said Frank. "So, who haven't we spoken to, as an individual, I mean."

"You've got the list. Just pick a male name off it at random, and off we go."

As they left the pub, Don raised a hand in farewell to the manager behind the bar. "Thank you," he called. The manager didn't look up. "You see? That proves it's not a real pub, Frank. It's just a beer shop that happens to have chairs in it."

IT ALWAYS SURPRISED DON to find places like this, so close to the shopping centres and Tube stations of suburbia. The Rees brothers lived less than ten minutes drive from the Hollow Head, but they lived at the end of what was more of a country lane than a proper road.

It's a kind of indecent exposure, thought Don; like an X-ray, or an archaeological excavation. A reminder that a suburb isn't a town: suburbs don't grow out of the country, the way towns do, they're a tablecloth of concrete and tarmac, thrown over the countryside, covering up whatever is beneath. And sometimes, the tailoring isn't as neat as it might be, and a bit of old table peeps through a hole in the cloth.

The house looked rustic, too. Bigger than a normal suburban house, probably five beds, sitting in the middle of quite a large plot, it didn't, however, look remotely prosperous. It was rather ramshackle, and surrounded by bits of old machinery, skeletal vehicles and tin-roofed outhouses.

Ah yes, thought Don: that's what it reminds me of— a tenant farm. Plenty of land, no cash.

Lee Rees met them at the front door with a smile

and a firm handshake. He had the same easy manner as his brother, and Don wondered what on earth the brothers had disagreed about so fundamentally that it had made two such friendly, relaxed people unable to talk to each other. Money? Hard to believe there could be much dosh in this place, or in the car business, though he supposed the land might be worth a fair bit. Maybe his brother wasn't keen on hot dogs, either.

Inside, the house was exactly as Don had expected it to be from seeing the outside: homely, untidy, full of junk, not as clean as it might be. In short, screamingly womanless. Rees led them through to the kitchen and set a kettle to boil on the old range.

"Mr. Rees—Lee, if I might?—we've talked to your brother already, as I expect he told you?"

"Nope," said Rees.

Don feigned surprise. "Oh? Well anyway, we did, and I have to tell you he seemed rather nervous. And my colleague and I got the impression that he was nervous on your behalf, rather than his own. What do you say to that?"

"I can't think why he would be. I certainly didn't kill Chalkie."

"Okay," said Don. "But is there any reason why your brother might think you did?"

Rees poured boiling water onto tea bags in three chipped mugs. "I couldn't say, I'm afraid. You'd have to ask him."

The bald man's relaxed air had evaporated slightly, Don noted, as he was forced to talk about his brother. Time to change tack.

"You understand, Lee, that whatever we learn on an investigation, if it isn't relevant to the crime, is confidential."

"Yes, I suppose so."

"Good. So, when my colleague here asks you about Chalkie's sex life, you understand that you can tell us anything you might want to, without fearing that you're breaking a confidence, or dropping anyone in it."

Lee Rees looked at Frank, his eyebrows raised. Frank cleared his throat a couple of times, and said: "Right, well. Yes. You see, we were wondering if you knew anyone who had had an affair with Yvonne Wood? Anyone connected to the darts team."

He's thinking about it, Don decided, watching Rees pour milk into the mugs. He's thinking about it hard. "Mind if I smoke?"

Rees emerged blinking from his reverie. "Not at all," he replied, absently, handing Don an ashtray. "Well, look—I don't actually know anything, all right? I mean, I don't concern myself much with gossip. I take the view that people's own business is their own business, you know?"

"Sure," said Don, thinking: *But…?*

"But the person who would probably be most able to tell you about that kind of thing would be Brian, the skipper."

"We've already spoken to—" Frank began, but Don interrupted him.

"Right, thank you, Lee, that's very helpful. Very helpful indeed." I must give the lad some training in reading between the lines, he thought. He's depressingly straightforward at times. "We'll get out of your way, then, soon as we've slurped down some of that tea. Well, you never know when you're going to get the next cup, do you? Be a shame to waste it."

"Sure," said Lee.

Frank looked a little puzzled, but he said nothing.

Good boy, thought Don. They took a few token sips of the over-strong, almost macho brew, and politely declined the offer of a ginger nut.

As Rees was showing them to the door a few minutes later, Don turned to him. "Answer me this, if you will. Your brother throws at number two, you throw at number three. So—does that mean he's the better player?"

Lee Rees gave his head a little shake, and ran a little smile over his lips. *He's not biting, then,* thought Don, who hadn't really expected him to.

"Well, Inspector," he said. "That's something else you'll have to ask the skipper, isn't it?"

FIFTEEN

"BACK AROUND TO Brian Gough's place, then?" Frank asked, apparently having finally caught on to what Lee Rees had been saying beneath his words. "His wife was certainly making faces when we talked to him before. You remarked on it yourself."

"No, not yet. We'll talk to one of the others first—I want to *triangulate* the skipper."

Frank nodded. "Get him pinned to the board, then watch him wriggle."

"Exactly. I don't want to go rushing in. If he was having an affair with Chalkie, he's a married man, rather staid and pompous—put that lot together, and I reckon he makes a good candidate."

"To avoid exposure."

"That's right, so let's approach with caution. I don't want to spook him, until we feel more confident about having him." Besides which, Don didn't really feel up to a major, possibly pivotal confrontation with a serious murder suspect. He was feeling a bit tired this afternoon, as the light began to thicken and fade; a bit listless. And his eyes had started to itch. Was it possible to get hay fever in the winter?

Meanwhile, Frank was saying something about how hard it was to imagine a stodgy, dour fellow like Gough having an affair with a woman as lively as Yvonne.

Don reckoned that what Frank meant was—Gough looks like a husband, and Chalkie looks like a goer. But he didn't use language like that, of course, not young Frank. He would no doubt consider *goer* a thoroughly crude and unnecessary term. Which didn't mean, evidently, that he was without his own prejudices.

"They do have sex, you know, Frank, even in Yorkshire," Don said. "They must do, God knows there's enough of 'em."

THE DI TOOK A WHILE to decide who they should see next, while his DC drove in circles. This struck Frank as decidedly unscientific, not to mention wasteful of time and petrol. Still, fair dos, it was an important decision, perhaps; he was beginning to see that the order in which you interviewed people could be almost as crucial as what questions you asked them. Could actually, in some cases, *determine* what questions you asked them.

All the same, penny to a pot of peas, when Don faffed about like this, he wasn't engaging in a methodical dissection of the conflicting alternatives...he was just figuring out who he could be buggered to talk to, depending on what sort of mood he was in. In the meantime, Frank drove, and looked forward to his supper. They were going to cook some Thai thing they'd seen on the telly, copied the recipe down off the teletext. Debbie was keener on hot stuff than he was, but he didn't object to a bit of an experiment on a Saturday night, now and then. They'd had Tex-Mex a couple of weeks ago, from a recipe leaflet the supermarket had been giving out. That hadn't been bad.

At last, the envelope was opened, the piece of paper

rustled, and the winner announced. "Who's this bloke they were calling Superdart the other night, Frank? At the match."

"Clive Callow. His wife, Di, is a suspect as well."

"Clive Callow." Don took out his mobile phone. "He didn't look especially super the other night, did he?"

"Won his singles."

"Did he? Well, all the same, Superdart suggests rather more than an ability to win a leg of 501 in a pub friendly. In my book, it does."

"He used to play for the county, apparently."

"Really? Oh well, now you have piqued my curiosity. I look forward to having a natter with this boy."

After a brief conversation, Don put the phone away and told Frank: "Yep, straight around there. You know the way?"

"I'll pull over and have a quick look at the A-Z. He's in, then, is he?"

"No, that was his wife. He's at work, I gather. Tell you the truth, I was caught on the wrong foot a bit. I thought it was a daughter who answered the phone at first."

"She's got a young voice, you mean?"

Don lit a cigar. "Not exactly. It was more the tone— rather shy, uncertain. Like a kid might be who wasn't used to answering the phone to strangers."

When Di Callow opened the door of her large, comfortably spacious council flat—in a mansion block which was nearer to north London proper than it was to the suburb of Cowden—she did indeed strike Frank as shy; almost painfully so. She ran her hands over her hair continually, and seemed unable to meet the police officers' eyes. *Either dead shy or else a murderer.* She was a bit younger than her husband, Frank reckoned; he'd have been pushing forty, she didn't look much past thirty; a short, frail woman, all skin and angles, with a great ball of frizzy hair that seemed too big for her narrow shoulders and thin neck to support.

Yes, she was alone in the flat today, she explained— though getting anything like a sentence out of her was hard work, as her voice kept cracking in a dry throat, and she had to pause to swallow. She and Clive had three children, none of them jointly. The eldest was away at university, the middle one worked on the buses and had a shift today, and the youngest was on a school trip abroad.

Frank persevered with his attempts at small talk, while he and Don settled themselves on a huge, yellow sofa in the middle of the living room. "You don't work Saturdays yourself, Mrs. Callow?"

Colouring like a greenhouse tomato in a heat wave, she told him that she worked in public relations. Her accent, he thought, was Northern Irish, or had been at some time; it was hard to tell, mind, through all the throat clearing and swallowing. "Nothing glamorous, very junior, just clerical stuff really."

"Must be very interesting work," said Frank.

"Oh, well—not really," she replied. He didn't bother to contradict her, even for the sake of politeness; he couldn't imagine anything duller than public relations. Bunch of coke-snorting parasites, telling lies for a living.

While they spoke—or while he spoke and she choked—Frank took in his surroundings. It struck him that, in a flat which contained a lot of pricey consumer goods—CD player, DVD, computer games console and so on—the sideboard over by the balcony window seemed a little out of place. Not the piece of furniture itself, but its burden; this was a sideboard groaning with non-alcoholic drinks. True, Frank and Debbie's own sideboard rarely held more than a bottle of Scotch and the odd cheap liqueur brought back from holiday— except at Christmastime, obviously but this one was covered with bottles, cans and cartons. It's just that none of them contained any booze.

He wondered if Don had noticed, and if so, what he made of it. But Don was silent, and as far as Frank could tell was staring into a space that was located somewhere else. Frank wondered what he should do, since it looked like he was in charge of this interview; how did you get anything useful out of such a shy woman? If he went in with his boots on, would she be startled into indiscretion—or just dissolve into tears?

He opened his mouth to say something—anything, really—when Di Callow suddenly leapt to her feet. "Oh dear, I'm so sorry!"

Frank got up too, startled; even Don rose from his seat.

"I haven't offered you a cup of tea! I am sorry!"

"That's all right," said Frank. "We've not long had one." They all sat down again. "I'll tell you why we're here, Mrs. Callow—"

"It's my husband," she said.

"I beg your pardon?"

"I mean, it's my husband you need to speak to."

"Right…well, we will speak to him, certainly, but this is something that perhaps a woman would be better able to help us with. Women are more observant than men, aren't they?" He forced a laugh that sounded phoney even to him. "Well, that's what you women are always telling us, anyway!"

She said nothing, but she did swallow noisily three or four times, so he assumed she was listening, at least.

"The thing is, we're trying to figure out how many of you at the pub knew about Yvonne and Brian Gough."

She reacted to that much as he had expected: with a spasm of blushing and gulping. "I think—I don't know."

"You didn't know about them?" said Don. "Or you don't know what you should say?" Frank was so relieved to hear Don speak, that he almost missed the precise form of words the DI employed; a construction designed to elicit information, not to give it away.

Di Callow nodded, swallowed, and said: "Yes."

"Well, that's fine," said Don, standing up. "That's very helpful, thank you."

Yes, thought Frank, as he wrote down the shy woman's instructions on where to find her husband, a well-phrased question: one to which almost any answer gave confirmation of what the detectives believed they already knew about the relationship between Gough and the deceased.

In the car, Don said: "No shortage of suspects in this one, Frank."

"How do you mean?"

"Meaning, I wonder why she thought we were there to talk to her husband, not her? Did you notice that?"

"I did, yeah, but then I thought—well, maybe she's so under the thumb she automatically defers to Clive in any dealings with authority."

Don shook his head. "Possible, but I reckon there was more to it than that. Anyhow, we'll ask him."

CLIVE CALLOW'S WORKPLACE was a stall on a street market in Camden. A multi-coloured, hand-painted sign on the awning read: *Tapes, CDs, New'n'Used.*

As they navigated their way toward him through the omni-directional foot traffic, Callow waved his mobile phone at the detectives. "Wife rang to say I should expect you," he said.

"Did she?" said Don. "Reckoned you needed warning, did she?"

"Well, you know what they say, Inspector—fore-warned is foreskinned."

If Callow was disturbed or offended by the implication in the DI's remark, he certainly didn't show it. He was a tall man, with—it seemed to Frank—an extraordinary quantity of teeth, and an equally extravagant quantity of curly, ginger hair spilling down almost on to the shoulders of his fleece jacket.

He shook hands with both officers. "You don't mind us talking to you here?" Don asked. "Us being cops, you being a market trader?"

Callow laughed. On the evidence so far, Frank thought, this man began and ended every sentence with a rattling, exhaled laugh. He seemed like a friendly geezer, relaxed and open. "On the contrary! If people see me talking to the cops, they'll assume all my stuff's nicked."

"And that's good?" said Frank.

"Of course it is," said Don. "Then they think they're getting a bargain, right?"

"Right," Callow agreed.

"They call you Superdart, Clive, is that true?"

"Well, that's only a joke, really." The smile broadened, revealing even more teeth. *Has he got two sets in?* Frank wondered.

"A joke referring to what?" said Don. "You're a bighead, are you?"

"No, all it is, years ago I used to play super league, turned out for the county a couple of times. I was even thinking of going semi-pro for a while."

"So what happened?"

"In a word—dartitis."

"Ah," said Don, with a sympathetic grimace. "And what a nasty little word that is."

"What does it mean?" Frank asked, believing he smelled a wind-up.

"Essentially, it's an inability to let go of the dart," Don explained. "Golfers get something similar—though that's their own fault for playing such a bloody stupid game—and so do tennis players, spin bowlers in cricket, all sorts. The yips, they call it in golf."

"What causes it?"

Don shrugged. "They don't know."

"They bloody do in my case, mate," said Callow. "A bottle of vodka a day, every day for five years."

"Ah," said Don, and *Ah!* thought Frank, picturing in his mind the alcohol-free sideboard.

"Yeah, I'm an official alcoholic, me. Got the paperwork to prove it." He shouted over to a neighbouring stallholder. "Isn't that right, Sammy?"

A six-foot ten-inch West Indian greengrocer wearing a Scotland rugby shirt called back: "Isn't what right?"

"I'm an official alcoholic, aren't I?"

"So you say, pal, though I've never seen you perform yet."

"You don't try to hide it, then?" said Frank.

"Why should I? It's a disease, not a sin. Besides, the more people I tell about it, the less likely I am to lapse."

"You go to AA and all that, do you?" Don asked.

Callow shook his head. "No. Not for me. Nice people and all that, nothing against them, but I just couldn't stick all that religious crap, you know? If there is a 'supreme being,' like they reckon, then the bastard's let me down quite badly I'd say, wouldn't you?"

"I saw something on BBC Two—" Frank began.

"Did you?" Don interrupted. "I bet you did! Great one for the culture, my colleague."

"—about an Alcoholics Anonymous for atheists."

That brought a bigger laugh than usual from Callow; a laugh of humour, rather than of punctuation. "AAA? No thanks, mate, too many bloody initials for me. Don't trust initials. You know—VAT, EEC, what have you." He lit a filtered-tipped cigarette from a lighter hung around his neck on a leather thong. "No, I get by on my own, with my family and friends. And we've got a very good GP, he helps a lot."

Don asked, "How long ago was all this, your darts career?"

"Ten years, ish. I've been teetotal for a while now, more than a year."

"So you're on the comeback trail?"

Callow blew out a lungful of smoke, and said: "No way. I just play for fun now. All that other stuff, the serious darts, that's all behind me now. Lost all that with the booze, along with so much else."

Frank glanced at Don, and saw that the DI didn't believe Callow's words, either; the man's eyes said he was lying—he still had his dreams, Frank would've put money on that.

"No more dartitis problems?"

"That disappeared along with the DTs. At least, I hope it did." He tapped his head. "Touch wood."

"So how did you end up playing for the Hollow Head?" Don asked.

Callow shrugged—not very convincingly, Frank reckoned. "No special reason. I know the Rees brothers, done a bit of business with them once, they said their team was looking for a decent player." He paused, laughed, and added: "But they couldn't find one, so they got me instead."

"They both invited you, did they?" said Don. "Jointly?"

"God, no! It was Luke—Bushy Bro, they call him at the pub—not his brother. They don't do nothing jointly, those two."

"You know about this falling out they're supposed to have had, then?"

"Oh, yeah, you couldn't really miss it."

"What was it all about, do you know?"

This time, Callow missed off his pre-speech chuckle, replacing it with an exaggerated sigh. "Nobody really knows, except the boys themselves. It happened years ago, apparently. They were pretty close before that, by all accounts."

Frank started to speak—he wanted to ask "By all *what* accounts?"—but an almost invisible twitch of Don's hand stilled him. Sure enough, after a moment's thought, Callow continued. "Look, I want to tell you a few things up front, right? Because I've got nothing to hide. I didn't kill poor Yvonne—she never did me any harm, she seemed like a nice enough woman. And my wife didn't kill her either, despite her famous temper. My wife's temper, I mean."

Involuntarily, Don and Frank exchanged astonished looks. Frank had a horrible feeling his mouth was hanging open, and he concentrated on trying to get it closed.

"Temper?" said Don. "What, your Di?"

The laugh was back in service, but it sounded more effortful than before. "Right, yeah, well, that's one of the things I was coming to. Look, put simply—I don't drink any more, but she does. She took it up while I was drying out, if you want to know. There are—well, there are reasons for that, that don't take a genius to work out. Thing is, she's a small-built woman, never had much of a head for drinking, so she gets totally pissed on about three glasses of white wine. Consequently, she can get a bit...you know, she can get a bit mouthy."

"Mouthy," said Don.

"Right, yeah—the language comes out, you know. She takes offence when there's none meant, that sort of thing. But that's all it is, just noise. She'd never hurt anyone. Doesn't last long, anyway—she reaches falling-over point pretty fast."

"Okay. I see. I appreciate you telling us about that. And what were the other things you wanted to mention?"

Callow was actually sweating now, Frank noticed. In February, in north London. "Just this, basically. When I was younger—when I was playing a lot of darts, and drinking, and generally living the life, I was a bit of a lad. No violence as such, let me stress that, but it'll all be on your computers, no doubt, so I didn't want you finding out later and thinking I'd been less than honest with you. I've got nothing to hide, see, like I said."

"Fair enough," said Don. "Now—one more very important question."

The market trader took a deep breath. "Go on."

"Do you deal any vinyl?"

After a second's delay, Callow's laugh exploded into the cold air. "Only for very special customers, Inspector—like yourself, of course! What are you after?"

"Oh infinite things, Clive, items without number. But specifically, Wreckless Eric's double album. You know the one? My copy's more or less worn out."

Callow took a tiny notebook from his back pocket, and wrote in it. "I'll keep an eye out. It does turn up, now and then."

Don caught Frank's eye, and nodded. *What?* thought Frank. Am I supposed to order a record, too? I'm quite happy with modern technology, thanks. He raised his eyes at his boss.

"My colleague," Don said, as Callow put his notebook away, "wanted to ask you something."

"Ah…" said Frank.

Making no attempt to hide his irritation, Don said: "He wanted to ask you something about Brian Gough."

"Oh, right," said Frank. "What sort of relationship would you say, Mr. Callow, existed between Brian and Yvonne?"

Callow smiled. "If you didn't already know, you wouldn't be asking."

"Suppose we're only guessing," said Don.

"Then you guessed right."

On their way back to the car park, moving slowly through the crowd of bargain-hunters and tourists, Frank said to Don: "He seemed very open, didn't he? A useful witness."

Don snorted. "Witness? He's just gone top of my suspects list. Stands to reason, Frank—he wouldn't have been so honest if he didn't have something to hide."

SIXTEEN

BY HALF-PAST THREE on Monday afternoon, Don was feeling thoroughly fed-up with the whole business. They'd done nothing yesterday—Sunday had been a day of rest, by divine decree: the DCI had specifically forbidden the authorisation of overtime payments "where not demonstrably vital to the outcome of an ongoing investigation," and Don didn't work unpaid overtime on principle. Of course, if Yvonne Wood had been a child, there'd have been no difficulties; every officer in the division would have been working around the clock, paying for their foreign holidays for years to come, ensuring that the TV pictures told a story of relentless busyness. Half the nation's police budgets these days went on pandering to self-righteous, self-appointed, ill-informed parents' groups, milking the myth of the random child-killer for all it was worth. Nobody gave a toss about single adults any more. If they were foolish enough to get themselves killed, they didn't even rate a couple of hours overtime on a Sunday afternoon for a tired DI and his stolid assistant.

Not that it made a lot of difference, in all fairness— one day missed. This wasn't the sort of case where you were racing against the clock, trying to locate the crucial footprint or the lipstick-stained fag-end before the rain washed them away. This investigation was, as he'd told Frank Mitchell at the beginning, one which would depend on the old dialectic, rather than on forensics or DNA matches or brilliant feats of detection. You just had to talk to people, and try and listen to what they said no matter how boring they were, and then compare what they said to what everybody else said, and eventually you would come up with a suspect. And once you had a suspect…well, then the hard work began.

Thus, the tired DI and his stolid assistant had taken Sunday off, and had spent most of Monday back at the office, catching up on the previous week's paperwork and phone calls. And as the day dawdled on its way, grey and cold and slow, Don's impatience grew. He wanted to get this thing done and put away. The fact was, he'd been letting Frank set the pace too much. No blame attached to Frank—he was the junior officer, he did as he was told—but it was true, Frank was young, a new father, he was a bit *soft,* let's face it. A good lad, no doubt about that, but inclined to let things drift. It was time for Don to take charge of this case, grab the bloody thing by the scruff of the neck and get it killed off once and for all.

Fact of the matter: he just didn't want to be *doing* this any more. He wanted, suddenly he wanted it very much, to get the rest of the interviews done as quickly as possible and then he could go home and sleep for a week. What sensible man would choose a job that involved being lied to non-stop for the whole of your working life? Or worse, being bored into a stupor by idiots droning on forever, and knowing that you have to stay awake in order to spot the moment when they start lying, or prevaricating, or contradicting themselves.

And now here I am, on a cold, dark Monday after-

noon, talking to this berk, when I could be at home in bed.

Sean Hall was a civil servant, but when Frank had phoned his office, he'd been told that Hall had left work early on flexitime to practice for a darts match.

They'd found the thin, fair-haired man at a corner table in the Crown Inn, in central London, sitting behind a ham sandwich and a pint of lager, studying a book through his thick spectacles.

"I didn't realise the Hollow Head had a game on tonight," Don had commented, as he and Frank sat down either side of their latest suspect. Hall reluctantly put his book down, and Don checked the cover to see what type of literary masterpiece had so engrossed the civil servant: a catalogue of out-shots, detailing three, two and one-dart check-outs for every number counting down from one hundred and seventy, the maximum possible finish. Don wasn't impressed; in his experience, truly great players didn't need to learn their outs off by heart from books—they knew them instinctively.

"No, it's not the Head—their game's been postponed, because of…you know. I'm playing for this lot, tonight. The Crown 'B' Team."

"You play for two different pubs?" said Frank.

"I play for five teams. Three winter, two summer. Not any two in the same league, obviously."

We had words for people like you when I was playing, thought Don. *Ringer,* was one: a guy turning out for a side that he didn't really have any connection with. Illegal, in some leagues.

"So you're playing darts, what, two or three nights a week?"

"*Every* night of the week," said the Ringer. "If there's no match, I play pub games."

"Not matches, you mean?" said Frank. "Just for fun."

Hall sniffed. "If you like. I prefer to think of it as useful practice."

Can't have much of a life beyond the oche, Don thought. "You're not married I take it, Mr. Hall?"

Behind his glasses, Hall's eyes hardened, and he busied himself with his sandwich. As the silence threatened to grow to the point where someone might have to make something of it, Frank spoke. "Did you get those new darts? The ones you were talking about at the match the other night."

"Yeah, I did. Want a look?" Happy again—or at least, not actively sulking—Hall dug into a briefcase next to his feet and brought out not one set of darts, but four, all in their individual leather cases. Don caught a glimpse of several more books, with titles like *John Lowe on Darts* and *One Hundred and Eighty!* "I'll be playing with these tonight. Twenty-five grammes, with a longer shaft. A lot of the pros like them."

"Well, good luck," said Frank. "Hope they do the trick."

The Ringer addressed the Detective Inspector with something that he presumably thought would pass as a smile. "I understand you're a bit of a darts man, yourself?"

But Don was having none of it. *Get this over with, get home.* "We're not here to talk about darts, Mr. Hall. As I should have thought was obvious, we are here to discuss with you the brutal murder of your friend Yvonne Wood." He lit a cigar, though he didn't really fancy one; he just had an idea that the Ringer looked like the sort of fussy little nonentity who found smoking objectionable. "Or was she a friend of yours, in fact?" *More than a friend; less than a friend—either would do for a motive.*

Hall waved Don's smoke away from his face. "Well, I'm not going to pretend otherwise—we didn't get on all that well, me and *Chalkie,* as they called her."

Don's opinion of the late Chalkie rose significantly. "Why not?"

"She didn't approve of me playing for more than one team."

"Oh," said Don, quite enjoying his cigar now, and wishing he had a nice pint to go with it. Bit early, though. "She was one of those old-fashioned types, was she?"

The sarcasm was lost on the Ringer. "Exactly! That's just what she was, Inspector."

Don leaned back in his chair and stretched his legs out. "Oh dear me, yes, I know the type. Believed in loyalty, eh? Believed in playing the game for the game's sake, didn't care for glory-chasers."

Now Sean Hall got the message. His mouth shrunk to the size of microchip. "If you care to put it that way. Yvonne was rather outspoken in her views, I have to say. Unpleasantly so. In fact, to put it frankly, she was bloody rude."

Keep talking, you little twat. Keep talking. "Bit high-minded about it, was she? Bit of a prig?"

"Well, I don't know about that." Hall had learned his lesson as far as the sarky DI was concerned; he wouldn't be caught out again. "But I certainly don't think I'd done anything to deserve such an attack."

"I'm sure you didn't," said Frank. "What exactly did she say to you?"

"Well, basically, that I should only play for one

team, dump the others. And she made it clear that in her view, the Hollow Head ought to be one of the teams that I dumped. Which wasn't very friendly, really, was it?''

''Not very,'' Frank agreed.

''And the thing is—what really got to me   she didn't just say it to my face.''

''No?''

''No. She went around telling some of the others in the team the same thing—the skipper particularly. You see? Stirring everybody up against me.''

''My word,'' said Don. ''Sounds like she really had it in for you.''

''She did. That's true.''

''And was she right?'' Frank asked. ''Did it ever cause problems, you playing for more than one team?''

''Well, there was just one time when I had a diary clash—two matches on the same night.''

''What did you do?''

The Ringer shrugged. ''I did what any serious player would have done in that position. The Head's game was just an ordinary league fixture against a much weaker side, whereas the other match was a cup quarter-final.''

''So you played in the quarter-final?''

''Obviously!'' Hall opened his eyes wide and spread his hands, at the absurdity of the question. ''But Brian Gough dropped me for the Head's next match. Which they then went on to lose, needless to say.''

''And you blamed Chalkie for you getting dropped?''

Hall nodded his head. ''Definitely. No question in my mind whatsoever. It was her, stirring it up. Brian wouldn't have done it on his own—he knows you've always got to put out your strongest team.''

''You do realise,'' Frank said, with a glance at Don, ''that you are talking yourself up as a suspect for her killing?''

Sean Hall's beer glass slipped from his fingers, landing on the table with a thump and sloshing an inch or two of beer onto his lap. ''What? Don't be daft! That's bollocks! Jesus, I wouldn't kill her over something like that! I wouldn't kill anyone.''

''Someone did though, didn't they?'' Frank pointed out. ''Someone killed Chalkie. It wasn't an accident, what happened to her.''

''And it was one of you lot that did it, Mr. Hall,'' Don added. ''We're certain of that. So one of you had a motive.''

Mopping at his wet lap with an off-white handkerchief, Hall said: ''You're assuming she was the target.''

Don was momentarily derailed by that. He hadn't expected that, and he certainly hadn't expected anything unexpected from this dull man. ''What do you mean by that, exactly?''

''Nothing. Only that, the way she was killed, whoever did it couldn't have known he was going to get her, could he? He could have got anyone using the Ladies that night.''

''All right, then, who do you think the target might have been?''

Hall dropped his damp hankie behind his seat. ''No, I'm not saying that, I'm only saying it *could* be. I don't know anything about it. But I'll tell you what, that team isn't the happiest little band in the world. Lots of ill-feeling all around.'' He shuffled his elbows forward on the table, and lowered his voice. *So,* thought Don, *he is interested in something other than darts: malicious gossip. Who'd have thought it?* "I mean, start with the landlady," Hall continued. "Thoroughly unpleasant woman, and I don't say that out of prejudice."

Don frowned. "Prejudice? What, against the Scots?"

The Ringer shook his head. "No, no. Against—well, I'm not the prejudiced type, is all I mean." He hurried on. "Then there's the skipper himself. He's a grumpy bugger, and he and Chalkie were thick as thieves." He held up his left hand and began counting off his fingers. "Those two weird brothers, not talking to each other. That flash geezer they call Superdart. That barrister, the black guy—now what's he doing there, have you asked yourselves that? Doesn't seem interested in darts at all, from what I've seen. And then of course there's Billy Page, poor old super-sub, I call him—"

Don interrupted. It was either that, or bang his head on the wall. "Yeah, you've made your point. But let's just assume for the moment that the killer—whichever one of you lot it was—did manage to get the right victim, what can you tell us about her relationships with the rest of the team?"

"Not a lot," Hall replied, proceeding without hesitation to give the lie to his words. "Apart from the skipper, she wasn't that close to any of them. She didn't get on with Cliff Overton, that's for sure. Bit of rivalry there, I reckon, what with them both having been around for so long. She kept her distance from Heather, the landlady. Most people do, to be fair. She seemed to be imposing herself on those two brothers a bit lately, but I wouldn't say they were particu-larly—"

"Which one?"

"Sorry?"

"The brothers. You say she was giving them a lot of attention. You mean both of them, or one of them?"

Hall chewed a fingernail for a moment, then shrugged. "Don't know, now you come to mention it. I know one's got hair and one hasn't, but to be honest you sort of tend to think of them as a pair, if you know what I mean. Not as individuals. Off the oche, I'm talking about—I notice them more when they're playing darts." He chewed some more, while Don counted to ten slowly and silently. "Could've been Luke, the hairy one. Though I wouldn't swear to it."

Don decided he'd had enough. This bloke could give obsession a bad name. He stood, buttoned up his coat, and without a word or a backward glance, left the pub.

"Right," said Frank. "Thank you, Mr. Hall. We'll let you get back to your book, then."

FRANK FOUND the DI leaning against the car, his hands in his pockets, his eyes on a journey to the centre of the earth.

"Well, he was surprisingly talkative once he got going wasn't he?" said Frank, as he waited for Don to move so he could get into the car. "I thought you got a lot out of him, in the end."

"It's quality that counts," Don replied. "Not quantity."

"Aye, right, I suppose so." Frank jiggled his keys. Don remained immobile. *Never mind,* thought Frank. *I was used to a lot colder up North.* "He certainly seems to know a bit about darts, anyway, our Mr. Hall."

Now Don moved—he span away from the car as if it was red hot, and turned on Frank with a look of deep disappointment. "Frank, he knows *bugger* all about darts! What are you talking about, all those books? All that twenty-five grammes crap? He's a pot-hunter, Frank. He's a mercenary. God, man, Sean Hall doesn't know the *fundamentals* of the game! Listen, darts isn't about stance and grip and all that rubbish."

All that rubbish you were going on about in the pub the other day, thought Frank. "It isn't?"

"Books of finishes, and quarter-finals, and trophies—it's got nothing to do with all that."

"It's more a mental game, is what you're saying?" Actually, now he came to think about it, bloody London could get cold enough, this time of year, thank you very much.

"Yes, yes, all that, but the point is, Frank, darts is about friendship. It's about playing the game for its own sake. Look, for instance, there's no handicapping in darts. Right? Not like golf. Now golf, that's a game designed for keeping people in their place, a game designed to ensure the continuation of hierarchies. That's why it's only played by second-rate businessmen and shit comedians."

"Right. Shall we get in the—"

"But darts—darts is a democracy. If you get beaten on the dartboard by someone who's not a quarter the player you are, you're *really* beaten—no handicap, no excuses. You see, Frank, darts is the only sport where there's virtually no element of luck involved. Anything else—football, tennis, anything—you get a lucky bounce and you're a hero. Or not. But with darts, you're on your own, and a millimetre either way makes the difference between winning or losing." Don ran his hands through his hair. "You don't know what I'm talking about, do you?"

"Oh, certainly. You're saying—"

Don rattled the door handle on the passenger side. "Let's call it a day, shall we?"

Frank bleeped the lock. "Yes, sir," he said.

SEVENTEEN

WHEN THE HAMMERING on his front door woke him early the next morning, Frank Mitchell, half awake, underwent a moment of strangeness which was to haunt him, on and off, for the rest of the day. As he struggled up through the dark fathoms towards the wakeful surface, just for a second he heard himself thinking: *Oh my God! It's the police!*

By the time he'd wriggled into his dressing gown and reached the hall, he was feeling slightly dizzy. "Morning, sir. I wasn't expecting you this early." Frank guessed the 'Sir' was appropriate, going by Don's face, but in any case it felt right to him just now, no matter what mood the DI was in.

"Couldn't sleep," said Don. "You coming, or what?"

Frank fingered the lapel of his dressing gown. "Perhaps I should get dressed first. Do you want to come in?"

"No." Don turned and walked back to his car. Frank assumed he had his car there, anyway. The fact was, it was pissing down, like rain had just been invented and they were giving everyone an hour's free trial; visibility was close to nil. Bloody chilly, too. *Lovely. Lovely start to a lovely day.*

It was only when he'd closed the door that it occurred to Frank to wish he'd asked Don why he was banging on the door with his fist, instead of using the perfectly good electric doorbell.

Debbie was at the foot of the stairs, her face still creased with sleep. She had her arms wrapped around her, fingertips clutching her dressing gown, doing the traditional female mime for "cold." Frank knew it had nothing to do with temperature, really; he'd seen women in bikinis doing that with big towels on Greek beaches in mid-summer.

"Is something wrong?" she asked. "It's only just six o'clock."

"Oh aye," said Frank. "My boss's blood sugar has evaporated in the heat."

"Poor love."

He put his arms around her. "Him or me?"

"Actually, I was thinking of me. Hear that?" He did; the baby crying. "Shall I put the kettle on?" said Debbie.

"No, he says he'll not come in. I'll just shave and get me socks on and then I'll be off." Ten minutes later—he wasn't leaving the house without cleaning his teeth, not even for Don Bloody Packham—he kissed his wife and baby, grabbed his coat and closed his front door behind him.

Don was standing by the side of the car, in the pouring rain—not exactly not noticing the rain, Frank thought, just not caring about it. Wait a minute, though—Frank's detective skills told him that a dripping DI Packham wasn't the only odd feature of the scene before him.

"Sir," he asked, as he and Don got into the back seat of the car, "why are we in a taxi?"

"Because it's too far to walk."

Why do birds fly south in winter? Frank thought, a line that hadn't entered his head since primary school, twenty years before. "Yes sir, but what I mean is...well, has your car broken down?" He was speaking quietly, so as to avoid providing free entertainment to the taxi driver. Don, predictably, was not following his colleague's lead in this matter.

"Oh, what," said Don, sarcastically. "I suppose *you've* never forgotten how to drive, hey?"

No, thought Frank—I definitely haven't. In fact, I didn't know that anybody ever had. I didn't know such a thing was possible. I don't even know whether you're joking or not. "I would have picked you up."

"And what would have been the point of that? Two journeys instead of one?"

Frank let it drop. Perhaps a change of subject would help. "So, who are we seeing this morning?"

"Who do you think? The only suspect we haven't already seen—Billy Page."

"Right." Fair enough; it had been a daft question. Or would have been, at a more civilized hour of the... *Oh, blimey!* Frank checked his watch. A long way short of half-six in the morning. "Look, sir, the thing is—I haven't had any breakfast this morning, what with one thing and another. And I was up all night with the baby—"

Don looked Frank full in the eyes, for the first time that day. "Joe all right?"

"Joseph's fine, thank you. But I was thinking, it's still early, why don't we stop at a café, get something inside us other than wind?"

Don frowned. "You and your sodding breakfasts, Frank. You're obsessed. I shall have to have a word with Debbie about that, I reckon you've got an eating disorder coming on.''

Nevertheless, Don didn't argue as Frank directed the driver towards an all-night café. Nor did he object when Frank paid off the taxi. ''No point paying him to sit out here while we're eating. We can always pick up another one later.''

''Uh-huh,'' said Don.

The Eat-Inn was a pleasant refuge from a cold, dark, wet winter morning—warm and lively, full of people ending their working day with bacon and eggs and orange juice and tea and coffee and toast and marmalade and cornflakes.

''Wonder if they have fish fingers, chips and peas when they get up, night workers?'' said Frank. ''Washed down with a pint of beer or a glass of wine?''

Don didn't answer. He didn't eat either. As Frank dug into a bowl of porridge, feeling it fill him out and warm him up like cavity wall insulation, Don merely sipped at a cup of black coffee, his expression suggesting that it was brewed from the stuff they put in hospital drips, or perhaps the active ingredient in a mercy-killing kit.

THROUGH JUDICIOUS DEPLOYMENT of the porridge, a round of toast and jam, two small pots of tea, and two visits to the loo, Frank managed to spin their meal out until a quarter to eight, but only by blank-facing Don's evident, and growing, impatience. Eventually, he could hold out no longer, and they left the café. By the time they'd hooked a cab, and driven the few minutes to Billy Page's semi, a few blocks from the Hollow Head, it was nudging eight o'clock. *Almost respectable,* thought Frank. *If you're the Gestapo.*

Page opened the door to them wearing a towelling bathrobe, though Frank, looking at the man's eyes, hair and shaven chin—and comparing them with how he himself must have looked just a couple of hours earlier—felt sure that the suspect had already been awake when they'd rung his doorbell.

"Sorry to call so early, Mr. Page. We were keen to catch you before you left for work."

"You've had a wasted journey then, haven't you?"

"Sorry?" This *was* Page, wasn't it? There couldn't be two people in one suburb with such hairy nostrils, could there?

"I don't work," Page explained. "Early retirement. I used to work in computers."

"Very nice."

"Well, you lot would know all about that, wouldn't you—early retirement? Come on, then, you'd better come through. I was just washing up." He sat the two policemen down at a plastic-topped table, amid the debris of his breakfast, in a knocked-through kitchen-diner. "Is that one with you?" he asked, nodding at Don, who was staring into space, doing his celebrated impression of a disused warehouse. "He looks like he's retired already."

Frank said nothing, in place of what he wanted to say: *Of course he's with me. What did you think, he was a poltergeist?*

"I suppose you'll be wanting a cup of tea?"

"Very kind of you, sir."

Page grunted as he hefted the kettle to check its water level, then lit the gas flame underneath it. "I wondered when you'd get around to me. Beginning to think you'd forgotten me."

"No, not at all. Lots of people to see, we'll get

around to you all in the end.'' Frank didn't think it would be politic to admit that they had, as things turned out, left Page to last.

''Well, you should have come to me first off.''

''Oh?'' Was this going to be a confession? If so, please keep it until we've got you in front of a tape recorder!

''Oh yes, definitely. I know more about that lot than anyone.''

''You've been in the team a long time then, have you?''

Page poured boiling water into three mugs. ''Not that long, six or seven years. But I keep my ears open. I take an interest, unlike some.''

''Well, that's very helpful, sir. And what have you heard?''

''Okay.'' He splashed milk into the teas, and distributed them. ''Sugar's on the table. Well, for a start, you do know that the skipper was knocking off the deceased, do you?''

''Indeed? That's very interesting. You know this for a fact, do you?''

''Wouldn't have said it otherwise. I'm not a gossip. No, I've seen them out together.''

''Out? In Cowden?''

''Not likely! No, up West. Saw them queuing for the cinema once, in a wine bar another time.''

''And they looked like a couple?''

''If you count having their tongues down each others throats, yes.''

Unless Frank was sorely mistaken, that sounded very much like the final confirmation of Brian Gough's motive that they'd been looking for. He didn't bother looking at Don, though; knew he wouldn't be any use this morning. Best not to draw attention to him unnecessarily. "And how about you, sir, did you get on with Chalkie?"

He wasn't an overly expressive man, this hairy, middle-aged darter, Frank thought—except when he's angry, he corrected himself, remembering the scene with Gough at the darts match last week. Now, Page ran a palm over his chin, and thought before he replied. "I believed I did, until recently."

"I see. What happened to change your mind?"

"Well, look—I'm not saying I'm Barney Barneveld, you know? I'm not the best player in the league. But I've been playing serious darts since I was nineteen, I know my way around a dartboard. I'm not bad, yes?"

Another one obsessed with his precise place in the pecking order. "What, and Chalkie said you *were* bad?"

"No, no, not like that. The thing is, I've been dropped—dropped from the Hollow Head team."

"I saw you at the match the other night."

"Sure, but I didn't get a game, did I? Look, I always turn up to the matches, that's the professional thing to do, but I don't know why I bother any more, because I haven't hardly had a game all season."

"What's the prize?" asked Frank. He wasn't sure where the question had come from; he only knew it was one which, suddenly, he couldn't help but ask.

"Prize? What prize?"

"For the team that wins."

Page shook his head, clearly baffled. "A cup, of course."

"That's it? Just a cup?"

"Well, a cup for the pub, and individual trophies for the players. Like those over there."

Frank looked behind him, at the dresser in the dining area, upon which stood more than a dozen well-polished trophies. Most were in the shape of cups with jug-ear handles, others were wooden shields with miniature dartboards set in their middles. None of them was more than four or five inches tall, and all looked to be made of cheap materials, cheaply engraved.

"Why do you ask?" said Page, still frowning.

"No, no reason. Sorry, Mr. Page—carry on, please," said Frank, remembering that when he'd first worked with Don, the DI had told him no motive was too small for murder, once you understood what was important to the people involved. Well, yeah, fair enough—but a four-inch high, fake silver cup with *Lge Wnrs 99* stamped on it? Surely not!

"Well, all right. I was a bit put out at being dropped so often, you know? So I asked Chalkie to intercede on my behalf. Speak to the skipper."

"Hold on, this was before or after you knew they were lovers?"

Interestingly, Page had to think about that. *Perhaps he really isn't a gossip, then,* Frank thought. "It was before I knew, but after I suspected."

"Right, got you."

"But that wasn't why I asked her. Nothing to do with that. She had influence, generally, in the team. Always has had—all the time I've been there, anyway. She'd been around for ages, you see."

"Yes, so I understand. And she refused to put your case to Mr. Gough?"

"She did—point blank. Wasn't even polite about it. You know, pretending she'd think about it, or anything."

"Did she give you a reason?"

Page nodded. "Oh, yes. She said the skipper always picked the strongest team, and if that didn't include me, then tough luck. But that was crap."

"Yes?"

"Yes indeed. You know what was really behind it? Female solidarity."

"Female…?"

"Definitely. You see, they've given my place to a bloody woman. A girl, really. If you can believe that."

"That would be Gail Webb?"

"Right. I mean, what's all that about? Dump an experienced league player, and replace him with some *girl*."

"Is she no good, then?" Frank asked.

"She's only a girl!" Page replied, in the evident belief that this was a full and complete answer to the officer's question.

Frank made sympathetic noises through his teeth, while he wondered how he might put the next question. "So what do you think is behind that, then?" Subtler than *Is the skipper screwing her, too?* he reckoned.

"Don't ask me," Page replied, as if the thought hadn't crossed his mind.

Quite possibly it hadn't, Frank decided. He wasn't a gossip, just as he'd said; and more to the point, he wasn't—this time in contrast to what he claimed—terribly interested in other people. Which made him, perhaps, more reliable as a witness than most. He didn't make up stories about people, or speculate about what they're up to, even when it would suit his own purposes.

Which means that if only bloody Don'd wake up and ask him a couple of penetrating questions, we might get something really useful…

"What about Heather Mason?" said Don, startling both the other men into small, involuntary jumps.

"What about her?"

"She's a woman, too. Do you begrudge her a place in the team?"

"No, that's different. She's the landlady, fair's fair. I mean, she makes the sandwiches for the matches and everything. Anyway, I didn't lose my place in the team until that girl came in, that's my point. Besides, apparently Heather's a lesbian."

Frank could vaguely, sort of, make out the logic of that—presumably, lesbians counted as honorary men for darts team selection purposes—but then he replayed the sentence in his head, and heard the key word. "Apparently?"

"That's what Chalkie told me."

"When did she tell you?" And how did she know? And did this explain the curious remarks various people had made about the fearsome landlady over the last week? Frank glanced hopefully at Don, but no luck—Don had gone back to Don Land.

Page shrugged. "Month or so back."

"Before you and her fell out?"

"Definitely! We weren't on speaking terms after that, you can believe me!"

"And how did she know that Ms. Mason was a lesbian?"

Page looked at Don, as if to make sure he wasn't listening. "Look, I wouldn't want this getting back to Heather. I mean, this is only hearsay, isn't it? What you lot would call hearsay."

"She won't hear it from us," Frank reassured him, more or less confident that he was speaking for both of them. "And you're only telling us what Chalkie told you, aren't you? You're not making any claims for the veracity of the information."

"I suppose so. Well, according to Chalkie—Yvonne, I should say; sounds bloody stupid calling a murder victim *Chalkie*—she said that Heather was after her."

"After her?"

"Yes, you know. After her."

"I see. And Yvonne had turned her down?"

Laughing, Page replied: "You can bet your life on that! If there's one thing Yvonne was, it's heterosexual."

At which interesting, and—Frank thought—highly promising point in the interview, Don stood up and walked out. Out of the room, out of the front door, down the drive. Without a word.

Leaving Frank no obvious option but to make his excuses—make *both* their excuses—and follow.

As they walked towards the nearest main road, Don said, "You know, the best evenings of my life have been spent playing for pub darts teams."

"Yes sir?"

"Thank Christ the teams I played for weren't a miserable bunch of bitching, moaning bustards like this lot."

"Yes, sir. What shall we do now?" Bit early for lunch, he was thinking. *I hope.*

"I've got some paperwork to see to," said Don. "Back at my place. You go back to the nick and sort out what we've got so far. Get it into some kind of order, for heaven's sake. We're getting nowhere on this, starting tomorrow morning we need to get a grip on things."

Frank didn't bother to sigh, let alone say anything; not even to himself; not even when Don had given him a curt *See you,* and wandered off. He supposed he was getting used to DI Packham. Was that a good thing, he wondered; or an incredibly bad, frightening thing, which required urgent medical attention?

He had his car keys out of his pocket before he remembered that he didn't have the car. Frank allowed himself a modest chuckle, then, as he realised that he was standing upstream of Don, as far as the traffic flow was concerned, and would therefore get a taxi before his boss did. He stuck his hand out into the road, and whistled into the traffic's roar.

EIGHTEEN

"WE'LL GO OFF-MANOR," said Don, on the phone to
Frank, half-past seven on Wednesday morning. "Don't
want anyone from the office barging in on us. I want
to spend all day on this, no interruptions."

"Right you are. Where do you have in mind?"

Don gave Frank the name of an all-day pub not far
from Pinner, well over the borough border into Harrow,
and was there waiting for him at nine o'clock. He liked
this place; one of the surprising pleasures of the suburbs was that, just every now and then, you came
across something like this that gave you a glimpse of
what the older suburbs must have looked like back in
the nineteen-twenties or thirties. It was an old pub—
sixteenth century building, the site probably in use as
an inn way before that—and it had simply stood there
all those years, selling beer, not changing much, while
the world around it did whatever the world felt it must.

A hundred and fifty years ago—maybe even a hundred—the village green which faced the pub to the west
would have been the centre of a community of people
who were quite certainly not Londoners. The city was
a good ride away, and many people, Don supposed,
must have lived their lives out around here without ever
visiting it.

Today, of course, this place was part of London—

administratively, culturally, and to all intents and purposes geographically; it was linked to London by a seamless river of tarmac and brick. Across the road from the old inn, looking south, plastic-framed double glazing and up-and-over garage doors stood in ranks which marched all the way to the capital, interrupted only by parks and flyovers. But turn your seat away from the concrete, and you were looking at woods to the north, the green to the west, and a row of old cottages to the east.

Borderlands, thought Don. And it was pretty obvious which of the worlds, old or new, the pub considered itself part of.

Sitting at a table by the window, overlooking the pub's parking area, Don felt a little thrill of pleasure and anticipation as he saw Frank's car arrive five minutes later. He was going to enjoy today; he was already enjoying today. To spend a day in a lovely, semi-country pub, with a friend whose company you valued, in pursuit of justice. What more could you ask for?

A good night's sleep had finally shaken off that cold virus, or whatever it was that had been dragging him down lately, and this morning he had awoken with his mind full of what a great team he and young Mitchell were. Once they sat down and applied their very different, highly complementary minds to the problem of Yvonne Wood's murder, he had no doubt that they would have it sorted out in no time at all.

"Good man, Frank," he said, shaking the DC's hand. Then he decided that a handshake wasn't altogether sufficient, so he slapped him on the shoulder at the same time.

Frank looked a little dazed as he mumbled: "Morning, Don."

Ah well; probably been up all night with the babby again. Changing nappies or boiling milk bottles, or whatever it was parents got up to. Slinging them over their shoulders and thumping them to make them burp—he'd seen that on telly. Blimey, it was a wonder any of the poor little buggers ever survived into their teenage delinquency years. Why not let them burp in their own time, if they needed to? Still, he supposed they knew what they were at, these parents; they'd been doing it for thousands of years, after all.

"I got a pot of coffee in, Frank—hope that suits you? I remembered from last time I was here that they did excellent coffee."

Don poured. Frank sipped. Don looked on anxiously, like the wine waiter at an embassy ball. "You're right," said Frank. "That's very nice indeed." He drank some more. "Oh aye, just the job, that is. Smashing."

Don clapped his hands together. "Good! We're going to need some decent fuel today, we've got a lot of work to get through. Mind you, I reckon we're almost there. Don't you? Tell you what Frank, this'll be a feather in your cap, when we wrap this case up."

"My cap? What about your cap?"

"Mine?" Don laughed. "I'm afraid my cap is too battered to carry any feathers these days. No, don't worry about that—I don't." He took a gulp of coffee, and lit one of his small cigars. "Right then. Let's start with the post mortem report."

Frank flipped through a sheaf of papers, and found the one he wanted. "She wasn't assaulted. Well—apart from being killed. Unconsciousness would have resulted instantly from the blow caused by the block falling on her head, and death followed a few minutes later. They now reckon that blow did not actually kill her—though they're not willing to say so a hundred percent.''

''The second wound.''

''Right. Which they believe resulted from her head striking the floor of the Ladies.''

''Striking or being struck?''

Frank shook his head. ''They won't commit themselves on that.''

''They don't like giving hostages to fortune. Too many appeal court overturns in recent years. What do they give us on state of the deceased?''

''A healthy woman for her age.''

''Daft expression that, isn't it? When you're talking about a corpse.''

''She wasn't pregnant, no sexually transmitted diseases, no cancer, nothing like that.''

''Okay,'' said Don. ''So the PM doesn't really tell us anything we didn't know from the scene. All right then, let's review the suspects, one by one.''

''In batting order?''

''Why not,'' said Don. ''That's how I think of them anyway, lining up on the oche.''

Frank selected a neatly typed sheet from the pile before him, and clicked his ballpoint into standby mode. ''The skipper, then: Brian Gough. Dour sort of geezer, isn't he?''

''He's a Yorkshireman, Frank, that goes without saying. He's one of those blokes who's always got a clipboard under his arm—even when he's in bed asleep, probably. He treats his leisure the same as his work, everything meticulously organised. Doesn't seem to get any real pleasure from running the darts team, but then I suppose you can't always tell with other people. What's his motive for murdering Chalkie?''

''Obvious—his affair with Chalkie.''

''And we're certain such an affair took place, are we?''

''I think we have to be,'' said Frank. ''Provisionally, at least. The evidence comes from several sources.''

''I agree. Okay, obviously we'll have to confront him with that before too long. And we're saying he killed his mistress because—why?''

''If he is the killer, then presumably Chalkie was about to blow the gaff. Gave him an ultimatum—me or the wife, time to choose, or else I'll tell your wife myself and let *her* make the choice. I understand that's standard procedure in cases of adultery,'' Frank added, with a small sniff.

''Fair enough. Makes sense. Now—we're definitely saying that Chalkie was the intended victim, yes? It wasn't a random killing?''

Frank sipped coffee and pondered. ''I reckon so, yes. My earlier point still stands: due to the location, we can assume that the killer knew the victim would be a woman. Now, okay, we could be looking for a crazed misogynist, but I think that's stretching it a bit. I mean, none of the suspects look the part for that role, do they?''

''Well,'' Don said, with a chuckle, ''we'll deal with Billy Page in his turn. But no, I think you're right. We should continue on the basis that Chalkie, unnoticed, goes out to use the loo; the killer, equally unnoticed, slips out after her and sets the booby trap while she's inside the cubicle. If it ever was random, it was no longer random by then. At that moment, when he set the trap, he knew he was going to get Yvonne Wood, specifically. Okay: who's up next?''

"Bushy Bro—Luke Rees, the one with the hair.''

"All right, now, let's deal with those two together— because that's how they strike me. It's hard to think of them except as a pair, wouldn't you say?''

"It's ironic, really,'' said Frank.

"Why so?''

"Well, I think you're right, as far as the outside world is concerned they *are* a pair. They look alike, except for the hair. They're similar ages, they work together, live together, drink together, play darts together. And yet they're not together, are they? Because they never talk to each other.''

"Perhaps,'' said Don. "But my experience of families is that hate keeps them more tied to each other than love does. Fact of life—hate is a stronger force than love.'' He regretted the words as soon as they were out of his mouth, even before he saw the curl of distaste on Frank's own lips. *I shouldn't be filling his young head with that kind of cynicism. It's not fair on the lad.*

As a distraction, he suggested that they continue their darts lessons. Frank seemed amenable to the idea, though he did take quite a while gathering his papers together, restoring them to his briefcase, and carrying it—and the coffee pot—to a table near the dartboard in the back room of the pub.

"Remember what I said,'' Don instructed the DC as he toed the oche. "Darts is a mind game. You don't throw the dart, you just let it go.''

"Understood. So you see the brothers' feud itself as a possible motive in some way?''

"I think it might well be. We've heard that Chalkie

was taking an interest in them, and we know she was a bit of a stirrer. Enjoyed getting a reaction out of people, albeit she was friendly enough, and loyal enough, in her own way.''

"So perhaps she found out what nobody else seems to know—the original cause of their rift.''

"Yeah, could be. And maybe whatever it was they fell out over was something so shameful that they simply couldn't bear for it to become common knowledge.''

"They?'' Frank said.

"Together or singly—there's nothing in the rules says two people couldn't have carried out this killing. One setting the booby trap, the other keeping lookout.''

Frank paused with his second dart in his hand. "No, I disagree. Seems to me, if they've just killed someone together, using a plan that they'd have had to agree on beforehand, then you'd think their feud would be pretty much over from that moment on, wouldn't you?''

"Unless they're playing it cunning—act normal, to deflect suspicion.''

"Okay, but there's a more practical difficulty, too. You've got two men, who everyone knows aren't even talking to each other, and they both disappear to the bogs at the same moment—people would have noticed that, and remembered it later.''

Don nodded, as Frank at last released his arrow. *Not a bad follow-through. He's learning.* "Yes, fair enough. One of them, then, acting alone to prevent disclosure of a damaging or embarrassing secret. Which, don't forget, could still be a *joint* secret—just that one of them's willing to do something about it, and the other one isn't. Or else, one of them beat the other one to the punch.''

After throwing his third dart, and retrieving all three from the board, Frank said: "Trouble is, from what we've heard of Chalkie, I don't really see her as a blackmailer, do you?"

"No you're right, not a blackmailer in the conventional sense. I don't see her demanding money with threats. But I reckon she could be a bit of a tease." Don threw twenty-five, treble nineteen, bull's-eye, to leave himself a two-dart finish.

"Well done," said Frank. "Was that deliberate?"

"You're supposed to say *Nice darts, mate.*"

"Nice darts, mate."

"Thanks, but it was a fluke. I was going for the nineteens with the last one."

Frank stepped up for his next turn. "Do you mean 'tease' in a sexual sense?"

"No, poor thing. I should say she was anything but a tease in that area of her life. Too desperate to be loved. I was thinking more that she liked to wind people up. I can see her finding out a secret, taunting someone with it, making out she was going to tell all, even if she didn't really intend to."

Frank turned around; he was frowning. *Not everyone thinks as straight as you and your nurse,* thought Don. *More's the pity.* "To what end?" said Frank. "What did she get out of it?"

"Oh, I don't know, Frank. A woman who spent her life trying to please married men, and ultimately never succeeded. Maybe she just liked the sensation of being in charge, for once. And it could be that one of her victims took her threats seriously, and decided on a pre-emptive strike."

"I'm not sure," said Frank. "It sounds like calculated cruelty, the picture you're painting of her. I don't see her like that.''

''All right.'' Has he really never encountered a cruel woman? When he was growing up, did his mum and his grannies and all his aunties and schoolteachers really treat him with the same tenderness as his Debbie does? You *are* a lucky little sod. Still, thought Don, your saving grace is that you know it. ''You have to admit though, she did have strong opinions on things. And she wasn't afraid to express them. On Sean Hall being a ringer, for instance.''

''Bringing this back to the brothers, for a moment,'' said Frank. ''What *kind* of thing do you reckon they're likely to have fallen out over?''

''Easy,'' said Don, missing his out-shot by about three inches. ''Bugger! Women or money, Frank, got to be one or the other.''

Frank stepped up to the mark, and was just about to let loose his missiles, when Don spoke. ''Don't aim too hard, Frank. You don't aim with your eyes, you aim with your mind. You *project* yourself into the treble twenty or the double top or whatever, and you simply *place* the dart in there. *Place* it there, with the minimum of effort. The perfect darts player, Frank, you wouldn't be able to see him move at all. One second he'd have the dart in his hand, and the next it'd be in the board, and he wouldn't have so much as blinked, let alone grunted like a Yank at Wimbledon.''

''I wasn't grunting,'' said Frank, with his back to the DI. ''I was clearing my throat, in case a minute quantity of phlegm in my trachea might upset the cosmic balance of my throwing arm.''

''The aforementioned Ringer,'' said Don, pouring

some more coffee. "Sean Hall. Now, he's a good'un, if you ask me."

"Meaning a bad'un?"

"Dead right. An obsessive dart player—and like any other obsessive, not entirely restrained by normal ideas concerning right and wrong, let alone important and not important. And he's got a clear motive—anger."

"Because Chalkie tried to get him out of the team?"

"Great motive, seething resentment, for a murder which, while certainly premeditated, needn't have been *long* premeditated. Suppose, on the night of the killing, Chalkie has another go at him about his lack of team loyalty. Right? So the Ringer drinks, broods, drinks some more, and follows her out to the ladies meaning to remonstrate with her as she emerges from the bog. But then he sees the doorstop…"

"What, and suddenly decides to kill her?"

Don shrugged. "Or just give her a fright. Could be either."

Frank poured himself another coffee. "Cold. I'll get some more."

"I'll get it," said Don. "I think the barmaid fancies me."

When Don returned from placing his order, Frank said: "What bothers me, about all of them, is that they're not experienced criminals. None of them, as far as we've been able to discover, has any history of violence. But one of them has just committed a murder, and yet, when the uniforms took their initial statements, they were all in a more or less calm state."

"Delayed reaction?" Don suggested.

"Okay, but since then—they'd surely be more nervous, more agitated, than they have been."

"So what are you saying?"

"I'm not sure. Nothing, probably."

Don't go coy on me, son. "Go on—follow your thought through."

"Well, okay. I suppose what I'm getting at is that maybe we're looking for someone who is used to hiding their feelings."

"In that case, there's no problem. We know at least one of them was exercising his organ in a prohibited manner. Think about it, Frank, an adulterer spends all his time acting. Acting to the wife, acting to the mistress who he's no intention of leaving his wife for. Acting to friends and colleagues. Or, and this brings me back to Sean Hall, it could be someone who is so obsessed with one thing that he's a kind of mild psycho. He doesn't even *have* any feelings to hide—not normal feelings."

That's it! Don had to struggle to contain an impulse to rush off and arrest the Ringer there and then. But no, better not overreact, stay calm, think it through. He concentrated on throwing his darts, but only managed a feeble score of half-a-crown: twenty-six. "Bed-and-breakfast," they used to call it, in pre-inflationary days. He'd have liked to have played better today, for the lad's sake; he was rusty, that was the trouble. Couldn't imagine why he hadn't kept up with the game these last few years. Hell, there'd been a time when darts was his whole life.

Ha! Just like Sean Hall!

"What are you chuckling about?" Frank asked, suspiciously.

"Nothing, mate, nothing. Just cogitating upon the solemnities of youth."

"I thought the expression was *follies* of youth."

"Ah well, see, that's because you're young."

"Oh, right," said Frank. "That'll be it."

"Let's turn to Superdart, Clive Callow. The Comeback Kid. Nice bloke, I liked him. Admire him too, overcoming his disability like that, that takes character."

"You mean the alcoholism?"

"What? No, Frank—the dartitis! Very serious condition."

"If you say so. And do nice blokes kill people?"

Don took the question seriously, suspecting that it had been meant that way. "Well, some detectives will tell you that some of the nicest men they've ever met have been murderers. But personally, I reckon that tells you more about the detectives than the criminals. No, I can honestly say I've never met a murderer I'd want to have a game of arrows with."

"We're ruling Callow out on those grounds, then?"

Don laughed extravagantly, causing a disproportionately large ripple of disturbance to spread through the pub's scattering of early morning customers. "No, quite right, Frank. They say there's a first time for everything. It's not true, in my opinion, but there is certainly a first time for many things, and this could be one of them. But what's his motive? He didn't strike me as the angry type."

"He is the only one of the suspects who's known to the police computer."

"Yeah, but he told us about that straight out, didn't he?"

"Told *us*," said Frank. "Sure. To prevent us finding out later and wondering why he hadn't mentioned it. But that doesn't mean he wanted the whole world to know about it."

"Yes, fair point. It was all a long time ago, though. So how would Chalkie have known about it?"

"Don't know that," Frank admitted.

"What precisely was he done for, anyway?"

"Usual juvenile stuff, car crime mostly. Taking without consent; he did a month in a young offenders' for car theft."

"His wife, now—Di—she's easier to find a motive for."

"The boozing."

"I know we haven't seen it ourselves, but from what he says she's a bit of a Jekyll and Hyde, depending on how much she's imbibed. Now, if Chalkie had caught her in the wrong mood, almost any slightly objectionable remark could have set her lashing out. And then, who knows, she could have forgotten all about it when she was sober, which would explain why she didn't immediately confess."

"We've done Di Callow out of order," said Frank.

"Oh dear, how dreadful! Sorry, Frank—no, you're right, we should stick to our game plan. All right then, who's next?"

"Coming in at number six, Heather Mason."

"Ah, the Hollow Head's jovial guv'nor! Well, quite apart from being a particularly nasty person, and possibly bright Orange—"

"Eh?"

"Orange. That stuff about the Queen."

"Oh, right."

"Actually, that's a thought. Yvonne Wood wasn't a Catholic, was she?"

"No, don't think so. No religion mentioned."

"Okay then, apart from all that, and Heather being unpleasant enough both to kill someone and to keep quiet about it afterwards, we just have this claim that she made a sexual advance to Chalkie which Chalkie rejected. And did so, no doubt, knowing what we know of the deceased, in a fairly brusque manner. Still, no point speculating about that, we'll just have to put it to Heather and see what colour she turns.''

"Orange, maybe," said Frank, lining up his throw.

"Don't look at it!" said Don, as Frank's first dart bounced off one of the wires separating the segments of the dartboard, and stuck into the floor with an impressive *twang*. "Don't follow it down with your eyes, just keep your eyes focussed on the..." His voice trailed off, as he realised that the young DC hadn't so much as twitched, and that the advice of his coach was in this instance entirely redundant. Good lad! Don felt a flush of pride, and he wondered for a moment if this was a lesson which—maybe, you never know—Frank might one day pass on to young Joe.

"Gail and Stuart Webb," said Frank, having completed his turn with a not-discreditable two-dart score of forty. "Very clear motives there—she thought, probably incorrectly, that he was having an affair with Chalkie; and he thought, possibly correctly, that Chalkie might tell people about his secret betting. Both main motives in one package; rage over adultery and fear of exposure."

"Neat enough, sure, but I think we can rule out Gail by using the Mitchell Test."

"The what?"

"Could she have kept quiet about it afterwards, having committed a crime of passion? I'd say no. She's the honest sort." *Lovely nose, too,* he added, but not out loud. *Definitely not a liar's nose.*

"I think I'd go along with that. What about her husband?"

"He's more likely to be able to cover up, I'd say; if you're keeping a gambling habit secret from your wife, you've got to be pretty devious to begin with."

"True enough," said Frank. "Right, so, the final team member is Kevin Lewis, the barrister."

"Ah yes, the newcomer. Now he interests me. And not just because I like the idea of nicking a barrister for murder."

"But we don't know anything about him, really, do we? No hint of a murder motive."

"Exactly!" said Don. "No hint of a motive for the murder, no hint of a motive for even being in the bloody pub in the first place, let alone becoming a regular in the darts team!"

"Well, he says he went into that particular pub by chance, and that he plays darts as a break from the stresses of the office."

"I know, cheeky sod—mindless pursuit, indeed! But he was cagey, wasn't he? Didn't want to tell us anything about himself. I think we need to press him a bit further, Frank. Put him on the list for another visit."

"I didn't realise there was a list," said Frank, putting his darts down and picking up his notebook.

"There is now."

"You're saying he's keeping secrets? So he's another fear-of-exposure merchant, then."

"Absolutely. A professional man, a barrister especially, must fear exposure more than most people do. Assuming there's something to expose, I mean."

"Yeah, but again—how would Chalkie have found out? Lewis is new to London, him and Chalkie moved in different worlds."

"There'll be something there, you mark my words."

"All right. Now, moving on to the non-players. Billy Page, that's a nice simple motive, if a bit...er..."

"Petty?"

"No, no, Don, no, I wasn't going to say petty. Honest I wasn't. A bit old-fashioned, maybe. Not approving of women playing darts."

"The irony there is that he thinks he was dropped to make way for a woman, but from what the mysterious barrister says, it was actually *him* who pinched Page's place."

"Proves my point," said Frank. "He's so obsessed with this anti-women thing, he can't see any other explanation."

"And he blames Chalkie for it."

"There again, I think if he was that far gone, he'd have killed the woman who'd supposedly taken his place, instead."

"Hmm, probably. Tell you what, put him on the Unlikely Possible list."

Frank sighed, and turned to a fresh page of his notebook. "Are there any other lists I don't know about?"

"I sincerely hope not, if you're doing your job properly."

"That only leaves the old guy, Cliff Overton."

"He's definitely worth talking to again."

"You really fancy him for the killing?"

"No, not especially. Though it's pretty obvious he and Chalkie despised each other. And were in competition with each other, both being of the same Hollow Head vintage. Overton sees himself as a sort of father of the team—even though I'm willing to bet he's never thrown a dart in anger in his life—and he certainly saw Chalkie as a dangerous challenger for his throne."

"But he didn't kill her?"

"I don't think so. Oh, I'm sure he's glad she's dead, but I don't see any reason he would have killed her now, rather than at any time in the past however-many-years. Even so, I want to talk to him. He's a nasty little shit, self-righteous and bitter, and after all those years of hanging around, I'll bet he knows more than he's saying. He just needs persuading to cough it up."

"Tell you what, then," said Frank. "I'll put him on the Nasty Little Shit Who Needs Leaning On list. All right?"

NINETEEN

SOMETHING THAT DEBBIE had said a couple of days ago had been strolling around Frank's brain ever since, getting to know the place, rubbing itself against the furniture.

It had never been his habit to talk about his work to his wife—home time was too short and too precious for that—but since joining CID, his habit in that regard had changed to some degree. Perhaps it was the increased responsibility, especially on days when Don wasn't offering much in the way of managerial leadership, and the more solitary nature of the plainclothes job; perhaps, thought Frank, the more your shoulders carry, the more you feel the need now and then to stop and shift the weight around.

For whatever reason, anyway, he'd been discussing the Hollow Head murder with Debbie after their evening meal, as they sat on their big sofa, watching a quiz show with the sound turned down, and he had explained the difficulty over alibis; that every one of the suspects had, theoretically, had an opportunity to commit the crime, but that none of them had seen— or, at least, noticed—any of the others leaving the bar in the direction of the yard.

"But you've only got their word for that," said Debbie.

"Well, yes, obviously one of them's lying."

"No, that's not what I meant. Obviously the killer's lying, but isn't it possible that someone else is lying, too? That the killer *was* seen leaving the bar by one of the witnesses, but that person is keeping quiet about it."

"It's possible, I suppose."

"The thing is, I just can't believe that all that night, nobody ever noticed anyone else getting up to go to the loo. At least, I can't believe that none of the women noticed."

"You mean women are nosey?" said Frank, skilfully ducking the resultant slap.

"Women are interested in people, yes. Okay, you give a man another man to talk to, and a corner to sit in, and a pint to drink, and he won't notice Elvis Presley walk through the room wearing a tutu."

"I didn't know Elvis was like that," said Frank.

"But women keep their eyes open—they like to know what's going on around them, who's moving where, who's talking to who. And of course we always go to the loo in pairs, as men never tire of pointing out."

Frank thought about that, while he watched the silent quiz show. A caption across the screen said *Answer: Beheaded.* He wondered what the question had been. "I see what you're saying, sure, but the point is on a night like that, people would be popping off to the loo all the time. Even the most *inquisitive* woman couldn't be expected to take note of every individual trip for the whole time period."

Now, however, enjoying an excellent pub lunch with Don—quiche with spinach salad for Frank; steak and kidney pie, buttered new potatoes and steamed broccoli for the DI—he began to wonder. Could one of the witnesses be keeping quiet about what he or she had seen; in effect, giving a false alibi to the killer?

"You said yourself that more than one person could be involved in the killing."

"Did I?"

"When we were talking about the brothers."

"Oh yes, so I did," said Don. "But think about what this means. One of the suspects-cum-witnesses sees the murderer following Chalkie out to the yard—"

"Or sees Chalkie following the killer out to the yard," Frank interrupted. "Unwittingly, I mean."

"Either way, this Witness X then lies about what he or she has seen, presumably in order to shield the killer. Why would anyone do that? There don't seem to be any potential money motives in this case at all. Just personal motives—which, by their nature, are unlikely to affect more than one person."

"Blackmail?" Frank suggested. "The witness blackmailing the killer?"

"Not impossible, certainly, but you're then assuming that within a small group of ordinary people, you've got two individuals who are willing to commit very serious crimes—murder on the one hand, blackmail and withholding evidence of murder on the other. I know we're supposed to live in a cynical, individualistic age, Frank, but that's going it a bit, isn't it?"

"All right then, how about love? Witness X is in love with the killer, so she—or he, I suppose, but more likely she—is unwilling to drop him in it. Doesn't want to see him sentenced to life. People'll do funny things for love, no?"

Don pushed his plate away—it was almost supernaturally empty, Frank noted, as if it had been licked clean by a dog—and picked up the lunch menu, encased in a red plastic folder decorated with golden tassels. "You having a pudding?"

"Don't think I'll bother, thanks."

"You don't mind if I do." He signalled to a barmaid. "One of those sticky toffee things, please love, and another pot of coffee. Ta."

"Or," Frank continued, "it could be mutual interest."

"How do you mean?"

"Well, like—'You keep my secret and I'll keep yours'."

"Again, that supposes we're dealing with two people who are into something dodgy, and are willing to let another human being die to prevent news getting out. I find that hard to swallow."

Only because it's a bloody darts team, Frank thought. *If it was the local branch of the Young Conservatives, you'd nick the lot of them without turning a hair.*

"You don't reckon this is worth pursuing, then?"

Don swallowed a mouthful of his pudding, and made a noise more commonly heard in films shown late at night on Channel 5. "Bloody good, this—you sure you don't want one?"

"Sure, thanks." Frank poured the coffee.

"No, I don't dismiss this Witness X stuff out of hand, Frank, not at all. You've got a very clever wife, as well as a very beautiful one. Though how you can afford two wives on your salary, I do not know."

Frank said nothing. He wished he hadn't mentioned that this idea had come from Debbie, but if he'd said it had been his—well, that would have been lying.

"If nothing else, it certainly gives us a fresh way of

looking at the case," Don continued. "And it's not a bad theory, when all's said. Definitely worth a walk around the park."

"But," said Frank, "if it's true, how do we prove it? Only by catching the killer, presumably, which makes it pretty useless as a shortcut."

"We *can't* prove it, in all probability. But that doesn't actually worry me. I've thought all along in this case, we can get confessions provided we're sufficiently certain of our ground, in our own minds. And that goes for Witness X, as much as for the murderer. It's that sort of case, Frank—they're that sort of people. Give them a good shove, from a position of real confidence, and they'll fall over."

"So if we can convince Witness X that we know who she is, then assuming she actually exists..."

"Right. In which case, who's the likeliest candidate?"

"Heather Mason?" Frank suggested. "When you think about it, the landlady of a pub, surely she's going to be keeping at least half an eye on comings and goings, just out of professional habit."

"Yes, you're right. We were maybe a bit too quick to take her at her word when she said she hadn't seen anything." Don lit a cigar, his pudding plate now as dog-licked as his pie dish. "So who might she be covering up for?"

"A woman, presumably, if she's a lesbian."

"*If.* That's only gossip. And besides, we haven't heard a hint that any of the other women in the case are that way inclined."

"A woman that she's got a crush on? A straight woman, I mean."

"Okay, we'll ask her. You ready to roll?"

"Ready," Frank replied.

"Right—on the way, ring Brian Gough, and ask him to meet us at the Hollow Head, immediately. Time we had another word with him, too."

THE HOLLOW HEAD was hosting a small, post-lunch crowd when Don and Frank arrived there. The landlady nodded a surly greeting; the skipper, sitting at a corner table studying a flowchart, was polite enough, but made it clear that this meeting had seriously disrupted his busy timetable. "We've got an important home game tomorrow night, you know. Lot to do, and only me to do it."

"You've got a match on a Thursday?" said Don.

"Rescheduled. Because of this business." He nodded his head towards the Ladies. "The other captain's idea, not mine."

"Well," said Don, "I fear you might have to play a sub for that one. We're expecting to make an arrest very shortly."

"Indeed? Well that's—that is good news."

"Is it? Tell me, Brian, how long had you and Yvonne Wood been having it off?"

Frank watched the skipper's face carefully, but detected no sign of surprise. He understood why, when Gough said: "Right, I thought it might be that. Here." He handed his mobile phone to Don. "Just press send—my wife is waiting to talk to you."

Don took the phone, and stepped outside into the car park. Gough returned to his paperwork, apparently unconcerned. When the DI returned to the bar, a few minutes later, he gave Frank a thumbs-down sign from behind Gough's back.

"Now then, Inspector. My wife confirms that she knew about me and Yvonne, yes?"

"That was the gist," Don admitted.

"And that she knew about it two days before the murder? Thus robbing me of any motive for killing poor Chalkie?"

"Why did you choose then, particularly, to tell her?" Don asked.

Gough looked shocked at the question, as if it were indecent in some way. "I *didn't* bloody tell her, did I? She found out."

"How?"

"The usual female ways," said Gough, distaste twisting his mouth. "Going through my bloody pockets like a spy. Credit card receipt for…for personal items, if you must know."

"I have to say, Mr. Gough," said Frank, "you don't seem terribly upset by the sudden death of your lover."

Gough cleared his throat. "Well, yeah, of course I was upset. Don't get me wrong. But at the same time, to be brutally honest…well…"

"It was rather convenient," Don said.

"Your word, not mine," replied Gough, primly.

Don sighed. "Go on, Mr. Gough, you can go. We won't need you any more today."

"That's all right. I have some matters to see to here, concerning the—"

"I said *go!*" Don's shout quietened the pub. "Go on, sod off home to your wife, you miserable little turd." As the skipper hastily gathered together his papers and fled, Don added: "And if she murders you, don't bother ringing 999, because we don't give a toss!"

As the background noise returned slowly to its nor-

mal levels, Frank put away his notebook, and said:
"That seems to be him out of it, then. And it fits in
with his wife acting so odd when we went round to
their place the other day."

"I suppose so. Right, let's have a word with sweet
Heather." He called over to the landlady, who was
polishing glasses with a stained cloth. "Ms. Mason,
would you join us, please?"

"Okay, I'm trying to run a pub here, if you haven't
noticed. I haven't got time to sit around nattering."

Don took a deep breath and let it out slowly. Somehow, Frank didn't think this was a technique he'd
learned on an anger management course. More likely
he was pumping himself up than calming himself
down. "That's fine, Ms. Mason. I wish to discuss with
you the love that dares not speak its name. Yes? So
I'll just do it from over here, shall I? *You can hear me
all right, can you? Or shall I speak louder?*"

Once Heather Mason had settled herself at the corner
table—and once her mutterings had subsided sufficiently to allow questions to be heard over them—Don
wasted no time in coming to the point.

"You made a pass at Chalkie, and she turned you
down. Did you kill her as a result of that rebuff?"

"Okay, Jesus, keep your voice down!"

"I am keeping my voice down, Heather, but it's
likely to rise inexorably if you don't answer my questions with prompt and transparent candour."

"I'm not a lesbian, if that's what you're saying."
Frank had to lean towards the landlady to catch her
words. He could have told her that that kind of whisper
can be heard more clearly a few yards away than it can
close-up. But he didn't.

"You made sexual advances to another woman,"

said Don. "That does sound somewhat Sapphic, you must admit."

"Okay, I'm admitting bloody nothing, and *you*—" She dug an elbow into Frank's ribs—"mind what you're writing down about lesbians and suchlike. That's how rumours start."

"This particular rumour," said Frank, "started because Chalkie told people that you'd tried to chat her up."

"Okay, yeah. I did that—but it was all a wind-up, see? I only did it to upset her, to get her going. And it worked!" She was no longer whispering, Frank noticed. "If you must know, I've got a boyfriend."

There followed a long moment of silence during which, Frank thought, every eye in the pub seemed to be fixed on Heather Mason, and the air seemed to be filled with a single, unvoiced thought: "You're *joking!*"

"Right," said Don, at last. "We'll leave it there for now, Ms. Mason. Thank you for your assistance."

As they got back into the car, Frank could still hear the silence of the pub; could see, through a small, unfrosted stretch of window, the landlady still sitting at the corner table, her face a study in blushing pride.

"DO WE BELIEVE HER?"

Don shrugged. "Ugly people get laid, Frank. The species would die out pretty soon, if they didn't."

"And she made a pass at Chalkie just to wind her up?"

"Yeah, there's more to that than she's told us, I agree. But we weren't going to get it from her today. It'll keep. I want to tick a few more names off the list, first, if we can."

WHEN CLIVE CALLOW opened the door of his flat, Frank noticed at once that his usual smile was missing. He also noticed a bottle of vodka in Callow's left hand. "Ah, gents—is this urgent? Only…"

"We were hoping to have a word with Mrs. Callow," said Don. "Sorry if we've chosen a bad moment."

Callow leaned against the doorframe for a moment. "You might as well come in. You'll have to take us as you find us, I'm afraid."

His meaning was instantly clear. Di Callow was asleep on the sofa; a plastic bucket alongside her contained a small quantity of yellow, watery vomit.

Her husband put the bottle of vodka down on a table, and spread his hands. "She'll be out for a while. That's how it takes her—a couple of stiff drinks, and she's on her back within minutes. Fancy a cup of tea?"

"No, you're all right," said Don. Frank caught his eye and could see that they had both come to the same conclusion: if this was what drink did to Di, then there was no way she could have got drunk enough to murder Chalkie, while remaining in control of herself long enough to manhandle the doorstop into position and then return to the bar unobserved. "While we're here, Clive, perhaps we could ask you a couple more questions?"

"Yeah, no prob."

"You knew the Rees brothers from the old days."

"Sure. I told you that."

"You did some business with them?"

Callow said nothing.

"Look, Clive—we're not investigating car crimes from the distant past, you understand? Whatever you tell us about that, as far as we're concerned it's just background.''

Callow nodded. "Fair enough. Yeah, years ago I did some business with Lee that was a bit on the dodgy side.''

"'A bit on the dodgy side' being chirpy cockney street market slang for supplying them with stolen cars?" said Don.

"*One* stolen car, *once*. It wasn't a career for either of us, me or Bushy. Just an opportunity that came along and being stupid and young we took it. Never again.''

"And his brother?"

"Well, see, he didn't know about the stolen car until years later. I mean sure, they used to be close, in the old days, but there was always secrets between them, even then. They weren't joined at the hip, you know, they had separate lives. So, anyway, when I reappeared on the scene—"

"Invited onto the darts team by Bushy?"

"Right, well that caused a big row between them. Like, Baldy was saying to his bro, *So, you're going back into the bent motors game, are you?* And Bushy's response was, like, *If you don't trust me, then sod you!* And they've never spoken since. See? My fault, in a sense.'' Callow sighed, and sat down heavily on a dining chair. "But then, most things are, I find.''

"But you get on all right with both of them, these days?''

"Well, yeah, pretty much. It's hard to explain, but it's as if their argument is with each other, not with me. You know? Fact is, they both know I'm not involved in anything dodgy now, so I reckon to them I'm just like a symbol of something that'd been simmering for years. Maybe all their lives. You think about it;

they've never married, always lived together, always worked together…there's bound to be tensions." He attempted a smile, which won more points for effort, Frank reckoned, than for execution. "They'll get over it eventually."

"You socialise with both of them, separately?"

"Lee I see mostly at the darts; Luke and I get together occasionally."

"At their place?"

"The house? No, haven't been there in ages. I don't imagine the atmosphere's too nice there, what with everything."

"When we asked you before whether you knew what their split was about, you told us you didn't," said Don.

"Yeah…yeah, I know. Sorry about that." Clive Callow stood up, walked over to the sofa, and bent down next to his wife. *He's checking her breathing,* thought Frank. "Thing is, gents, I've got enough stuff of my own to lug around, without getting involved in everybody else's hassles. But when you came here today, I just thought—to hell with it, better out than in."

"All right," said Don, with a glance at the pale creature on the sofa. "We'll let you off."

TWENTY

"BIT OF A LET-DOWN, really."

"What is?" Frank asked, as he started up the car. "And by the way, where to next?"

"We'll go and see Stuart Webb. See if he can give us a horse for the three-thirty. And failing that, see if he's got any tips on how to get one's oven showroom-clean and sparkling like the morning sun."

Frank looked at the DI out of the corner of his eye. He'd seemed fine this morning, full of the joys, but ever since Brian Gough had punctured the adultery motive with a single phone call, Don'd been a bit—well, a bit *over-lively*. His voice was just a little too loud, his delivery just a touch too fast. He was smoking, which ought to be an encouraging sign; but on the other hand, he kept lighting them, taking a few puffs, and stubbing them out, which didn't seem normal. All in all, Frank just wished his boss would slow down a bit. That's all—just *slow down*.

"What's a let-down? Di Callow?"

"No, I never really fancied her for it, did you? I'm just as glad to have her off the list, really."

"Along with the skipper and the landlady," said Frank, mainly just to see what sort of reaction he'd get.

"Yeah, well…I'm not nearly so glad to see them out of the frame. Nor am I convinced they *are* out of it yet, if it comes to that. It's just that they're no longer the main faces on the wanted posters. For now. No, what I meant about a let-down was Superdart's explanation of the feud.''

"Bushy versus Baldy.''

"I was expecting something a bit juicier than that, I have to say.''

"He's telling the truth, is he?'' said Frank, pulling up in plenty of time for a red light.

"Come on, Frank! You're not required to slow down half an hour before the lights change, you know—I would like to get to Webb's house before nightfall, if possible.''

"Just trying to behave like a responsible road user,'' said Frank.

"Why, for Christ's sake? You're a copper!'' Don lit another cigar. "Yes, I think Callow's telling the truth about why the brothers aren't talking to each other. The way it came out, you know? Sounded genuine to me. He's not a happy man, is he, Clive Callow? Considering he spends every working day surrounded by records.''

Frank couldn't see why being surrounded by records ought automatically to make a person more or less happy, so he didn't comment. Instead, he concentrated on driving in accordance with both the spirit and the letter of the Highway Code.

Stuart Webb was not pleased to see them, and said so. He did let them in, though, after Don had offered to interview him *under more formal conditions,* if he'd prefer.

"Look at it from our point of view, Stuart. You're a secret gambler—''

"I have a few bets! You make me sound like the

victim in one of those Victorian things they show at
Christmas!''

"You may object to my melodramatic language,
Stuart, but the fact remains that you gamble, and that
you don't want your wife knowing about it. Chalkie
found out, and a little while later she was dead. You
have no alibi. You have failed to convince me and my
colleague of your innocence. I'll be absolutely honest
with you, pal—right now, you are the leader of the
pack. If I can't come up with anything better by this
time tomorrow, I'm going to nick you anyway, just to
keep my bosses quiet. Let you take your chances with
the Crown Prosecution Service.''

Interesting, thought Frank. The guy must know—
anyone who's ever read a book or watched a TV show
must know—that whatever Don says, we're not really
going to arrest him without any evidence, no matter
how strong his motive might appear. He must also
know that if we did have some evidence, he'd be under
arrest already. And yet, look at him now: pulling his
fingers through his hair, eyes darting this way and that,
steam almost emitting from his ears as he racks his
brain for something he can give us to get us off his
back.

"You want to talk to that barrister," said Webb.
"That black chap. Two separate occasions, at darts
matches, he was pumping me for information about
Yvonne Wood. Not that I knew anything to tell him,
as it happened, but he wasn't to know that. And presumably, if he's been asking me about her, he'll have
been asking the others, too.''

"That's very interesting, Mr. Webb. Why didn't you
mention this before?''

"Because, Inspector, believe it or not, there are still

some people in this country who don't take pleasure from sticking their noses into other folk's business.''

Maybe, thought Frank. More likely, it's because up until now you weren't feeling sufficiently desperate to give your memory a thorough search.

From the car, Frank rang Brian Gough. ("You do it, Frank," Don told him. "I can't face talking to that pompous prat twice in one day.")

Gough's initial blend of nervousness and irritation soon evaporated when he realised that DC Mitchell wanted to ask him about another suspect, not himself.

"Yes," said Frank, putting away his mobile. "He confirms that Kevin Lewis had been asking questions about Chalkie. He didn't think to mention it before because he didn't think it was relevant—he just assumed Lewis fancied her."

"Maybe he did. But I hope it's more than that."

Don got through two more small cigars as they sat in the car outside the Webbs' house, trying to figure out the implications—if any—of this new piece of information.

"From the start," Frank pointed out, "we thought Lewis was being secretive about his background. Now we know that, despite the impression he deliberately gave us, he was sufficiently interested in the deceased to be asking around about her."

"But is it relevant...and if so, how? As far as we know, Lewis has no connections with Chalkie, the Hollow Head, or Cowden, going back more than a few months. He'd never shown his handsome face around here, until the night he happened to wander into the pub."

They pondered in silence for a while, until Don suddenly gave a yelp that sounded as if it was born of either inspiration or toothache. Frank hoped it was the former—he dreaded to think what sort of company the DI might make if he was in pain. "Have you got that darts team photo there, Frank? No, not the recent one: the oldest one."

Frank dug into his briefcase. "Here you go; this the one?"

"Ta..." Frank had expected his boss to study the picture, possibly to the accompaniment of more yelps. But in fact, Don merely glanced at it, grunted once, and pulled out his own mobile phone. "Start the car. I'll call Mr. Lewis, and tell him we're on our way."

At Kevin Lewis's chambers, they had to wait ten minutes for him to complete a meeting with a client— but Don didn't seem to mind. He spent the time humming. Frank did not recognise the tune, but then he didn't claim to be a connoisseur of music.

"Frank Sinatra," were Don's first words to Lewis, as the young barrister emerged smiling from his office. *"Songs For Swingin' Lovers."* He shook hands with Lewis. "Also, *Slade Alive* by the Slade. Bit of a controversial choice, that last one, I realise. But I think if you give it a fair listen—"

"Are you here to discuss music, Inspector?"

Don beamed. "I very much hope we're here to arrest you for murder, matey."

Lewis allowed his eyebrows to rise, but not to an unseemly degree. "Really? Well, well." He rubbed his hands together. "We'd better step into my office, then."

"Anyone you recognise here, sir?" Don held the 1979 team photo in front of Lewis's face as soon as they were through the door, cutting across an invitation to sit and the start of an enquiry concerning coffee.

His hands behind his back, the barrister leaned forward to inspect the picture. After a moment, he nodded. "Well, of course, the black chap is my father, as you have already deduced."

"Thought he might be related," Don said. "You have the look of him. Tell you what, we will have that coffee now, if you like. Only make it tea, okay? Me and my colleague, we're just about awash with coffee today."

Lewis spoke into his intercom, then took a seat behind the desk. Don and Frank sat in clients' chairs—Frank's positioned, carefully but not too obviously, between the desk and the door.

Steepling his fingers and closing his eyes, Lewis took a moment to gather his thoughts—or, thought Frank, having seen the same trick performed in court many times, to give the impression of someone gathering his thoughts. "My parents split up when I was quite young. My father was a senior sales representative for an import-export company; hence my rather peripatetic childhood. Father travelled a great deal in his work—quite apart from the frequent changes of address, I mean."

"And he took advantage of the traditional perks of the trade," said Don.

A young man knocked and entered, carrying a tea tray.

"Thank you very much, just leave it on the side." When the boy had left the room, Lewis continued. "I've no reason to believe that he was unfaithful to my mother on a regular basis, Inspector, but on this particular occasion—yes, he did have an affair, here in London, over an extended period of time. Not a one-night-stand, I mean. My mother found out, they were divorced. I stayed with my mother, of course, but kept in contact with Father over the years.''

"Did you meet his girlfriend?''

''No. My impression was that their affair did not last long, once my father was 'free'. This is often the case, as I know from my professional life.''

''So what brought you to Cowden eventually? Not coincidence, I'm sure.''

Lewis busied himself a while pouring tea. ''Father died not long ago, and amongst his effects I discovered a team photograph—a print identical to the one you showed me today. As you know, it carries a date and the name of the pub, the Hollow Head. I wished to…to settle some ghosts in my own mind. It was a long shot, of course, but I thought that someone at the pub might still remember her. I didn't dare think that she might still be drinking there.''

''She being Yvonne Wood? Your father's lover.''

''Having got talking with some of the darts players, I soon learned that this woman they called Chalkie had been involved in the pub darts team for many years, having originally taken an interest because her then boyfriend played there.''

''Your talent for the game is inherited, then.''

''Possibly.''

Don looked at the photograph. ''Chalkie had, naturally, changed a bit over the years, but she was still recognisable as the woman pictured here.'' Lewis sipped his tea and said nothing. ''And so, Mr. Lewis. Having identified her, you killed her.''

''I did not. I was not yet—I am still not—certain it was her that broke up my family. Not a hundred percent certain. I'm a barrister, remember, I know the difference between suspicion and proof. That's my bread and butter.''

"I notice," said Don, "that you do not deny that you *would* have killed her, had you been a hundred percent certain."

Lewis put down his cup; his hands, Frank thought, were remarkably steady. "You know better than that, Inspector. I advise all my clients never to comment on hypotheticals.''

Don stood. "Thank you for now, Mr. Lewis. I must ask you to make yourself available to us for further interview, should that prove necessary.''

"It's him, isn't it?" said Frank, as soon as they were clear of the building. "I mean, it's got to be, hasn't it?''

But Don shook his head. "I thought he sounded pretty convincing, Frank. It *could* have been him, I can quite believe that—but someone else got to the poor cow before he was ready to make his move. Anyway, I hope it's not him.''

"Why?" *Just because you share a taste in ancient music?*

"Simple—he'll never confess. I said earlier, the only way we'll close this case is to get a confession supported by a very good motive, or vice versa. And I'm still sure we can do that, if we can just present the right scenario to the right person. None of these people are truly cold-blooded killers, even if one of them thinks he is.''

"Okay. So who are we left with? You said you wanted to talk to Cliff Overton again.''

"Did I? I can't think why, tedious little tosser. No, forget him, Frank, we need to do this the old-fashioned way, how we should have done it from the start. We'll go back to the office, go over all the statements again, page by page, word by word. Somewhere amongst that lot, someone must have said something that clashes with what someone else has said. Or someone must've contradicted themselves. We've just got to find it.''

Frank didn't like the sound of that. Not that it wasn't a sensible course of action—just that it was so un-Don; so pukka CID.

THE FOLLOWING NIGHT, in the Hollow Head, Don watched the players warming up. They formed a conga line stretching from the board, right around the playing area, and out into the bar, each man or woman throwing three darts—at the bull, usually, or at the treble twenty—then returning to their drinks or their cigarettes, before rejoining the end of the queue.

He and Frank had spent hours the previous afternoon and evening, going over and over the various witness statements, but had found nothing significant—or nothing that struck them as significant, anyway.

So much for the old-fashioned way. Back to Plan A...

As he leaned against the counter, Heather Mason stretched past him to reach a clutch of empties. On an impulse (and why not? Nothing else seemed to be doing much good), Don said: ''What you told us yesterday, Heather. I'm afraid I'm going to have to ask you to prove that—as things stand, you killing Chalkie because she turned you down still looks pretty good to me.'' Frank arrived at that moment, and nodded to them both.

The landlady sneered. ''Prove that I'm not a lesbian? What, you want me to give you a blow-job in the public bar? Well, you wouldn't be the first copper who's asked me for that favour.''

I bet I bloody would! thought Don. Has this woman really no idea how unattractive she is? ''That would be delightful, Heather, but for the moment, I just need the name of your boyfriend.''

She stood still, put the glasses back down on the bar, and ran her tongue around the inside of her lower lip. Don watched, fascinated; every face tells a story, he thought. She isn't really frightened that we'll nick her if she can't prove she has a boyfriend, and most of her instincts tell her to tell me to sod off. But one part of her is breaking ranks. The pride of a plain woman: *she wants to boast.*

''Okay, none of your business, but I've got nothing to hide. I happen to be going out with Luke Rees.''

''And on the night in question,'' Don began, promising his subconscious it could do all the boggling it fancied at a later date, provided it allowed him not to show anything on his face right now.

But Frank interrupted. ''Right, well, he's quite a catch, Heather. And single, of course.''

''Aye, well,'' she said, with a levity so uncharacteristic as to be almost grotesque. ''You can't have everything, can you? Anyway, okay, that's why I told Chalkie I fancied her—to put her off the scent.''

''You didn't want her knowing about you?'' Frank asked. ''Why?''

''Just that Chalkie was the kind of person who liked to know things. You know?''

''And what did she do with the things she knew?''

She shook her head. ''Nothing, I'm not saying that— she just liked to know things.''

''And to spread them?''

Heather Mason gathered her glasses once more, and as she left the policemen, she said over her shoulder: "Okay, I'm not the sort of person to call a dead woman a shit-stirring little cow, so you needn't bother asking me to."

"Why did you interrupt me?" Don demanded—but immediately wished he hadn't as he saw the expression on Frank's face. The boy was obviously aghast at his own cheek.

"Sorry about that. It's just that—well, look, what she just told us, it makes Bushy Bro a bloody good suspect, doesn't it? I mean, we know now who she would cover up for, if anyone."

"If anyone," Don stressed.

"Sure, yeah. But supposing she is giving him a false alibi—well, she doesn't know that we know. So I thought, you know, best leave it like that."

"All right, I see what you mean. Heather doesn't know we've brought in Debbie Mitchell, the legendary consulting detective of Cowden. And now we've cracked that aspect of the case, all we've got to do is find out the whole entire complete bloody story. Seriously, Frank: what's Luke Rees's motive? Was the garage going back into the stolen cars business? If so, how did Chalkie find out?"

"From Di Callow when she was drunk?" Frank suggested.

"Which puts Clive Callow back in the frame." Don rubbed at his forehead with two knuckles. "Oh Christ, don't complicate things. Let's stick with Bushy Bro for the moment. What else is there? The affair with Heather isn't a motive for murder, surely? I mean, yeah, he'd be dead embarrassed to be seen with such an awful woman, but it's not as if either of them are married or anything.''

A cry of *Game on!* brought cheers from the bar tables, followed by loud *shushings* from the playing area. Don shrugged; no point trying to talk while the match was on, they'd be overheard in the respectful silence which the whole pub adopted each time a player stood up to the line. ''Might as well watch this,'' he whispered. ''Maybe the killer will reveal himself by means of a fiendish breach of darting etiquette.''

The game was a close one, between two evenly matched sides, the Hollow Head emerging victorious only in the last leg of the night—the all-in, in which every player from each team took turns to throw their three darts. By the time the final dart hit its target, the warning bell for last orders had gone.

As the losers lined up at the bar to buy their victorious opposite numbers the traditional half-pint, Don hoisted himself halfway up a bar stool and clapped his hands together.

''Ladies and gentlemen, nothing to be concerned about, could I have your attention for a moment, please. For those who don't know, I am Detective Inspector Don Packham of Cowden CID, and I would be grateful if those of you who were *not* present here on the night of the murder of Yvonne Wood could please drink up and leave as quickly as possible. The rest of you, I am going to ask you to stay behind for a short while.'' He and Frank had discussed the wording of that request in some detail. They couldn't order anyone to stay, but they hoped that most if not all would realise that the alternative was likely to be a more formal interview at the police station. ''So, if any of you need to phone home, to say you'll be a little bit late, please do so now. There's a pay phone on the bar, for those who don't have mobiles.''

He jumped down, as around the room groans of resignation and annoyance began to fill the air. ''Let them make their calls, Frank, then it's as we planned, yes? Get them all sat at the tables over there, and we'll bring them over one-by-one to the far side, there.'' The bell rang, and Don cursed as he realised he'd missed his last chance to refill his glass. ''I'll lead them through everything again, in detail, while you check it against their original and subsequent statements. Any inconsistencies, and you—''

''Who's he phoning, then?''

Don turned around. ''I beg your pardon, Mr. Overton?''

The old man pointed towards a dark corner of the room, where Luke Rees was talking quietly into a mobile phone. ''Who's he got to phone? His brother's sat at that table right there, and he hasn't got a wife.''

Irritated—by the man as much as by his interruption—Don began to wave Overton away.

And then he stopped, turned to Frank, and smiled. ''Told you we needed another word with Cliff, didn't I, Frank?''

''Sir?''

''Go on over to Bushy Bro, and ask him if you can borrow his phone. And bring it back here.''

Frank frowned. ''You can use mine, if you—''

''No, no, Frank. Yours is out of order. Remember?''

Frank did as he was told. Don could see Luke Rees wasn't keen on the idea, but after a moment the DC returned, carrying the phone.

''Right,'' said Don. ''Now let's see what we shall

see.'' He pressed the redial button, and held the instrument to his ear.

A woman's voice answered: ''What did you forget this time, your head?''

''Good evening, madam,'' said Don. ''Sorry to trouble you. My name is Detective Inspector Don Packham of Cowden CID. May I ask to whom I am speaking, please?''

TWENTY-ONE

IN INTERVIEW ROOM number three at Cowden police station, Luke Rees said: "It's rather a complicated story, I'm afraid."

"As so often," said Don, "in tales of love and sex. This is a tale involving both, I assume—love *and* sex?"

"In a way, yes. Though to be honest...well, like I said, it's all a bit complicated."

Rees was being interviewed under caution, but not under arrest. It had been made clear to him that he was free to leave at any time, and that he was entitled to consult a lawyer before being interviewed, but he had insisted that he "just wanted to get it over with." Given that it was now well after midnight, Rees would have been within his rights to refuse to be interviewed until the next day, thus forcing Don to either arrest him or let him go. Swallowing a yawn, Frank rather wished Bushy Bro *had* refused; it had been a long day.

You wouldn't know it by looking at Don, mind; he looked as fresh as toothpaste.

"Don't worry, Luke, we'll take our time," said Don. "Let's start with this famous feud between you and Lee."

Rees assembled a roll-up with swift, practiced movements, and stuck it in his mouth—then, on second thought, took it out again. "Sorry, is it okay to smoke in here?"

"It's strictly banned," said Don, leaning over the table and lighting Rees's cigarette.

"Ta. Right, the famous feud. Well, it's not a feud, really, just a silence. As for how it started, well, years ago, when I was much younger, I did something really stupid."

"The stolen cars?"

"*Car,* single." Rees drew on his cigarette. Frank thought, for the first time, that he saw some calculation in the mechanic's friendly eyes. "You know all about that, then. Well, you'll also know that it was a one-off. No kidding, you could go over that garage now with a microscope, you wouldn't find anything wrong. It's been clean as a whistle from that day to this."

"This once-in-a-lifetime piece of larceny; your brother wasn't in on it?"

"Bloody right he wasn't! Lee went mad when he found out. Never took his eyes off me for a year or more after that. Made it plain he didn't trust me."

"But your relationship recovered eventually?"

Rees let smoke trickle out through his nose. "Well, yeah, more or less. I mean, nothing was said, but it was obvious he never quite trusted me again. Which you couldn't blame him for, I suppose."

"Then, three years ago, you ran into Clive Callow again."

Rees nodded. "Okay, so Clive's told you all about that, I won't be breaking any confidences. Yeah, well, Clive wasn't drinking any more, and I thought it would do him good to get back into the game, so I introduced him to the Hollow Head."

"And Lee wasn't pleased?" said Don.

"Lee went *mental*. All about how I was I putting the business at risk by getting mixed up with characters like Callow. I thought he was talking bollocks and I told him so: Clive's as straight as a die these days, has been for years. Anyway, by the end of the day, Lee wasn't talking to me, and then the next day, I wasn't talking to him, and…well, before you know it, three years have passed. In silence." He scratched head and smiled. "Daft, I know. But that's how it is. Things sort of *ossified*. We were still working together, obviously, but I started spending more and more time away from the house in the evenings and weekends."

"And you met someone," said Don.

"Right. Met a girl, Carol, last autumn. Welsh girl, from Harlech. Fell in love, basically. Before then, neither of us—me and Lee, I mean—had ever really thought of marriage." Rees paused for a moment, looking, Frank thought, slightly puzzled. "I don't know, it just never came up. We had girlfriends and that, but nothing serious."

"You had each other," Don suggested.

"I suppose, yeah."

"So you and Carol got married?"

Rees grinned. "Yup. Well, no, not technically. But we set up home together, a flat south of the river. We plan to have children eventually."

"And what was your brother's reaction to that?"

Frank guessed the answer even before Rees drew in a deep breath and said: "He didn't know. He still doesn't know."

"I see," said Don. "Your wife, didn't she think it strange that she never met your brother?"

"No." Rees shook his head. "See, she's never heard of him."

Don nodded, and Frank could tell that nothing Rees had yet said had come as a surprise to the DI. Which was good news, presumably—and probably explained Don's current equanimity. "Tell us how that worked, Luke."

Rees smoked, clearly gathering his thoughts. "You've heard about bigamists, who live two completely separate lives, in different places, and get away with it for years? Well, I was like that. Only instead of two wives, I had one wife and a brother."

"You mean you *commuted*," said Frank, unable to stop himself from interrupting, "between Lee in north London and Carol in south London?"

"Exactly. Yeah, that's exactly it—I commuted. I worked at the garage most days, then most evenings and weekends I was at home with Carol."

"And your wife didn't find this strange?"

"That's the thing, you see," said Luke, in a voice that sounded, to Frank, rather more enthusiastic than was healthy under the circumstances. "Provided you keep your story simple, it's surprisingly easy to keep it straight. Carol doesn't know about the garage, she thinks I'm a jobbing mechanic, doing jobs here and there all over the country. And the fact that Lee isn't talking to me makes it easier—he couldn't ask me where I was disappearing to without breaking the silence, which I guess he was too proud to do."

"All right," said Don, lighting a cigar. "I see how it could work. But the question is *why?* Why the secrecy?"

"Ah, well." Rees held up his hands. "To be honest, I suppose I'm guilty of pride, too. Fact is, I just didn't want anything to do with my brother after we fell out.

But I was stuck with him, obviously, because of the business.''

"You could have left, and got a job elsewhere. You're a skilled mechanic.''

"Why the hell should I? I built up that business as much as he did.''

"So you didn't tell your brother about your wife simply because you're not talking to him. Okay, but why didn't you tell your wife about your brother?''

Rees stubbed out his cigarette. He'd been smoking fast, Frank noted, dragging down rapid, urgent lungfuls. "To put it bluntly, I reckon I was ashamed. Or embarrassed, at least. I mean, let's face it—two grown men behaving like kids, it's nothing to be proud of, is it? It was easier just to start afresh, with a whole new life.''

"Two whole new lives,'' Don commented. "Except for the darts team, of course.''

With a laugh, Rees said: "I wouldn't give up my darts, Inspector! Not for anything. You can understand that.''

"Let's move on, then. Where does Yvonne Wood come into the story? And Heather Mason, for that matter?''

Rees swallowed, and rubbed a bead of sweat away from his upper lip. *They turned the heating off hours ago,* thought Frank. "Chalkie found out I was married—''

"How?'' said Frank and Don together.

"Well, not exactly *found out,* but she was that kind of woman, she could *smell* a married man a mile off. Like a tiger smells its prey. I'd been living with Carol just a week or so, when Chalkie started going on at me.''

"How do you mean?"

"She wouldn't leave me alone, Inspector. Flirting, making little comments, double entendres...see, she was never interested in single men. Never. But her sixth sense told her I wasn't a single man any more, and it was like suddenly I'd become visible. So, what I did was, I pretended to start an affair with Heather. To put Chalkie off, like."

"How," Frank interrupted, "do you *pretend* to have an affair with someone?"

Don nodded. "Heather seemed to think it was real. Did you sleep with her?"

"You're joking!" Rees shuddered, and Frank decided at that moment that he really didn't like this man very much at all. He hoped they'd end up nicking him for murder, he really did. "Yuk, what a thought! No, I had to kiss and cuddle a bit occasionally, but I told her I was engaged."

Don rubbed his eyes. "Wait a minute—to keep your marriage secret from Chalkie you told Heather about it?"

"No, look, I told you it was complicated. I didn't tell Heather about *Carol*. Right? I told her I *had* been engaged, and that it was a big secret, she mustn't tell anyone—not even my brother, because it was one of his ex-girlfriends that I'd been engaged to. She can keep a secret, in her line of work, you've got to be discreet, haven't you? Then I said to her that once I was finally free of this supposed fiancée, which would be any time now, then we would be together properly."

"You and Heather."

"That's it. I said I wasn't willing to sleep with her until then, because it would be deceitful, and I didn't want to sully our relationship. Yeah, look, I can see in your faces what you're thinking. And believe me, I know, it *was* pretty revolting. But you two just do not know what Chalkie was like! I was desperate, I won't deny it.''

''Doesn't sound like much of a long-term solution,'' said Don.

Rees shrugged. ''Best I could come up with. If I could convince Chalkie I *wasn't* married after all, I just had a girlfriend, then she'd lose interest. I hoped.''

''But it didn't work,'' Don suggested, and Frank held his breath—he knew what was coming next. ''Chalkie wasn't fooled. Which is why you killed her.''

''On the contrary,'' said Luke Rees, leaning back and folding his arms across his chest. ''It worked like a dream. I didn't kill her. I'm sorry, mate, but you've got the wrong man.''

''It's him,'' said Don, the following morning in the police canteen. He'd slept surprisingly well during the few hours between releasing Luke Rees and returning to the nick for this early meeting with Frank. He didn't feel a lot better for it, though; his eyes were heavy and his shoulders ached. Face it, he was too old for late nights and crack-of-dawns. And what didn't help matters—he reckoned he'd lost a murderer, by going in too soon.

''I think you're right,'' said Frank, who also looked tired, Don thought, but in a young man's way; temporarily, rather than cumulatively. ''He was that cocky at the end, like he was sure he'd got away with it. But we haven't got enough to charge him, have we?''

''No. So much for my theory about confessions. And without a confession we haven't got anywhere near enough circumstantial evidence, even if Heather does say she witnessed him go into the Ladies. Which she probably would, when she finds out he lied about his 'fiancée'.''

''That theory could still hold, though. Maybe we just haven't got the whole story yet.''

Shut up, Frank, thought Don. *Nobody loves an optimist—especially at breakfast-time.* Out loud, though, he said: ''I suppose there is one thing still missing from this case—money.'' And as he said it…he began, just a little bit, to believe it. He sat up straighter, and closed his eyes to concentrate.

''Does there have to be money?'' Frank asked. ''We've got secrets, fear of exposure, infidelity…''

''Yeah, all of which might add up to murder—but not to *this* murder, Frank. Think about it, this is a cross between premeditated and non-premeditated. A hybrid. Right? On impulse, Luke follows Chalkie out to the Ladies. That could lead to a crime of sudden anger, frustration. But then there's the business with the doorstop. Now, that is premeditated. There were a few minutes there, before Chalkie walked into the booby trap, when he could have changed his mind about killing her. In a true crime of passion, you don't get those few minutes, that's the point. So if this isn't a crime of passion, it can't have a crime-of-passion motive—QED.''

''Okay,'' said Frank. ''So where is the money?''

''The business,'' said Don, vocalizing the thought in the same moment it entered his head. ''Got to be.'' He stood up. ''Hold the fort, Frank—I'll be back shortly.''

HE WAS BACK three hours later, wearing what Frank thought of as his funeral suit—though Debbie, when he'd told her about it, had suggested 'denouement suit'—and with his hair freshly cut. Frank knew what that meant; or at least, what Don thought it meant. He just hoped the DI was right.

"Is Luke here, Frank?"

"Yes. Formally charged with murder, and awaiting interview in the presence of his lawyer."

"Right then." Don let his head drop, like a hanged man, and took in a series of what sounded like painfully deep breaths, which he slowly exhaled through his nose. "Let's go."

That's it all right, thought Frank: the black suit, the haircut, the breathing exercises. Mr. Packham believes he's got his man.

"Mr. Rees," said Don, after the tape-recording formalities had been seen to. "I have two new matters to put to you. Firstly, I intend to speak again to Ms. Mason, landlady of the Hollow Head, concerning what she might or might not have seen on the night of the murder."

Bushy Bro had nothing to say to that. He must have guessed it would happen, Frank supposed, and decided that on its own, an alteration in Mason's statement would not be enough to put him on trial.

"And secondly," Don continued. "I have this morning discussed with your brother, Mr. Lee Rees, the contents of your parents' wills. Now: I expect you would like some time to consult with your solicitor." Without waiting to find out if that was, in fact, what Rees wanted, Don announced that the interview was suspended, and he and Frank left the room.

"Give them ten minutes," said Don, lighting a cigar in the corridor outside. "Lawyers know when the game's up, even if murderers don't."

"It's No Smoking here, sir," said a uniformed sergeant as she passed them, pointing at the large, fluorescent sign on the wall which confirmed her words.

"It's all right, Sergeant," said Don. "I'm not inhaling."

The door to the interview room opened. "We're ready for you, Inspector," said the lawyer, his face unreadable. "My client wishes to make a new statement."

"Everything I told you before is the truth," Rees began, once the tape recorder was running again, "except for one thing."

"Quite an important thing," Don pointed out.

Rees tried a smile, but it didn't amount to much more than a tightening of the jaw muscles. *He's done it,* thought Frank: *this really is going to be a confession, just like Don predicted!*

"As you know, Lee and I are joint owners of the garage business and the house. Our parents were obsessed with the idea that families should stick together, them both having lost all theirs one way or another. And as you've heard about their wills, you'll know—"

"That neither of you can sell your share in either property, unless you both sell up simultaneously."

Rees gritted his teeth and nodded, as Frank exchanged an exultant look with Don. Now it made sense! The other motives—the feud, the desire to make a fresh start with the woman he loved—they were real, too; but this one, the money, this was the one that made murder worthwhile.

"Worse than that, Inspector. If one of us leaves either property—which is defined as having a principle address other than the house, or a significant source of income other than the garage—then that brother's share automatically passes to the remaining brother. Without compensation.''

"Pity you didn't take legal advice," said Don, and Frank was amused to see Rees's brief nod his head emphatically. "I'm not sure you could be held to a will like that, not these days."

"Maybe. Who knows? If Lee and I had still been talking to each other, we could probably have worked something out. But then, if we'd still been talking, I'd probably still be living there." Rees massaged his bushy hair with rough fingers, and groaned. "I suppose Mum and Dad thought that if and when we got married, we'd have all lived together in the old house. That's how they did things, in their day."

"But as things stood," said Don, "if your brother knew—or could prove, since he must have had his suspicions—that you were living elsewhere, effectively in a marital home, he could have had your inheritance off you in a flash."

"Right, exactly. Even if I did go to court to fight it, a case like that could drag on for years. We'd have ended up selling the properties anyway, just to pay the bloody lawyers' bills."

Rees's lawyer coughed, twice. Frank, Don and Rees all looked at him expectantly, but it seemed he had merely been clearing his throat.

"Well, Chalkie was suspicious, like I told you. That charade with Heather—" he shuddered "—didn't fool her for a moment, and then Heather came up with that bright idea about pretending to be a lesbian. Stupid cow. That only made Chalkie more suspicious."

"She kept after you?"

"You can bloody bet she did! Just wouldn't leave me alone, every time I went in the pub. She kept saying

You've got someone, haven't you? And I'd say, 'Look, me and Heather, that's none of your business, that's private'. And she'd laugh and say, 'No, not *Heather,* I mean you've *really* got someone'. Then, that night after the match—''

"You phoned home," said Don. "Because there was a lock-in, so you were going to be late."

Rees blew out his cheeks, shook his head a little from side to side. "That's right. Just like last night. I only figured it when your mate here asked to borrow my mobile. I leave my phone in my jacket pocket when I go out to the bog or whatever, can't be bothered to lug it around all night. It's mostly regulars at the Hollow Head, nothing gets nicked, and I was always discreet. But I have to ring her when there's a change of plan, you see—I have to. She worries, what with me being on the road so much."

"Pursuing your career as a peripatetic mechanic, you mean," said Don, with not quite enough censure in his tone to suit Frank.

Self-pity clouded Bushy Bro's face, as he continued. "It's been difficult at times. But I'd never leave my wife sitting in the dark, worrying about me, the way some men do. Anyway, that night, Chalkie must have done exactly what you did—rang redial."

"How did she know you'd got a mobile," Frank asked, "if you were always so careful not to be seen using it?"

His face reddening, Rees snapped: "Don't you *listen?* She never took her eyes off me, all night! She *knew* I was lying, and she was going to catch me at it, sooner or later."

"All right, Luke, calm down. Mr. Mitchell wasn't

taking the piss, we just like to fill in all the spaces. Carry on, now.''

''All right, sorry. Well, she waits until she sees me heading for the bog, follows me out, grabs me by the elbow. She says *So, who's the lucky lady with the Welsh accent, then?* I didn't twig about the phone, I thought, Jesus, she's been following me! She knows where I live! Or she's hired a private eye, or... whatever. I know that sounds paranoid, but honestly, I can't say it often enough: you don't know what she was like. She was *addicted* to married men. Like she was trying to get through every married man on the planet, or something.''

''What was your reply?''

''I just told her to sod off, said I don't know what you're talking about. She laughed—I mean, fair enough, she could see the sweat running off me in rivers, in the middle of bloody winter. She says, 'Okay, I'll ask your brother,' and she turns to go, giggling like a *fucking schoolgirl*.'' Rees's lawyer touched him lightly on the arm. ''All right,'' said Rees, much more quietly, dabbing at his lips with the pads of his fingers. ''All right. I told her, look, I'm really busting for a pee, just wait here for me, don't do anything, we'll talk in a moment.''

Don interrupted. ''At this stage, you'd already decided to kill her?''

Rees looked at his lawyer; the lawyer shook his head.

''I've no comment on that,'' said Rees.

''But you *did* then kill her? You followed her into the ladies, quietly set the trap...?''

Rees looked at his lawyer; the lawyer gave a tiny shrug.

"I went into the Gents, vomited, and when I came out, she wasn't there. For a moment I thought... But when I calmed down, I had a peek into the Ladies, and saw that the cubicle was closed. I could hear that bitch, still giggling to herself."

"So you set the trap with the doorstop," Don said, his delivery firm and deliberate, "which killed Yvonne Wood."

Luke Rees put his palms flat on the table in front of him, and took a deep breath. "Yes. I killed her."

"Thank you, Luke. What did you do then?"

"I didn't stay around to see it—you know—actually happen. I went back into the pub. Tried to act normal. About five minutes later, Heather—wondering what Chalkie was up to I suppose—went out back, found the body..." He closed his eyes, and made sobbing noises; though Frank couldn't see any actual tears. "I couldn't believe I'd done it. In fact, I think that's how I managed to get through the rest of the night, I think I just convinced myself I hadn't done it."

Don waited for a moment, allowing the tape to capture the sudden silence of the small room, and then spoke to the solicitor. "I think we're done for now. Your client will—"

"Mr. Packham." Rees looked up at Don. "Could you give my brother a message? Could you just tell him...just tell him 'good luck'. Just say *good luck,* please, from me."

"In his new hot dog venture, you mean?" said Frank, enjoying the bafflement on the killer's face.

"CYNICAL BASTARD," Don said, once the prisoner had been returned to the cells. "*Tell my brother good luck...* He's already playing the penitent. He'll look a picture in the witness box. Pity he isn't bald—juries hate bald men.''

''Won't do him any good, though, will it?''

''No, I don't suppose so. Right, Frank.'' Don put his overcoat on. ''We'd better go and have another chat with Heather, don't you reckon?''

''Do we need her, now? We've got a full confession. Anyway, it's not clear she actually knows Bushy killed Chalkie, even if she might have suspected it.''

Don lit a cigar. ''The thing is, Frank, I was just wondering. Do you suppose Chalkie was actually dead when Heather found her? Or did the lovely landlady wait a moment or two before dialling 999?''

Frank stood for a while, not moving, feeling tired. Then he sighed, and said: ''Right. Right, yeah, I see your point. I'll bring the car around.''

''Well done, by the way, Frank. You did well.''

''Thanks,'' said Frank, wishing very much that he was at home with his wife and baby. ''Thank you.''

A GOLDEN TRAIL OF
MURDER

A BEN TRIPP MYSTERY

JOHN PAXSON

Old-time ranchers like
Carson Woolsey aren't the
kind of men who die in a
Montana blizzard—they're
just too tough. So when his
frozen corpse appears in a
melting snowdrift during the
spring thaw, Ben Tripp agrees
to look into the matter—
and finds murder.

After another murder and
a close call that Tripp takes
personally, a trail of murder
begins to emerge, as wild
and dangerous as the land
itself—a place where
nature's riches clash
with cold hard greed…
sometimes with deadly intent.

*Available May 2003 at your
favorite retail outlet.*

 WORLDWIDE LIBRARY®

WWMAGTOM

**New York Times
bestselling author**

TESS GERRITSEN

**and
Favorite Harlequin
Intrigue® author**

DEBRA WEBB

**Bring you two full-length
novels of breathtaking
romance and heart-
stopping suspense, in...**

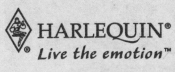

Available in June 2003
wherever paperbacks are sold.

HARLEQUIN®
Live the emotion™

Visit us at www.eHarlequin.com

PHDI

Sometimes the last man on earth you'd
ever want turns out to be the very one
your heart secretly yearns for....

#1 *New York Times* bestselling author

NORA ROBERTS

**brings you two passionate classic tales
about the thin line between love and hate.**

ENGAGING
THE ENEMY

Coming in May 2003
Available at your favorite retail outlet.

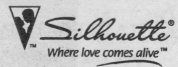

Where love comes alive™

Visit Silhouette at www.eHarlequin.com   PSETE

HARLEQUIN®
INTRIGUE®

Travel with Harlequin Intrigue bestselling author

JOANNA WAYNE

into the American South in a new series as she unlocks...

HIDDEN PASSIONS

What would you do if you'd just married a man who might be a murderer...? Nicole Dalton turned to the only man who could help her—Detective Dallas Mitchell. But would their past relationship prove more deadly to her future happiness?

ATTEMPTED MATRIMONY
On sale in June 2003

Look for more sultry stories of *Hidden Passions* coming soon.

Available at your favorite retail outlet.

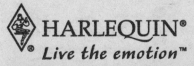

HARLEQUIN®
Live the emotion™

Visit us at www.eHarlequin.com

HIHPAT